DEFIANCE

A **STRANGE ANGELS** NOVEL

LILI ST. CROW

razOr bill

An Imprint of Penguin Group (USA) Inc.

Defiance

RAZORBILL

Published by the Penguin Group
Penguin Young Readers Group
345 Hudson Street, New York, New York 10014, U.S.A.
Penguin Group (USA) Inc., 375 Hudson Street, New York, New York 10014, U.S.A.
Penguin Group (Canada), 90 Eglinton Avenue East, Suite 700, Toronto, Ontario, Canada M4P 2Y3
     (a division of Pearson Penguin Canada Inc.)
Penguin Books Ltd, 80 Strand, London WC2R 0RL, England
Penguin Ireland, 25 St Stephen's Green, Dublin 2, Ireland (a division of Penguin Books Ltd)
Penguin Group (Australia), 250 Camberwell Road, Camberwell, Victoria 3124, Australia (a division
     of Pearson Australia Group Pty Ltd)
Penguin Books India Pvt Ltd, 11 Community Centre, Panchsheel Park, New Delhi – 110 017, India
Penguin Group (NZ), 67 Apollo Drive, Mairangi Bay, Auckland 1311, New Zealand (a division of
     Pearson New Zealand Ltd)
Penguin Books (South Africa) (Pty) Ltd, 24 Sturdee Avenue, Rosebank, Johannesburg 2196,
     South Africa

Penguin Books Ltd, Registered Offices: 80 Strand, London WC2R 0RL, England

10 9 8 7 6 5 4 3 2 1

ISBN: 978-159514-392-1

Library of Congress Cataloging-in-Publication Data is available

Printed in the United States of America

For Christa Hickey, true blue.

Acknowledgments

Thanks again to Mel Sanders, Christa Hickey, Miriam Kriss, and Jessica Rothenberg. Special mention must go to Lea Day, Bookweasel and Research Helper extraordinaire. Last but not least: You, dear Reader. Let me, once again, thank you in the way we both like best.

Let me tell you a story…

Plus in mora peliculi.
—*Livy*

CHAPTER ONE

Stick to the *plan*, Christophe had said. *Stick to the plan and everything will be fine.*

So I had.

I'd laced up my boots—knee-high red Doc Martens, good for everything from dancing to running to kicking ass—and put on the dress. It was a silvery baby doll number with spaghetti straps, and with my hair up my nape felt indecently bare. Even my *knees* felt naked. My mother's locket felt naked, too, hanging out against my breastbone instead of tucked under my shirt. I was even wearing *earrings*, for God's sake, cute little diamond studs Christophe had insisted I needed. I'd picked out a gauzy silver scarf sewn with little seed pearl things, hoping it would take the emphasis off my lack of cleavage.

Nathalie even managed to get me into a bra that didn't have "sports" in front of its name. An actual underwire. With padding. Another case of someone insisting and me going along with it, but with Nat I didn't mind. At least she took all of the mystery out of shopping for bras. I'd always wondered about that. Even though there was no real need, with my chesticles impersonating gnat bites.

I mean, seriously, is a baby doll dress for the breastless? *I don't know.* I only ever wore a skirt when Gran made me dress up for church, and even she quit it the third or fourth time I left Sunday school and somehow got rolled in mud and whatever gingham or flowered cotton she'd put together for me was torn all to hell.

I never told her it was the other kids. I know she suspected, though.

Nathalie had actually got some foundation and powder on me too, high-end girltastic stuff she'd dragged me to some huge store downtown to buy on one of our sneakabout-during-the-day excursions. The effect was okay. My skin was pretty much behaving these days; any zit I felt pressing up under the surface never seemed to break free. I sometimes got a small red spot, but nothing like it used to be.

You'd think that would make me feel better.

It didn't.

I hit the dance floor, wincing a little bit as the DJ looped feedback through the throbbing of a useless song about someone playing poker with his face or something. Sometimes hyperacute senses are so not worth it, even when you can concentrate and tone it down a bit. When I finally hit my blooming—the point where I got the speed and strength of a *djamphir* reliably, instead of in emotion-fueled bursts—I'd be able to tone it down as a matter of course. But for right now, I was stuck.

One good thing about this, though. I like dancing. Or at least, hopping up and down on a crowded floor, people hemming me in. I never thought it was anything I'd be happy about, especially since I've got the touch. You'd think that many people in one place *think-*

ing would drive me crazy. But when they're all happy and sweating and dancing, it's like white noise. It can help you relax.

When you're not watching out for bloodsucking fiends who would just as soon kill you as look at you, that is.

I stayed on the periphery, far enough into the crowd to get some cover, close enough to the edge that I could get away in a hurry. This rave was being thrown in a huge weird building called Pier 57, full of chemical fog and cigarette smoke. And other kinds of smoke, too. Glow sticks and bare flesh and sweat, it smelled like menthol and cigarettes, the musk of weed, and an indefinable tang that's all youth. Plus the smothered salt smell of sex in dark corners. There were enough hormones in here to fuel a rocket out to Orion.

I raised my arms when the crowd around me did, colored lights flashing. It was a migraine attack of red blue orange yellow, except for when they got fancy at certain points and made it all blue and green, or all orange and yellow. The music would crest, then whoever was doing lights would flick off everything but the mirrored ball, a tiny bit of spots to make everything glitter, and the black lights to make lipstick and synthetic fabrics glow oddly.

With the touch loose inside my head—just a little, not enough to drown me in a wash of sensation from every random stranger bumping against me—I drifted, letting my body slide through like a little fish in a bunch of water weeds. A minnow. Something too small to catch.

At least, I hoped I was too small.

Stick to the plan. Well, I was sticking to the plan.

The problem with vampires is that they *don't* stick to plans.

The first shard of hate, sharp and bright as an icicle under full sunlight, jabbed into my head. I kept moving, edging for the outside of the crowd. If I timed it right, the wheeling movement of the dancers—because if you watch a time lapse of a dancing crowd, they do always go in a wagon wheel—would take me right to the best exit Christophe had shown me on the layouts, his arm warm and comforting over my shoulders and his voice just a murmur in my ear. *Don't worry. You're fast enough and trained enough, or I wouldn't send you in.*

The thought made me flush all over, the healed fangmarks on my left wrist tingling slightly. At least he'd let me *do* something, not like some of the others on the Council. Hiro was having kittens about me being involved in an actual operation. Bruce just got That Look, the one that said I was Too Young and Too Irresponsible and Too Precious and the Hope of the Order.

It made me want to punch something.

If tonight went south, I might even get to.

The taste of rotting, waxen oranges slid across my tongue, paying no attention to the fact that I was chewing on a wad of spearmint gum. Gran called it an *arrah*—an aura. I was calling it danger candy nowadays. I always felt like spitting it out, but spitting would only make it worse.

Plus, spitting on a dance floor is damn rude. I was raised better.

I slipped my hand into the tiny net purse hanging at my side. Nathalie said it ruined the line of the dress, but I had to have someplace to stash lip gloss and the little thing I pulled out now, reaching up as if to brush a stray brown curl back and fitting it over my ear. It looked like a wireless headset for a cell phone, a sleek silver one. I pressed the button and let some of the curls hanging from my updo fall over it.

Noise-canceling earphones are a blessing. I just wished he'd given me two of them. Or earplugs. Earplugs would've been just jim-dandy.

4

"We read you, Dru." Christophe's voice, as crisp as if he was standing right next to me, overriding the attack of the music. Now it was some retro whitewashing of an eighties song, about a girl named Eileen and how she needed to come on, over thunking, thudding bass. "We have a visual. Primary team, move in."

This was, he'd told me, the most dangerous part. Before the other *djamphir* infiltrated the building, while I was still dancing. I was just about to break free of the crowd and head for the exit when another bright shard of hate lanced through my head.

I drew back instinctively, and the exit I'd been planning to take suddenly had a flicker of movement around it. "Shit." I wasn't even aware I'd said it.

"What?" Christophe didn't sound worried, but I could almost see him sitting at a sleek black desk in Mission Central at the Schola Prima on the Upper West Side, tense, his head cocked and the aspect slicking his hair down and back, the fangs peeping out from under his upper lip. His fingers would be poised over a slim black keyboard, and his blue eyes would be cold and far away, completely closed off. He would be coldly handsome, and I would almost feel . . .

No, I was never afraid of him. Not really. But it was easy to see how I could be, when he looked like that.

I had other problems right now. "Primary exit's blocked. I'm using secondary."

"Dru—"

But I was already moving. It wasn't a mistake, because the flickers at the door resolved into three teenage-looking males. One blond and two dark, all of them cute enough to get a second glance from any reasonable girl. If she was smart, the girl would see the hard edges of their smiles, or the nasty glitter in their dark eyes, or even just the way they moved. And she would run like hell.

But normal people don't look too closely. They glance, slot you into whatever hole they think you fit in, and bebop along right into the jaws of whichever slice of nasty is looking to feed. Dad and August used to argue over whether or not people *wanted* to know about the Real World, about the things that went bump in the night. Neither of them ever won the argument.

Me? I'd had nothing to say. I'd just been a kid.

I was still following the plan. I headed for the secondary exit, Christophe muttering in my ear as he sent the secondary and tertiary teams to their backup positions and gave the primary new orders. There was an odd echo to his voice, as if the signal was getting bounced around or he was outside.

I wished he was a little closer than the Schola, to tell the truth. But he was my control for this run, and Mission Central was where he belonged, coordinating. I drew in a nice deep breath, trying to force my galloping pulse to slow down. We were about to serve the vampires hunting the rave scene a really bad plate of kickass, Christophe had finally judged me competent enough to work inside a very limited seek-destroy operation, and the thought was comforting. Like I was doing something *real*, for once, instead of just training. Even if this was the closest thing to safe you could get when dealing with vampires.

That was when everything went bad. Because another quick movement near the secondary exit caught my eye, and the bass hit a smashing, rollicking rhythm. Everyone raised their arms, the crowd's mood turning on a dime into a breathless anxiety under all the roller-coaster fun, and I realized the secondary was a no-go too. My scarf fluttered a bit, seed pearls rasping against my suddenly damp neck.

Unfortunately, I'd just stepped out of the mass of normal kids and into a clear space, a sort of walkway for anyone who needed to escape the dance floor. I should have kept moving as if I was heading for the bathroom. When you freeze and stare at a rave, you stick out.

The lead vampire at the secondary exit lifted his head. His eyes shone flatly, the black of the hunting aura eating the irises and spreading into the whites, oddly like oily rainbows on wet pavement. The older ones have those black oily eyes pretty much all the time, but it takes a while for the younger ones to develop it.

He sniffed, aristocratic nostrils flaring, dark curls falling over his forehead.

Oh shit. "Secondary exit blocked," I muttered. "Switching to Plan C."

"Wait." It wasn't often I heard Christophe sound baffled. "What's plan—"

The curly-headed vampire stopped sniffing. His head moved a little, and he looked right at me. His lips moved, and I knew what he was saying.

I swear to God I heard him, too, a whisper bypassing my ears and sliding right into the center of my brain.

"*Svetocha.*"

The name for what I was—part vampire, part human girl, poisonous to suckers and all kick ass once I bloom and finish getting trained.

If I survived tonight, that is.

I swallowed hard, wished I hadn't. "Plan C is where I improvise," I said through the sudden thickness of danger candy, and bolted.

Chapter Two

You'd think I'd feel good about being able to turn a Chelsea warehouse rave into complete and utter chaos in under fifteen seconds.

I didn't.

I went over the bar in a flying leap, my boots barely kissing its glass surface. There was no liquor here, just overpriced bottles of tap water and energy drinks in shiny cans. The bartender, a beefy guy who was probably pretty upset at being stuck here instead of at a real bar, held a baseball bat the size of a small tree. He was yelling something, but I couldn't hear him over the fire alarm and I was already past him anyway. The crush toward the doors set off by my yanking the jury-rigged alarm—I hadn't actually been sure it would work— might keep the suckers off me for a few more moments.

Instead of hunting helpless humans tonight, they were going to be hunting me. I was hoping I wasn't as helpless as I felt right at the moment.

Dad's voice, showing up like it always did when I needed to

figure out what to do next, and fast. *Don't think about that, Dru-girl. Thinkin' slows you down. Move.*

They had to have somewhere to bring things in behind the bar. I saw the door and dove for it, a splintering crash behind me audible through the wall of noise masquerading as music plus the whoop of the alarm.

The suckers had hit the bar. For a moment I wondered and worried about the bartender, but I couldn't for long. I was too busy.

"What are you doing?" Christophe sounded calm. But I needed all my breath for running. "Never mind, *kochana*. I can hear you breathing. All right."

Hearing him, cool and collected in my ear, was comforting. I always work better with someone telling me what to do, I guess. At least when there were vampires behind me. It was like that when I was with Dad, too—with him doing the directing, I could just calm down and focus.

The door behind the bar flew open and I piled down groaning wooden stairs. The noise decreased, partly because the migraine attack they called "music" was cut short on a squeal of feedback. I found myself in a kind-of basement. Concrete walls, crates of bottled water, other shapes I couldn't identify.

They have to bring the supplies in somewhere, or else I just trapped myself. But I saw another set of rickety wide stairs and a ramp going up to a wide metal double-door thing, the kind you walk over on the sidewalk, on your way to somewhere else.

At least, people walk over them without thinking twice. I try not to. You never can tell.

It took me half a second to see it was padlocked.

Shit. But I was going too fast to care. And behind me, I heard a high glassy scream of rage that went straight through my head.

A *nosferat's* hunting cry. It speared through my temples and twisted, hard.

I yelled, too, put my head down, and drove for the doors. Terror is good for fueling the aspect. I felt it, like warm oil sliding down my skin, the world suddenly closed under a layer of clear plastic goop. I thought it was the world that slowed down until Christophe explained that no, it was just me going too fast. After I "bloomed" I'd be able to switch it on at will.

I couldn't wait. But for right now—

The padlock snapped. I hit the doors like a bomb, each step splintering as my Doc Martens slammed down. A flash of red pain, my yell cut off in midstride, and Christophe saying something in my ear but I couldn't hear it, the words were stretched out like taffy.

Not only that, but the shock of busting the doors open jolted the earpiece off. It went skittering away, and I leapt, boots hitting the pavement as the metal doors clanged down on either side. I'd just jumped up out from under the sidewalk like a human-sized jack-in-the-box, and the screaming started.

Now move that ass, Dru-girl! Dad's *don't worry about the ammo, worry about running* tone, like that time we were outside Baton Rouge and the zombies had shown up.

Oh, but it hurt to think about Dad. And zombies. And everything.

The crowd would provide some cover, but not enough. Neon ran against glass, streaking oddly because I was moving so fast, scarf fluttering and snapping in my back draft, pulled tight against my throat. This part of the city was alive and thumping, other nightclubs spilling out onto the street and people everywhere. There's a skill to running through a crowd, but you don't have to use it when you're streaking along like *djamphir* do. Instead, you just have to avoid hitting anyone.

You could really hurt someone or throw them out into traffic. But there's another reason you try to avoid hitting someone—because it'll slow you down. And you can't have that when a bunch of vampires are chasing you. The gum in my mouth had turned into a hard piece of flavorless glue. My teeth tingled as the aspect rose, slicking over me and spurring me on. My mother's locket bounced, cool metal kissing my breastbone.

At least in a skirt I could really move it. Jeans sometimes get a little tight. But I was booking so hard I was glad of every inch of movement the dress could give me. I jagged around the corner, hit the crosswalk, and leapt. A silver BMW hit the brakes, they had the green light, my boots thudded into the hood, and I used it like a springboard, crumpling the sheet metal. I heard the high screeching cry behind me. It drove glass spikes through my brain and tried to dig in, twisting and tearing, but I didn't slow down.

Training's good for that. When a situation occurs, Dad always said, you don't rise to the occasion. You sink to the level of your training.

I *did* snap my head aside and spit the gum free, wished I hadn't because my saliva immediately dried up and the taste of wax citrus was worse than ever.

Head for the Park, you can lose them in the Park. And that'll get you closer to the Schola, plus the other djamphir *can night-hunt around you. That's a great plan, really wunderbar, now let's see if it'll work.* The world stuttered and slid around me, like I was on a greased glass plate. Another hunting cry lifted, whistulating at the end like a kettle with a busted flap. The two groups inside the club had to be hunters, and there were others on the prowl tonight. They were calling in reinforcements. Two *djamphir* combat units and a logistical team weren't going to be able to handle this, and now that the *nosferat* knew they were after a *svetocha*, they wouldn't stop.

Which made getting the hell out of Dodge the best idea around. But it also meant heading for Chelsea Park was a *bad* idea, not enough cover, I had to think fast but there wasn't anywhere else to go except vaguely north and hope for the best.

Running. The air was made of diesel scorch, a stitch hovering just outside my ribs, ready to grab me as soon as the clear goop over the world snapped aside and I was left with just human speed.

That's not good, not good not good—

But I kept going. I had no choice.

The world rang like a wet wineglass stroked just right, and I heard an owl's soft passionless *who? Who?* A streak of white coalesced overhead, feathers shading themselves in like a fast-forward of a charcoal artist at work. The owl's yellow eyes took fire, and it wheeled in a tight circle overhead. Then it shot away like a rocket, and I held off the inevitable *snap* of the world taking back its usual slow speed with a tearing mental effort.

It was like being with werwulfen on one of their daylight runs that starts in the green blur of Central Park. Flashes smearing by, an openmouthed old lady, a group of college kids on the corner, a Chinese restaurant with a pirate ship on its sign, each just a compressed bullet of smeared information. The owl—Gran's owl, though it was my aspect taking animal form—nipped smartly to the right and disappeared into the open maw of a subway entrance.

Bad idea, Dru.

But I'd never doubted Gran's owl before. I flashed over the pavement, each step making a weird smacking sound, and saw why the owl was leading me there.

Because there were paper-cutout black shadows of *nosferat* leaping upstreet as well as down, and I'd be caught between them and the ones behind me like a rat in a cage if I didn't figure something out right quick.

I put my head down and streaked for the subway entrance. Just before I hit the top of the stairs, another howl lifted into the night. This one was pure and cold, digging through layers of humanity and tickling the furry thing on four legs that lurks under the thin veneer of civilization in you, me, *everyone*.

The wulfen were out, and they'd heard the *nosferat* making a ruckus. Thank God.

It didn't mean I'd survive this, but my chances just went up.

My purse bounced against my side and my fists pumped. The scarf slipped, seed pearls scratching at my windpipe. I clattered down the stairs, my feet only touching every fifth or sixth one. There was a half-turn, I almost hit the wall, leapt the iron railing in the middle, cleared the turnstile where you were supposed to swipe your card, and landed on the platform with a jolt. Almost overbalanced, scrambled, and I'm pretty sure I was giving the whole three people on the platform a good shot of my undies because the skirt was flipping and flapping like a flag in a high wind.

The train had just pulled in, a streak of butter-yellow light and screaming filthy silver. I nipped smartly through the doors as they closed and found myself in an empty, urine-smelling subway car. Orange plastic seats stood in neat, tired rows, and graffiti scarred the walls.

The claws of a side stitch tangled in my ribs, sweat standing out in great clear drops on my skin. At least my hair was still mostly up. Curls fell in my face, streaked with gold as the aspect blurred over my skin with warm, loving hands. My ribs flickered with humming-bird breaths, while my heart felt like it was going to kick out of my chest and do a cancan right there.

The train heaved away just as I caught flickers of shadowy movement near the turnstile. A flash of ivory teeth and wide black gelatin-gleaming eyes as the *nosferat* snarled, then the train plunged into the tunnel and the only thing I could see was my own reflection on the window. I looked scared to death, high hectic color blooming on my cheeks and the eyeliner Nathalie had talked me into giving me raccoon eyes. My mother's locket gleamed sharply, a chip of ice against my sweating skin. The stitch in my side retreated a little, but I couldn't stop gasping.

I tried to look everywhere at once. Reached up, touched my ear. Nothing but the sharp edges of a diamond stud met my fingertips. *Dammit.* I remembered the earpiece skittering away now.

I pulled my skirt down, tried to control my breathing. Pulled at the scarf to loosen it a little. I wasn't an idiot enough to think I was out of the woods yet. If they wanted me bad enough, they could certainly chase a train. I let out a high nervous laugh, grabbing a pole as the train flung itself into a long downhill curve.

Plan C wasn't turning out so bad. I was still breathing.

A thump from the car behind me brought my head up. Was it just subway noise, or . . .

I considered spitting again, the taste of danger candy was so thick. *Definitely* not out of the woods yet.

Were my chances better staying put or moving? Well, duh, moving. I headed for the front of the car, my legs about as starchy as rubber noodles. It felt like one too many hits of Dad's Jim Beam, the world turning to a loosey-goosey carnival ride. There was another thump in the car behind me, and I still couldn't tell if it was train noise or a *nosferat* looking to take my head off the hard way.

Huh. Is there an easy way to take someone's head off? It's one of those unanswerable questions, like why hot dogs come in eight-packs and buns come in tens. Someone had asked me that a while ago, *is there an easy way?*

My heart squeezed down on itself, hard. I shoved the feeling away. I couldn't afford to think about *him*. I needed all my wits in one basket right now.

I eyed the door. There was a release catch, and if I bailed, I could be pretty sure it would hurt and then I'd be down here in the tunnel. In the dark, or so close to complete dark it doesn't matter.

What a choice. *Nosferat* in a rollicking subway car, or bailing and possibly breaking something, then having to deal with *nosferat* and trains in a dark tunnel. "Stick to the plan," I muttered, digging in my tiny little purse. "Stick to the goddamn plan. Yeah."

Hiro wasn't just going to have kittens. He was going to have little baby penguins, too. And Bruce would just look disappointed. And Christophe . . .

He's on his way. You know he is. You've just got to keep your head attached until he gets here.

Easier said than done. The brakes squealed; I rocked sideways as the train slowed. Coming up on the next stop. My fingers closed on the teensy disposable cell phone just as a third thud, this one accompanied with a screech of tearing metal, came from the car behind me. I dropped the phone, glanced back, and saw the claws sticking through the back wall. They retracted, then maggot-white fingers squirmed through and started tearing at the back end of the car like it was tinfoil.

Run first, call in later.

I was suddenly, deeply glad there were no civilians in this car. The train jolted, slowing, and I grabbed for the door release.

Keep your arms and legs inside the ride at all times, sure. Worked great in an amusement park. Not so great right now.

The aspect blurred lovingly over me as I wrenched at the door, metal squealing and tearing along with the brakes. The station burst open like a flower, lit by fluorescents, a long flight of stairs going up. I kicked the door twice; on the second kick it exploded out and I grabbed the side of the hole it left behind. The door flew into a tiled wall, hit with megaton force. Dust and sharp tile shards puffed up. I leapt, just as the *nosferat* burst into the car.

My feet hit first, and training curled me into a ball. I rolled, shedding momentum and erasing some skin on my knee and my right arm, came up running. The scarf tore free, its little pearls scraping some skin loose as well. Hit the stairs at warp speed, my boots making an odd hollow ringing against the concrete. Slapping bootsteps behind me, too heavy and fast to be human.

In movies, the girl being chased looks over her shoulder while the thing comes for her. The urge to do that never occurs to me. For one thing, it'll slow me down too much.

For another, if I'm going to be hit, I don't want to know. I want to be running flat-out when it happens, not stumbling because I'm glancing back like a moron.

The world slowed down again, but grudgingly. I was too tired, I was terrified, but the edge of emotion that let me use superhuman speed was wearing off. Adrenaline can only take you so far.

I jumped the turnstile at the head of the stairs. Gran's owl was nowhere in sight. I was on my own here, and the *nosferat* was right behind me, footfalls echoing and its glassine snarl bouncing off the tiled walls. A half-turn and another short flight, and the night breathed over my hair, full of exhaust fumes and the smell of danger. Wax oranges filled my mouth, I swallowed again and wished I hadn't, and the touch blazed inside my skull.

My feet tangled together.

If they hadn't, the *nosferat* would have hit me. As it was, he went tumbling overhead as I fell, his claws kissing my hair and shearing a few curls as he twisted like a cat in midleap. I rolled, erasing more skin on my leg, gained my feet with a convulsive lurch, and stumbled back. The street was dark, residential, but I could hear the neon and the clubs pounding just a short distance away, a thunderstorm pulse.

The *nosferat* landed neatly, kneeling with one hand spread against the wet pavement. Fine rain misted down, and his black eyes gleamed in a streetlamp's uncertain light. He was blond, jewels of water hanging on his fashionable razor-layered cut. His clothes were worth more than a month's running money, Armani unless I missed my guess, and the shoes were alligator.

Bastard. Even gators don't deserve that. Especially when most of their meat was probably dumped back into the swamp to rot after the jerks got the hide.

I inhaled, my hands coming up and everything narrowing to a single point around me. This was it. This was what I'd been training for—facing a *nosferat* on a dark street.

Getting a little of my own back. Some revenge.

If I hadn't been playing bait tonight I'd've had a gun, or a pair of *malaika*. Even my silver-loaded switchblade would've been nice. But no, it was *mano a mano* for this.

Great.

The *nosferat's* lips curled back, ivory teeth glowing. Those teeth grabbed all available light, pulling it in from the darkened street and swirling it against his lips. The snarl made his pretty teenage face into a caricature of hatred. I loosened my knees.

If you've got a Plan D, Dru, now would be a good time.

I didn't. In a few seconds he was going to spring, I was going to do my best to stay out of his way, and I'd either be jumping to stay ahead of him—or very dead.

Another snarl, this one low and incredibly loud. It came from behind me on a hot draft, thudding through my bones like a bass beat from big speakers. I never thought I'd be happy to hear that sound.

Or feel a werwulf breathing in my hair.

Of course Christophe would have let Ash loose. He was like that—always two steps ahead. As long as he was taking care of things, I didn't need to worry.

Much.

The Broken werwulf slid a few steps to the side. His narrow head dipped, the silvery streak glowing just like the *nosferat's* teeth. Even on all fours, his shoulders bulked and reached the lower curve of my ribs. His growl didn't change in pitch, but it seemed to swell. Like his chest did. He got even bigger, bulking up.

Graves would have started muttering about mass-conversion ratios and irrationality.

That was the wrong thing to think. Because sick, furious heat welled up inside me. My hands, held loose and ready, turned into fists. The bloodhunger woke up, stroking the back of my palate. This was the other way to make the aspect come alive, with anger.

No, not just anger.

Rage.

A thin thread of heat kissed my upper arm. I'd scraped *hard* against the pavement, and I was bleeding. There was another way to fuel the aspect.

Bloodhunger. Why they call it that when it's technically thirst, I don't know.

I lifted one fist, licked along the meat of my palm, a flicker of disgust quickly shelved. The red fluid coated my tongue, hit the back of my throat, and the *nosferat* jerked forward. He blurred into motion, and Ash grabbed the pavement and flung himself forward, too.

But as fast as Ash was, I was faster. The aspect crackled into life, bloodhunger spurring me. I leapt, and I hung in the air for a long heaving second, the night turning soft, legs pulled up and left hand forward, the tips of my fingers tingling as my fingernails sharpened. My wrists ached, a sweet sharp pain.

When I bloomed, I'd have claws.

Someone *crunched* into me from the side. I tumbled through air, oddly weightless, and landed on something soft. We rolled, and I punched him twice before I realized it was a friendly.

I gained my feet in a convulsive lunge, my boots scraping wet concrete. Beside me, the werwulf shrank, hair receding, and Shanks cursed as he grabbed my arm. His eyes were orange lamps. He flung his head back and howled as the change ran over him again, fur crawling fluidly over his skin and his bones crackling as he bulked up.

I tore away from him. Out in the street, as if they were on a stage, Ash and the blond *nosferat* circled each other. The Broken werwulf moved with supple fluidity, the *nosferat* with jerky marionette grace. One of them would pause for a half-second, or twitch forward, and the other would counter with a quick movement.

Another wulf cry, this one very close and high up. Probably a rooftop; wulfen like to get some height while hunting. It meant the cavalry was coming up over the hill.

Thank God. I might survive this after all.

Shanks had dropped something with a clatter, two sharp wooden lengths. He'd been carrying *malaika*. Long, slightly-curved, hawthorn wood swords. Just the thing for killing a perky sucker.

No way. I can't be this lucky.

Except I could. Because the wulfen were looking out for me.

I was going to kiss Shanks—on the cheek—as soon as I got out of this. My hands closed around the hilts; I scooped them up and let out a short sharp cry. It hit a high soprano note, uncomfortably like a *nosferat's* crystalline scream, and if I'd had time to think about it, that might have upset me.

As if he'd read my mind, Ash dropped his shoulders and snaked in for the kill. The *nosferat*, as if sensing something amiss, actually hopped back like a frog. The *malaika* spun, sharp oiled wood cleaving air with a low sweet sound, and just before I landed, my left-hand blade sheared through undead flesh.

Well, technically not undead, because they can procreate. But it sounds good.

My feet hit pavement and I spun, right-hand blade flickering out like a snake's tongue. He was quick, bending back like an impossibly boneless gymnast. I heard Christophe's voice again.

Faster, but precise. Precision in everything, little bird.

To use *malaika*, you have to think in circles. More properly, you have to think about the disks the blades make when you spin them. Each blade is curved just a little, a slashing weapon, and they're supposed to be both shield and weapon.

Traditionally, a *svetocha's* weapons.

The *nosferat* darted in, claws chiming off my right-hand blade. The left sliced down, a pattern unreeling through my arms. You swing from the hip, just like in baseball. Not that I was any good with a bat except in the time-honored sport of home defense. That time with the zombies it'd been a baseball bat before Dad got to the ammo—

The blade bit deep. Hawthorn wood is venomous to *nosferat*, deadly just like the happy stuff in a *svetocha*'s blood. I could probably weaken this sucker just by exhaling in his presence, once I bloomed. But right now I was stuck with an unreliable aspect and my speed beginning to flag despite the spur of bloodhunger.

Ash darted in, and his claws flickered as they opened up the *nosferat*'s belly. The thing screamed, a high thin cry of hatred, and I brought my crossed *malaika* down. It was a risky move, and Christophe would freak out because I never pulled it off right in practice.

This wasn't practice. And this one time, I pulled it off. The blades turned into scissors, and they cut *deep* on both sides of the blond's throat. The sucker's cry cut off midway on a gurgle, its head lolling back and dangling from a strip of meat, and caustic black blood sprayed. I skipped back, both *malaika* still held at the ready. Ash fell back, too, still growling and flanking me. More footsteps, but I knew who they were.

The wulfen flowed down the street, some of them dropping from rooftops. Their lean dark forms spilled between shadows, and their eyes were orange and yellow lamps. They descended on the struggling *nosferat*, and the wet ripping sounds were enough to fill my throat with bile.

At least it got the sweet copperheat of my own blood off my tongue.

Ash moved closer. He wasn't growling anymore. The inky textures of his pelt moved as he did, the change rippling through him but not all the way. He still couldn't turn back into a boy.

On the other hand, Shanks could. He halted just beside me, shaking his head. His dark hair flew, settled into its usual emo-boy fringe across his forehead. "You *hit* me."

"Sorry about that." I didn't relax, staring at the knot of shaggy forms. They parted, and there was nothing but a jumbled collection of sucker bits, torn Armani, and a lake of black blood. "Really."

He massaged his jaw, shifting his weight from one long leg to the other. He'd probably bruise, but it wouldn't stay more than an hour or two. "Yeah, well. Congratulations."

For what? My arms relaxed a little. The tips of the wooden swords did not touch the ground, though. Christophe was real keen on that. "What?"

"Your first kill, ennit?" His shoulder bumped mine. His chest was narrow and pale under the open corduroy coat, hairless now that he wasn't under the Change. "And Reynard not around to see it."

Oh. I didn't want to think about it that way. My entire body sagged. Using superhuman strength and speed is no picnic sometimes. When you don't have the aspect to cushion you, things get real sore real quick. And you don't get the great part of adrenaline dump after a fight, the part where you feel like you've kicked the world's ass.

No, you get the morning after, when you wake up with bruises and pulled muscles in places you didn't even know you *had.* "You guys were on sweep?"

"Nah." He shook his head, subtracting the *malaika* from me with quick grace. I gave them up without a peep—if he was taking them, it meant the fight was over. The other wulfen slid out of changeform and became boys again, moving into a loose guard ring on the off chance that there were other suckers around. "I just got a few of the boys together. We decided to hang out at a safe distance in case things got interesting. You being bait and all."

I was so relieved I didn't even want to throw a fit over everyone thinking I couldn't handle myself. I twitched like I was going to hug him, but he stepped away.

I tried not to feel disappointed. I probably still smelled angry, and wulfen are cautious about getting physical. PDA isn't their thing unless it's rough, careless, or between kin. Instead, I tucked more stray curls behind my ears. "Glad you did. Did you bring Ash, or was it Christophe?"

"Bring him? Nah. Brought himself." Now Shanks looked amused, one corner of his mouth curling up. "I just figured you didn't want the door to his room busted again."

Well, that answered that question. It hadn't been Christophe at all. "Great." My shoulders slumped. I felt like I'd fought through both World Wars without a break.

Ash glanced up, a quick canine twist of his narrow head. He was oddly clean, no vampire blood on his fur. He proceeded to slump against me, almost throwing my off my feet. For such a big shaggy being, he was incredibly catlike and precise about placing his paws. And incredibly doglike when it came to leaning and gazing up adoringly.

Nosferat go fast, when they go. This one was just a bubbling mass of stuff that would vaporize into ash when the sun came up. He hadn't been particularly old, either. Just under a hundred years, if his corpse was reacting like that. All wet rot instead of dry-dusty.

I just killed him. Or I helped kill him, it's the same thing. The shaking was new. *He would've killed me. I just killed him first.*

I reached down, wrapped my fingers in Ash's fur. Braced myself. "Jesus."

"You gonna throw up?" Shanks looked down at me, his lean face shadowed. One corner of his thin mouth quirked up again. He looked just about too pleased with himself. "That's real common the first time."

Ash growled, but softly.

Now I was cold. My legs were naked, and the dress didn't cover much. Sweat on bare skin cooled in the faint night breeze. At least the dress was pretty okay—I hadn't bled on it.

Much.

My mother's locket was skin-warm now, resting against my breastbone and suddenly heavy.

I shivered. "Let's get the hell out of here."

"Sure. Wanna take the subway?" He laughed, a sarcastic little bark. "Kidding, kidding! Let's get you home."

CHAPTER THREE

The **Schola Prima** masquerades as a hoity-toity New York all-boy private school, but you'll never find the students slumming with their crested blazers thrown over a shoulder. I mean, sure, you'll see them, but you won't know they're from the Schola because they just look like attractive teenage boys in civvies, doing whatever mysterious things teenage boys do. If you ask them where they go to school—nobody asks, but if you *did*—they'd lie. And if you ever saw them taking on the suckers or anything else that goes bump in the night, well . . . you'd either be dead or traumatized by the experience, and you'd know to keep your mouth shut. Or you'd end up in a loony bin or something. That's not New York, that's universal. People just don't want to see, and the people in power collude.

Still, I think only in the Big Apple could you drop a huge white-pillared school for the half-vampire and werwulf hunters of the dark forces onto a big piece of prime parklike Manhattan real estate and have nobody even *care*.

I dropped down in the red-cushioned chair. To be properly insouciant, I should've put my feet up on the glossy conference table, but the skirt was short enough I didn't want to. Even if every guy on the Council was old enough to be my grandfather. Or older.

And none of them look a day over twenty-five. Most of them look about seventeen. Christophe muttered sometimes about being trapped in a teenage body, but I hadn't had the courage to ask him the million questions *that* brought up. It's just one of those things.

I wondered what I'd end up looking like once I bloomed. I couldn't even guess. If I had to be stuck in my own skinny, gawky, coltish body forever . . . well. It probably wouldn't be so bad.

I wouldn't mind a *little* more in the chest, though. But wild horses wouldn't drag that out of me. Ever.

"Unacceptable," Hiro said quietly. The word bounced off the table's shiny surface. His long caramel-colored fingers were wrapped tightly around a white coffee mug, knuckles whitening a little. He was pale under his coloring, and his mouth was set. He looked like a disapproving samurai. "If the wulfen hadn't been there—"

"They *were* there." I leaned my head back against the chair's high carved back. My hair was falling down, and my arm and leg were both scabbed over so the happy stuff in my blood wouldn't drive them all nuts. "Shanks isn't about to let me go out alone. Just like you guys."

Bruce sat ramrod straight in the chair to my left, his proud beaky nose lifted just a little. "How did they lose you? How did Reynard—"

"It wasn't his fault. I bolted because the suckers were covering both entrances, and they'd marked me before the combat units could do any penetration. I had to improvise." I wished I'd had a chance to change, but debriefing came first. And it was looking like they were calling the operation a failure, even though we'd lured the suckers in that slice of the rave scene out and killed them. "I lost my earpiece while busting out of the cellar, and—"

Hiro set his cup down and said something quietly that sounded like a curse. He leaned forward, setting his elbows against the table, and dropped his head into his hands. His shoulders actually shook under his gray silk shirt.

It was amazing. He was always so calm.

The coffee smelled good, but I didn't want it. I kept going. "—and I escaped. I was only followed by one sucker; stayed ahead of him long enough for Shanks and the others to move in. Ash was there, and Shanks brought my *malaika*. It actually went really well. And we're not going to have any more kids going down under sucker attacks from *that* bunch, too." Which was the important thing, right?

I mean, it was to me.

The Council room was long and windowless, the buffet up along one wall empty except for the silver samovar and a carafe of hot water for tea. It was always the same in here, right down to the uncomfortable, highly carved, thronelike wooden chairs. Bruce steepled his fingers in front of his chest. The sharply handsome lines of his dark face all conspired to make him a picture of disappointment. How he could look so official, even wearing blue jeans, was beyond me.

"You are far too precious to risk yourself in this manner," he said, for the fiftieth time. "You are the only *svetocha* we—"

Oh, Lord. Not this again. "I didn't *risk* myself. The operation went off successfully, at least as far as my part. I got my first kill. Aren't you even going to congratulate me?" I managed to sound like I was proud of killing, instead of half sick with a stomach full of nervous bile.

Hiro stood up, scraping his chair back and tugging at his cuffs to make his sleeves fall right. He must buy those shirts in job lots, because they're all he wears. Sometimes, if he's getting really American, he'll wear dark-wash jeans instead of the loose black trousers. But it's always a high-collared gray silk shirt and those weird black shoes, with the big toe separated from the rest of the toes and the grippy soles. I was working up the courage to ask him where he got them, Chinatown or something?

So far, there hadn't been a good time for that little conversation.

I was saved further lecturing by the door at the far end of the room opening. Christophe stalked in, his aspect sleeking his hair back and a colorless fume of rage boiling off him like heat-haze above pavement.

Blue eyes, burning like they were going to set fire to the rest of him. His face worked together well, every line perfectly proportioned to give him just enough handsomeness without going over the top into "too pretty to take seriously." When he was under the aspect, his hair was dark, lying close to the skull; when he relaxed, it sprang up and the blond streaks came through. I caught my breath.

Black sweater, a pair of jeans—no sucker blood on him. He was completely clean.

Good. My shoulders relaxed a little.

He didn't even break stride. "Bruce, Hiro. We have confirmed kills."

"Including mine?" I tried to find a more comfortable way to slouch in the chair, but nothing worked.

He brushed past Hiro, the aspect boiling between the two of them and Hiro's head jerking aside like he smelled something bad. Christophe descended on me, grabbed my shoulders, and hauled me out of the chair. It went over backward and landed with a gun-crack sound, and Bruce let out a yell and shot to his feet.

"Are you damaged? Are you *hurt?*" Christophe held me at arm's length, his fingers gentle but iron-hard. He checked me from top to toe, and his eyes narrowed when he saw the dried blood crusting on my arm and the scrape on my leg.

"I'm *fine.*" I said it a little louder than I necessarily *had* to, but I didn't try to shake him off. It went better when I let him reassure himself that I was okay. "Really. I did the scissors thing right, too. Shanks had *malaika.* Ash was there too."

"You are *never* playing bait again." A muscle flicked once in his cheek. "Never. Do you hear me, *moj maly ptasku?* They swarmed the club. They knew you were there!"

"Of course they knew. I've been going raving for two *weeks* to draw out this group of happy little bloodsucking assholes. We made *sure* they knew. Plus, they've done lure-and-kill at every rave from Chelsea to Newark we've been able to check." I leaned forward, but his arms didn't bend. "I'm fine, Christophe. Only one of them chased me. I got away and—"

He looked about ready to explode. "I should never have allowed—"

Oh, for Chrissake. "Allow? What's this *allow?* I was ready, wasn't I? Next time it'll be better. I got my first kill, Christophe! I used the *malaika*! Ash was there, too!"

Well, that was the wrong thing to say. His mouth turned down like I'd just offered him a plate of caterpillars. "I will not trust your safety to the Silverhead."

"Yeah, well, he's more faithful than *some* I could name." I shut my mouth, but it was too late. The damage was done. And I'd been sucking at keeping my mouth to myself lately.

Christophe's face slammed shut, almost audibly. The aspect fled, blond streaks moving back through his hair as if painted by invisible brushes. He examined me one more time, let go of me finger by finger. "I trust you're not flinging accusations, *Milady*."

That actually managed to hurt me. "Of course not. I just . . . god-dammit, Christophe, can't you be happy? I got away! I fought! I did what you've been training me for!"

"Nobody's disputing that." As usual, Bruce stepped in to smooth things over. He was good at that. I should be taking lessons. "You did very well. We're just worried for your safety, Milady."

I wished I could tell him to quit *calling* me that.

It was what they called Anna. Each time one of them used the word it was like a pinch in an already-sore spot. The word bruised me on a daily basis.

Christophe leaned forward. "You shouldn't have—"

Oh, he was *so* not going to Monday-morning quarterback me. "What, I should have just stayed in there and waited for them to move in and kill me before the combat units could get to me? Then I would have had to fight off six of them instead of just one."

"I was on the roof," he said quietly. "You don't think I'd send you in alone?"

Well, it was kind of comforting knowing he'd been there, and the sound of outside I'd gotten through the earpiece made sense now. But still. "You were supposed to! You were home control! You said I was ready!" *Ready for an easy operation, ready for the closest thing to safe you can get while hunting suckers!*

"You are ready, but not without me." His hands flickered forward, and before I knew it, they were cupping my face. He was so damna-bly fast. "I would not put my little bird in the jaws of a trap without being near enough to make sure it wouldn't close on her." Warm skin against mine, and he leaned in. He *did* smell like a Christmas candle, warm apple spice. It was familiar, and comforting.

He reeled me in. Our foreheads touched.

For the first time since the sun went down that evening, I felt safe. He breathed out and I breathed in, and the shaking in me went away little by little. I was vaguely aware of the others watching, but it didn't seem important. Nothing seemed important when he did this.

Except sometimes I wished he was someone else. Someone in a long dark coat, with the smell of wulf and wild and strawberry incense on him.

Which was, again, the wrong thought. My chest tightened, and a shiver went through me.

Christophe murmured something I didn't quite catch. I squeezed my eyes shut and tried to pretend it didn't matter. And also tried to pretend most of me wasn't running with soft lightning because he was so close. It was like my hormones had decided to stage a revolt whenever he got within a ten-foot radius.

And wasn't *that* confusing and unwelcome? Yessir, it was. Right next to being the best thing I'd felt since the night before Dad's dead meatless fingers tapped at the glass on our frozen back door, way up in the Dakotas.

The night everything went sideways and my life imploded.

He finally pulled away a little and pressed his lips to my forehead, a soft touch. "Nathalie and Benjamin are outside. I'll be along."

In other words, I was dismissed. Bruce was looking up over my head, his face set and a little embarrassed. Hiro had folded his arms and turned, staring at the samovar's gleam.

"What about the rest of the Council?" I tried not to sound petulant. Probably failed miserably.

Christophe's half-smile would have been chilling if his eyes hadn't been so soft. He never looked at anyone else like this, and it was a mystery to me how the same blue eyes could be so cold one moment and warm and giving the next. "Would you care to wait for them? I am certain there will be an argument about the night's events, at which I will be taken to account for risking your safety. It should be most entertaining."

He had a point. "Okay. I'll leave you to take care of that, then."

Christophe actually *grinned*. Without the aspect, his teeth were perfect, white, and wholly human. "I thought so. Happy to be of service, *skowroneczko moja*. Tomorrow, bright and early. More *malaika* practice."

"Great." I scrubbed at my forehead with the back of my right hand and scooped the tiny purse off the table. "Bruce, Hiro. Sorry to worry you." That was as far as I'd go.

Bruce nodded. His aspect had retreated, and he was just a cute Middle Eastern guy in a green cable-knit sweater and fashionably frayed designer jeans. "We'll celebrate your first kill, Milady. It's tradition, after all."

The sick feeling returned. "No. I mean, no thanks. It's okay. Really."

And then I got out of there, feeling Christophe's eyes on me all the way.

CHAPTER FOUR

"**The blood won't** come out of this." Nathalie sighed, tilting her sleek dark head to the side. She held the silver dress up with delicate fingers, as if it was made of tissue paper. "We'll have to go back to Nordy's."

"Not again." I groaned, dropping down in front of the vanity. A shower and half an hour of *t'ai chi* in the middle of the room had settled me down, kind of. I didn't even mind Nat watching, since she very obviously didn't look at me while I did the familiar movements. "I won't do it, you can't make me."

"You'd think I was taking you to an execution, not shopping. Jeez." She grinned over my shoulder, the water-clear mirror holding our reflections. I was flushed and tangled, rangy like my dad, my blue Rolling Stones T-shirt torn but the hole-worn jeans I'd shimmied gratefully into mercifully hidden. Nathalie, on the other hand, looked like she belonged in a catalog. Curvy in all the right places, she wore a set of rosy-pink silk pajamas. You could tell she was werwulfen just by the way she moved and the supple grace of her shoulders as she flicked the dress again, laying it over a straight-backed wooden chair in front of the stripped-pine desk. *"Really,* Dru."

"It's the same thing," I muttered.

She could even make a shoulder holster look like a planned part of her pajama outfit. The coffee-colored leather number carrying a 9mm that she had on today moved as she rolled her shoulders back once, settling them. She ghosted over the pale wooden flooring and picked up a silver-backed hairbrush. This was the part of the night I alternately dreaded and looked forward to most.

"I can take care of—" I began. But she took a handful of my hair and started brushing, just the last few inches and working up.

"It's traditional. Before Anna, each *svetocha* had an honor guard of wulfen girls, too. Good way for us to get out of the compound, get to see a lot of boys, and you know . . . it's bound to be lonely, being *svetocha.* I'm glad we like each other."

Yeah, well, the last girl that was around emptied an assault rifle at me. You could just open me up like a soda can. "So Anna changed all that?"

A shrug. "Slowly but surely, yeah. I think my aunt was around when it happened. She never talks about it."

I sighed. Thin blue lines of warding slid over the walls, complex patterned knots over the windows and the door. Refreshed every night, trembling under the screen of the visible, the wards were at least *one* familiar thing. I never went to bed without redoing the warding, no sir. Gran would be proud.

The fingers in my hair were soothing, and Nathalie could be trusted.

Christophe told me so. So did Shanks and Augustine. I suppose I could trust them, right? At least, Christophe hadn't been wrong yet.

I just . . . I wasn't as trusting as I used to be. I guess. Getting betrayed over and over will do that to you. Still, I liked Nat. She had her head screwed on straight, and—this was the important thing—she understood that I was gonna go mad if I stayed cooped up all the time. So she was teaching me how to play another "traditional" game, slipping out during the day and exploring. We'd started with little runs through the Schola grounds and graduated to shopping and sightseeing. With a wulfen around in broad daylight, I was as safe as possible, right?

And every single time she threw a handful of gravel at my window, inviting me to come out and play, it was easier to trust her a little more.

The brush slipped through my hair. Nat could take the curling mass and make it look elegant, put together an outfit that looked actually *fashionable* in seconds, and she was so damn organized she could have given any Marine sergeant a run for their money. And I had to admit, it was nice to have a girl around.

One who wasn't trying to kill me, that is. I've never had close girlfriends. Why bother, with Dad and me moving so much?

Christophe had actually argued me into having someone else around. *I would not choose one who couldn't be trusted. You'll enjoy it. It will help me worry less.*

That was the big argument, trotted out whenever he wanted to mushroom-cloud me into something. I let out another long heave of a sigh and felt the night's tension slip away from me. It was in the long dead stretch between three and four a.m., quiet time. Just like the shoal between three and six in the afternoon, when everyone in the hot part of the world is taking a siesta.

The Schola is oddly reversed. Nights were our days, because sunlight is safer to sleep in. My body clock was adjusting slowly. Sixteen and a half years of being diurnal is a hard habit to shake.

"You have such beautiful hair." Nathalie lifted a handful of it. "These highlights. My God. You'd look great with a shorter, layered cut . . ."

I glanced up at the pair of *maliaka* hanging in a leather harness next to the vanity. They'd been my mother's, and they were beautiful. I didn't know where the ones Shanks had handed me had come from. "No way." *Gran would kill me.* It was a habitual, instinctive thought. I hadn't had more than a trim in *years.* "If it's short, it ends up in my face all the time. Eating hair is so not cool."

She rolled her cat-tilted, beautifully expressive eyes. "That's what *product* is for. You kill me, you really kill me. Hey, I think we should paint your nails. Not pink, though. I'm thinking a dark red, because your skin tone—"

I shivered. "Not red. Besides, I don't have time." I glanced at the mirror. Her skin was perfect, poreless, and her sleek dark hair, parted on the side, looked like she'd just stepped out of the salon.

I, on the other hand, was a mess of reddish-purple bruising, scrapes, tumbled tangled hair, and red spots high on my cheeks as if I had a fever. My eyes were shadowed, darker than their usual blue, as if I was thinking of something serious. And that line between my eyebrows was back. Gran would've called it an I-want line.

I tried to make my face look like I wasn't Thinking About Unpleasant Things.

Her nose wrinkled. "You *make* time for self-care, Mil—ah, Dru. Jeez." The brush worked through my hair, slipping through the curls as if they always behaved. They did for her. It was like my hair was a traitor. She'd worked all the way up to the roots, and now started on another section.

I had to admit it was kind of nice. Like Gran brushing before she braided me up at night. Soothing.

I held up my hand. The pavement had erased skin all the way up my forearm. I was lucky I'd stopped bleeding by the time the boy *djamphir* showed up to bundle me in an SUV and get me out of the way. I'd been scabbed over good by then, thank God. Once I bloomed, I'd heal like they do—on fast-forward, shaking off damage like a duck's back sheds rainwater.

Right now, though, I was stuck with sucky human healing times.

"Ouch." Nathalie was all sympathy. "Good thing you're not going to scar."

Christophe has scars. Heat rose in my cheeks again. "Yeah, that'd be a bitch," I mumbled.

"It must burn them that the wulfen got there first. I hear the teams who managed to get inside the club were swarmed. Fifteen *nosferat*. Thank God the one after you was . . ."

"Young and sloppy?" *Fifteen of them? Christ.* I shivered. I'd only seen six. "Christophe was too tactful to say it."

"It'd be the first time he's been that." She grinned. Flash of white teeth. "I heard it was a young one you got, but plenty vicious."

"How do you hear these things?" But I knew. Shanks liked her. He got all weird when she was around.

Her face scrunched up. "The air itself brings me messages." A low sepulchral moan. "Ooooooo-OOOO-oooh!"

I snorted, laughing into my cupped hand. She kept brushing my hair, the strokes turning long once she had all the tangles out.

"Now, a braid in this, and we'll settle you down. I've sent for some hot milk. Just the thing to soothe the nerves." Soft and pleasant, her fingers slipping through the curls just as the brush did. The brush was an antique. Silver-backed, probably Victorian. I wondered if it had been my mother's too, like the *malaika*.

After dawn there would be a golden flood of sun through the skylights, spilling over the shelves and the mellow glow of the wood floor. The books were hers, and the bed had been hers, too.

I didn't mind. Sometimes I would take the books off the shelves and flip through them. Some had notations in the margins, faded schoolgirl's handwriting in blue ink. They were textbooks and studies of Real World things, and all of them were mine now.

After so many years of having nothing of Mom's but a photograph in Dad's wallet and a Holstein cow cookie jar, it was a little overwhelming. I was missing all Dad's and my old stuff, but having my mother's things . . . it was nice, and not so nice, all at the same time. Because it was like with all her things around me, I wasn't the same girl who had traveled around with Dad. I was someone else. Maybe who I could have been if she hadn't died.

If she hadn't been killed.

Nathalie's fingers were quick and deft. She had the whole mess braided in a minute and a half, and her braids didn't come out the way mine did. No, when she did it, it *stayed*. Just one of her many talents. I could almost hate her for it, if she wasn't so cool otherwise.

There was a knock at the door. Nathalie let the braid fall. On the way across the room she drew her nice little baby Glock, keeping it low and ready. She sniffed, too, audibly, as she glided on soft bare feet.

Even when she opened the door, her shoulders didn't relax.

CHAPTER FIVE

"**R**oom service," **Christophe** said pleasantly. "You take good care of her, Skyrunner."

"It's what I'm here for." Nathalie slid the gun back in its holster and took the tray. "Do you seek admittance to the lady's presence, Reynard?"

"Do I dare?" He grinned, rueful, and I touched the vanity's painted surface. Ran my fingers over the heavy silver comb, the wooden box holding tissues. It felt like sacrilege to set any of *my* stuff on here. "If the lady is so disposed, *mademoiselle.*"

"That's right, you mind your manners." Nathalie turned smartly on her heel and marched away. "Lock the door, will you? Here, Dru. Your hot milk. And look, sugar cookies. The kitchen thinks you deserve a treat."

"Sugar cookies?" That perked me right up. Milk and cookies, like I was five years old again. I didn't mind, tonight. It was actually . . . soothing. To think I was safe here, finally. At last.

"I think chocolate chip might've been a better choice, but the kitchen apparently had other ideas." Nat grinned, a flash of white teeth.

"I'm not even going to ask who does the cooking." I always wondered, though. What *was* behind that mask of billowing steam that hid the kitchen's interior?

"You don't want to know." Christophe slid the door shut. "The Broken is bedded down for the night. He's amazingly amenable. All Robert has to do is invoke your name, and he follows like a lamb."

Shanks had been slowly getting to know Ash, and they seemed to get along. Kind of. Dibs still refused to go anywhere near Ash if he wasn't wounded, and a lot of the other wulfen seemed to feel pretty much the same way.

Everyone was waiting for him to go mad and start killing people. Or run back to Sergej.

Nathalie actually shivered. The vanity had plenty of room, so she slid the tray onto it, bumping aside the brush and comb and silver-backed mirror. "Jesus."

"Quite." But Christophe was looking at me in the mirror. "How are you?"

I shrugged. It was like he just forgot about Nathalie standing there when he looked at me. I can't explain it, but if you've ever had it happen to you, you know. It's like someone is trying to look under your skin, like you're all alone with them no matter who else is in the room.

Like they're seeing nobody but you, even in a crowd.

I reached for the embossed teapot on the tray, but Nathalie got there first. She poured, taking a long deep surreptitious sniff.

Because wulfen can smell poison. Most of the time.

I rolled my eyes. There were three little porcelain cups on the tray, but I could bet Christophe wouldn't be taking a little warm milk.

He surprised me, though, by leaning over my shoulder to snatch a cookie. The draft of his apple pie smell was actually soothing. If he was here, nothing could get to me. "No weeping. If you've thrown up, you've done it privately. You're a little pale, and you smell of old blood and resignation instead of fresh spill and fear. All in all, you're taking this quite well."

Is that a compliment? What do I say? "Gee, thanks"? I picked up a cookie. Perfectly round, perfectly golden, perfectly browned on the bottom. It was kind of nice to bite into it and destroy the perfection. No shortening in *these*; I could taste real butter and crunch the sugar crystals. "Yeah." My stomach tried to close up, but now I was damned if I would let anyone know I felt like heaving. "I guess."

"Jesus, Reynard, how gruesome can you get?" Nathalie made little shooing motions with both cups. "Go *away*. Go sit over there and let her have a cup of milk."

That was another reason to like her. Christophe wasn't so intense when she was around. She was a layer of insulation, and she ordered him around with such cocky self-assurance I kind of envied her.

Christophe grinned, movie-worthy teeth glinting, and ruffled his fingers across the top of my head before grabbing another cookie and retreating to the bed. Where he dropped down, as if the whole place belonged to him, and proceeded to keep watching me.

I rolled my eyes. Nathalie fussed over me until I ate a few cookies and drank off enough milk to satisfy her. She roamed around unnecessarily putting the room to rights while I sat and ran my fingers over the vanity's edge, and when she came back to collect the tray I tried not to look relieved.

Sometimes when she pampered me I felt even more like I didn't belong here. Like someone was going to come in and tell me there had been a mistake and would I please leave now? And I'd find myself on the street outside the Schola, or sitting in that food court in the mall back in the Dakotas, shivering and trying to think of what to do next.

"I'll be back at five sharp this evening." She cast a significant glance at Christophe, winked at me. "Behave yourself."

He waved languidly. Nathalie retreated, the silver dress over her arm and the heavy tray balanced on one spread hand as if it was made of paper. I finished off the last cookie and moved the brush and comb around.

Nat swept the door closed. Christophe slid off the bed and padded across hardwood. He threw the locks, stood for a moment, and nodded. Didn't put the heavy iron bar in its brackets, though, just retreated to the bed and sank down again with a slight but very satisfied sigh.

I gathered myself up, as Gran would have said. *Come on. Ask.* I waited until I couldn't stand it anymore. "So has anyone found—"

He beat me to the punch. "If I had any news about the *loup-garou*'s whereabouts, Dru, I would have given it to you immediately. We're still looking."

"You wouldn't think the king of the vampires would be that hard to find." It was bad-tempered of me, I knew it. I just couldn't stop myself. "If Ash could find me, he could find Graves—"

"You seem to be the only person Ash is interested in finding." He didn't visibly hold on to his temper, but it was close. "America is a big place; *he* could have your friend hidden in Canada or Mexico, for all we know. Or even further afield. It's not beyond *his* power, and we don't even know that he would keep the *loup-garou* with him. We're looking. Finding Anna is challenge enough, but once we find her, we'll have more of an idea where your friend is likely to be." He let the sentence die. It was the same thing, said the same way almost every night.

I'd already tried tracking with a map of the US and a pendulum. Even with Graves's coat—I'd mended the rips and tears in it, sewn up the torn-loose sleeve—spread out under the map, it was no good. There was static interference, the touch just echoing inside my head and the pendulum moving erratically instead of swinging out and locking onto his heartbeat.

I should have known Sergej would have ways of keeping even someone with the touch from finding him, or finding someone he didn't want found. Of *course* he would. I hadn't quite worked up to using my own blood in a finding yet.

That kind of magic leaves traces someone could use to hex you right back. If things kept on like this, though, I might get the courage to even do *that*. Even if Gran had warned me to never, ever use the red stuff unless someone was gonna die for real, *no foolin', you mind me now Dru*.

She had all sorts of ideas about blood. Nowadays I wondered about that.

My hands turned into fists. Long narrow fingers, thumb on the outside so it don't get broken when you punch, the scar across my left-hand knuckles from that one time in Macon when Dad and I were taking care of a hotel that had a resident angry ghost. I could still smell the burning from that night sometimes, and hear the window shivering as I punched it, desperate for a way out with Dad right behind me and the holy water bubbling in its plastic container, reacting to the fury of a swollen, fiery thing that didn't like being dead—and hated everything that had escaped death so far.

We'd gone back during daylight and kicked the ghost's ass but good. Still, the whole place had burned down. It hadn't been a win, more like a draw. On the other hand, we'd both survived.

I rubbed at the scar. When I bloomed, would it go away? Maybe.

Maybe my hands would look different then, too. And maybe they'd all stop fussing over me and let me do something *useful* for once.

Not soon enough. "I hate this. I hate thinking of . . . What if he's *torturing* him? Sergej." The name sent a glass spike of hate through my head. Christophe didn't flinch, but his jaw set.

It was my fault Graves was captured. If it hadn't been for me, he'd still be living in the Dakotas. Sure, his life hadn't been exactly normal, but at least he hadn't been at risk of dying at the hands of a crazed king vampire, right?

Right.

Christophe took a deep breath. "It isn't likely. The boy is *loup-garou*, not wulfen. He won't be as easy to break as—"

"But all it takes is time, right? And it's been weeks. He could be anywhere now. He could even be . . ."

Dead. With no heartbeat for the pendulum to lock onto at all. It curdled in my throat. I didn't want to say it. Not here in this pretty white room.

Christophe uncurled from the bed. The aspect slid through him once as he approached me, disappeared. He leaned down over my shoulder, his face next to mine and his blue gaze holding mine in the mirror.

Seen this way, we had an odd similarity of bone structure. We didn't quite look related, but certainly like we came from the same country, especially with my hair pulled back. What was gawky on me was spare angular beauty on him. He leaned in close enough that his cheek was next to mine. And that made the skin on that whole side of my body heat up. The flush went all the way through me.

His tone was just the same, low and even, every word chosen carefully and the spaces between them echoing with a foreign tongue. "If he is dead, you cannot help him. If he is still alive, you will do him exactly *no* good by haring off and getting caught by Sergej your-self." His mouth turned down, briefly, before he continued. "Not to mention you could waste several of the Order in an assault to free you, because we would certainly throw everything we have into the attempt. Your task is the hardest, Dru. It is to wait and to train. I would change it if I could."

My chin jutted stubbornly. He read the mutiny on my face, plain as a billboard.

"Don't even think about it." The aspect ruffled through him again, blond-streaked hair turning dark and sleek, laying flat against his skull. The whispering sound of its shifting was like the ocean far away. "If I had to come fetch you, Dru, I would be very displeased. And despite what you think, every time I've gone up against my *father*"—his lip curled, fangs sliding free—"I've achieved no better than a draw."

I *was* about to point out that he'd rescued *me* from his father, but then I thought of how close a thing it had been. The snow and the cold and the wulfen and Graves staring through the crack-starred windshield through a mask of bruising and bright blood.

There. I'd thought his name again. *Graves.* I winced.

The aspect retreated, and Christophe's fangs disappeared. A *djamphir*'s fangs are meant for puncturing flesh, but they have al-most no growth in the lower fangs. A *nosferat*'s are bigger yet, and ugly, and big on both upper and lower jaw. They deform the entire mouth, so that when suckers hiss, they look like a snake fixing to swallow an egg.

"I swear we will find him. But it takes time." He straightened, apparently considering that to be that. "I'm on guard tonight. May I stay?"

I struggled with myself for a few seconds, gave up. "For a little while," I said finally, and his whole face changed. It wasn't the slow, dangerous grin he used when he wanted to scare someone. No, this was a genuine smile, ducking his head a little like he was pleased. And it warmed me right down to my bare toes.

Even if I didn't really want it to. But some part of me did, right? Some part of me must, given the way I got all gooshy inside and how my internal thermostat went out of whack whenever he got close.

I couldn't even figure out *why*. I mean, I didn't like him that way, did I? I'd told Graves I didn't. But here I was, and pretty much everything in me just wouldn't listen. I kept doing weird things whenever I got a whiff of Apple Pie Boy.

Even though I knew he probably smelled like that because he fed from the vein. Like a sucker. A "glutter," the wulfen called it—a *djamphir* that drank human blood.

They don't have to. But it kickstarts them, gives them greater strength and speed and accelerated healing. The tradeoff is the risk of the aura-dark, an allergy to sunshine that can induce anaphylactic shock. Still, some *djamphir* do it. They aren't supposed to . . . but they do, for that extra strength and speed. I hadn't worked out if Christophe smelled like that because he drank, or because . . . I don't know, some other reason. I couldn't figure out where he'd find the time to bite someone, hanging around and training me all the livelong night, but still.

And was I a coward, because I didn't ask? I had enough to worry about, right?

Right?

He stayed for a bit, and we talked about other things. Mostly about the paranormal biology textbook and where the tutor had left off, what the chemical processes were that allowed *djamphir* to sniff a victim's or a *nosferat's* blood and tell things about them—age, sex, sometimes even hair color. And what was the standard method for taking down a well-organized hunting pack of older *nosferat* instead of a Master and acolytes. Equals don't often pack up, because they're jealous and nasty even to each other, but it had happened sometimes and the Order knew how to deal with it.

I swear, sometimes I learned more from him in the last few hours of my "day" than from all the tutors. He never acted like my questions were stupid, or like I should have known everything in the first place, the way some of the other *djamphir* did.

So it got harder and harder, each dawn, to watch him walk out into the hall. Then to shut the door and know he was leaning against it on the other side and wishing he could stay inside while he heard me flip the locks and settle the bar in its brackets, the warding strengthening as I touched it.

But I kept sending him out each night. Because when I crawled into bed and dragged the long black coat up from underneath the covers—Nathalie always replaced it when she changed the sheets, and she didn't say a word—and hugged it, smelling the fading breath of cigarette smoke and healthy young *loup-garou*, I didn't want Christophe to see.

CHAPTER SIX

n the long golden time of afternoon, my window rattled. Tiny stones, flung with more-than-human accuracy, popping and pinging against the glass because the screen was gone. Later in the summer I'd figure out something to do with the screen, but for now it was sitting in a disused classroom a couple floors up, and I didn't mention it to Christophe *or* Benjamin.

Another sound, a soft exhalation, and a shadow in the window. I was up and waiting, sitting on the wide white-satin window seat. I jammed the switchblade with its silver-loaded flat into my back pocket and pulled the stamped-iron shutters aside. Late-spring sunshine flooded me, and I glanced back at the barred door. Benjamin was on guard duty out in the hall; it was his day.

I felt bad about it for a half-second. At most.

Nat's blue eyes sparkled, her sleek hair glistening in the sunlight, her blue Converse sneakers balanced on the ledge outside my window. She didn't wait, just fell backward out into space. She twisted, lithely, and landed in a pool of dappled shade, the gravel walk in the gardens silent under her feet. This postage-size garden was full of roses, and the apartments facing it were meant for *svetocha*. There were a couple baseball diamonds, a track and a polo field, and some other gardens inside the Schola's protective wall; it was a microcosm that almost blocked out the hum of the city daydrowsing outside.

I was out the window in a flash, leaving it partly open as I fell, too. A moment's worth of wind whipping my hair and a sudden nausea; the aspect boiled up and snapped over my skin like a rubber band. And I landed lightly as a cat too, braced and ready, my hands out just a little as if I expected a punch or needed to balance myself.

Christophe taught me that.

Nat was suddenly beside me, crowding me back against the wall. There were shrubs here, spiny and thorny things. "You're too loud when you hit," she whispered.

"Must be my fat ass," I whispered back, peering up at my window. It looked just the same, only half open. Like I needed some daylight air or something.

She grinned, tugging on her cropped, faded denim jacket to straighten it, and I had to stop the laugh boiling up in my throat. Daytime Nat was a pretty humorous creature. It was at night that her serious side came out.

Because night was more dangerous, I guess. What with all the suckers around.

We slid soft and easy along the strip of shaded shrubbery, and Nat held up one slim pale hand when we reached the corner. The blue Lucite bangle on her wrist slid down her forearm, and I wondered again how she could look so impossibly *finished* all the time.

Sometimes I even thought I should learn some of the girl stuff that looked so effortless when she did it.

Yeah. Then I woke up.

It wasn't exactly dangerous to be out during the day . . . but the Council, every one of them, up to and including August, would have kittens and penguins and little baby narwhals, too, probably, if they knew what I was up to. Still, I figured I was safe enough with all the sunshine. And with wulfen.

Pretty much the only people who hadn't tried to kill me were wulfen. I mean, unless you count Ash, and he'd been doing a pretty good job of not killing me since I shot him in the face with silver-grain bullets. Maybe that shot broke . . . Sergej's . . . hold over him.

Maybe not.

I winced inwardly. Every time I thought about things I just found a new way to mess myself up. Sometimes you just can't clap a lid on a thought fast enough. It gets there before you can tense up and sucker punches all the air out of you.

"Dru?" Nat, questioning. She glanced over her shoulder, her hand dropping. A brief flare of yellow slid through her irises, clearing instantly as she cocked her head. "It's clear enough. Let's go."

Getting off the Schola grounds during the day is a weird game of move-and-freeze, creep-and-duck. Some older students and some of the teachers, not to mention groups of wulfen, patrol during the day. Nighttime, the patrols are timed down to the second and every inch is watched.

At least, theoretically. There had been *nosferat* attacks before. The last one had been about a week ago just after dusk, but it hadn't gotten anywhere near me, for once. I'd just heard about it afterward, from Benjamin. Who Christophe had promptly shut up with a mild blue-eyed stare. Like I wasn't supposed to know there'd been a hell of a tussle with two teams of suckers bouncing around the Prima's halls.

I wondered what Christophe was doing right now. Sleeping? Maybe. If he found out I was out and around, we were likely to have another argument. I heaved an internal sigh at the thought.

There's only so much of being locked up a girl can take, even if there *are* suckers looking to separate her from her liver.

During the day, if you know the patterns and have a wulfen's sharp ears, you can slip around quite a bit on the Schola's green, hushed grounds. And you can work close to the high ivy-veined wall on the east side, and with ten strong fingers interlaced you can toss a not-quite-bloomed *svetocha* to the top of said wall. As soon as I was up and precariously balanced, Nat sprang up lightly, and we both went over. She landed gracefully, I almost overbalanced, and her hand flashed out to catch my upper arm.

"Your fat ass," she whispered, and this time I did laugh, catching it behind a cupped hand. I mimed mock-punching her, and she made a mock-terrified face, bugging her eyes. Then she pulled me down the slope. When we stepped out of the bushes and onto the sidewalk, I had to pick a couple leaves out of my braid and brush my shoulders off.

"Where we headed today?" I stuffed my hands in my hoodie pockets and looked down at my boots. She was always on me to wear something nice, but jeans, hoodie, and a black T-shirt were *it* today. I wasn't looking forward to tonight, when I'd be exhausted and the tutors would be on me . . . but getting out and breathing some free air was worth it. "I mean, anyplace is nice. I liked FAO Schwarz, although we probably shouldn't go back there until they've cleaned up. But *please* tell me we ain't clothes shopping."

"Surprise." She grinned again, a wide white smile. Model-perfect, but it didn't scare me the way Anna's polished flawlessness had. Nat and I had gotten along almost immediately from the moment she'd waltzed into my bedroom behind Christophe, set down her big slouchy leather purse, and stuck out her hand, not waiting to be introduced. *Nathalie Williams, Skyrunner clan. Don't send me home, it's boring as fuck-all there.*

I'd burst out laughing, Christophe had looked mystified, and from that instant we were pretty much friends.

Nat's usual speed was a brisk stride with her head up, avoiding eye contact like everyone in this city did, but with her jaw set and every line of her body proclaiming that you did *not* want to mess with her. My legs are longer, but I still had to hurry to keep up. It was kind of like trailing after Dad.

Another painful thought. Jesus.

"You're quiet." She produced a pair of big tortoiseshell movie-star sunglasses and slipped them on. No purse today, which meant we weren't going shopping.

Thank God.

"Just . . . thinking." It sounded unhelpful, even to me. I decided it was maybe safer to say a little more. Nothing I told her ended up coming out Christophe's mouth. Or Shanks's. "About my dad."

"Yeah?" She sped up a little, and I could tell she was aiming for a subway entrance. For a moment my skin chilled. "Good or bad?"

"Both. You know how when you're reminded of things, and you can't shut it off quick enough?" *Like, before it slips the knife in and twists? Like that.*

"Like a bad breakup?" But she sobered, her mouth turning down. "Yeah. I know."

"He was all I had." I stared at the sidewalk, glancing up every once in a while to check out the street. Nat took care of steering us both.

"Bound to be rough, with your mom gone and all."

I shrugged. "Yeah. I just didn't think about it, though. There was Gran, and then there was Dad. I didn't miss her. At least, not like he did. He missed her all the time. And now . . ."

"Sucks." She waited to see if I was going to say any more, and I was just about to panic when she changed the subject. "I figured you'd need a distraction today, and the boys were game."

"Shanks and the others?" I perked up a little. That was about all the self-disclosure I could handle for a day, and she wouldn't make a huge deal about it. "Are we going for a run?"

"Kind of. Don't ask, it's a *surprise*."

I gave an eyeroll, relaxing my clenched fists inside my pockets. Took a breath. "Jesus, fine. As long as we eat sometime afterward. I'm starving."

"For once. Don't think I haven't noticed you hitting the anorexia button. Bad for you. You need those calories for blooming, kiddo."

If I could just bloom and get it over with instead of hanging on the edge, that'd be nice. I snorted. "Me and my lard, right?"

"Skinny chick. I *wish* I had your problems."

No, you don't, Nat. But she was trying to help. And when you're a girl, you do that—say that you envy something about your friend. Build them up. It's like the insults boys trade, a kind of friend-currency. "I wish I had some of your hips, girl." Still, I meant it. She was curved in all the right places, and those catlike eyes were just deadly.

In more ways than one.

She grinned, finger-combing her perfectly sleek hair back. "I'll donate some of my hip then. You can have some tit, too."

"A tit transplant?" We both cracked up at that, and when she slid her arm through mine and pulled me down the stairs to the subway station I could feel the butt of a gun under her jacket, solid and reassuring. Goose bumps rose up all over me, but they faded by the time Nat swiped her MetroCard twice and we slid on through.

* * *

The north end of Central Park near the Pool was green and shaded. The group of about a dozen boys lounging around, a few of them monkeying up in any tree near enough that was big enough to climb, looked just like any other gang of toughs. One or two of them had hoodies, but most of them were just in T-shirts and jeans or khakis, boots and sneakers; the only thing giving them away was the fluid grace of wulfen. They move like they're shouldering through tall grass, different than *djamphir*'s eerie quickness. Sunlight coming through the leaves dappled them, and normal people's eyes would just slide right over their essential *difference*.

People are goddamn geniuses at not seeing what they don't want to see. It's like the great human trait, along with fighting over abstract principles and craving junk food.

Shanks hauled himself up as soon as we got close. Next to him, shy blond Dibs slowly rose from his crouch, running a hand back through his golden hair. Alex and Gerry tipped us salutes and gave wide toothy grins. The others muttered greetings, or just nodded. The excitement was palpable, what Gran would've called the high fidgets, and it ran along my skin like electricity.

"Took you long enough." Shanks jerked his head, flipping his emo-boy swoosh out of his dark eyes. I swear he has to buy his jeans in grasshopper size. Those legs are *unreal*. Plus his hands were a little big, and his feet, my God. He was like a puppy growing into its paws. A big, sarcastic puppy.

"You can just bite me," Nat returned cheerfully, slipping her sunglasses off. "I'll even mark the spot. Who's the lucky guy?"

"Our very own Dibsie." Shanks's grin stretched, if that were possible. He sized Nat up, dark eyes running appreciatively down her. "Mark that spot, Skyrunner. I'll set my teeth."

She waved her fingers, pale-blue polish glittering. "You *wish*, fleabag. Dibs, man, congrats."

Dibs was scarlet by now. He looked down at his feet, muttering something, and the other wulfen clustered around us. I knew most of them— Shanks's loose collection of friends and buddies, familiar faces.

Most of them had been there last night. But they didn't treat me any differently. Bobby T. gave me a thumbs-up, rolling his shoulders under his leather jacket; on Nat's other side slim dark Pablo crouched in an acid-green Lucky Charms T-shirt, the change rippling just under his skin. Gerry hopped on his toes once, twice, his brunet curls bouncing. They were all excited.

"All right, rules!" Shanks didn't have to raise his voice. Everyone just went still and listened. As wulfen went, he was pretty dom. Dominant, that is. Alpha.

Kinky, Graves said way back in my head. I shook it away, and Nat glanced at me.

Shanks just plowed straight ahead. A flash of orange went through his eyes, and his skin rippled a little, like little mice under the surface. "No cabs, no buses. Straight-up run. Midpoint's Coney and home base is back here, but *no* lying in wait." This was directed at Alex, who shrugged and grinned, his hair standing up in wild vital springing curls. "Jumping's legal, so's using the crowd. Change-form's only legal if it's sub rosa. Got it?"

Which basically meant it was a pretty regular daylight run, nobody could hang around home base or midpoint waiting to jump

Dibs, and we had to avoid being so weird it would make a commotion. My heart leapt, pulse settling into a high gallop. A disbelieving smile cracked my face. "We're playing rabbit?"

"Toldja it was a surprise." Nat bumped me with her hip. At least she didn't get all weird about touching me. Maybe it was okay for female wulfen, I dunno. Or maybe it was how I smelled that turned the boys off. Now that I was, um, fertile. And getting so close to blooming.

I almost hopped up and down like Gerry. I'd heard about chase-the-rabbit—one wulfen bolts and the others give a head start, then the hunt's on. It teaches the pursuers cooperation and tracking, and teaches the rabbit how to slip free of pursuit.

Plus, it's just plain *fun*. And this was the first time I'd ever been invited. They took me along on other runs, but playing rabbit meant I could keep up.

It meant I was part of the group. My heart just about swelled up like a balloon, and I looked down at my boot toes. I didn't want anyone to see my big stupid grin.

"Prize?" Alex piped up. "Come on, can't have rabbit without a prize!"

"Catch him before he gets back home and we'll do a flyby for pizza." Shanks tilted his head slightly. "Catch him before Coney, and we'll get beer with it."

I made a face. So did Nat. But the guys all rumbled their approval.

"How much time do I get?" Dibs was calming down, even though I could hear his pulse thundering, and little ripples raced through his skin. The Other was turning briefly inside him, making his eyes glow too. It's the thing inside them wulfen can tap for the changeform, the thing that has a line right down into the heart of a hunting beast.

It didn't scare me. I had so much else to be scared of nowadays that wulfen were looking pretty damn safe. Plus, I trusted them.

I trusted them all.

Shanks punched Dibs on the shoulder, but very lightly. "You've already wasted half of it, Dibsie. Get going."

Dibs stood there for a few seconds. A slow, very sweet grin lit up his entire face, and I blinked. In that one second, shy, blushing Dibs looked . . . well, almost handsome.

Then he turned on his heel and was gone, skirting the edge of the pool and vanishing into leafshade and sunshine. His hair blazed for a moment, but then branches moved to hide that gleam.

Shanks glanced at me. The orange in his irises fought with the fluid leaf-shadows. "Keep up, Dru-girl."

I snorted. "You haven't lost me yet, *Robert*." It was what Christophe called him, just like he called Dibs *Samuel* all the time.

It was Shanks's turn to make a little dismissive noise. He folded down, crouching, dark head cocked and the emo swoosh hiding his eyes. Readiness ran through the rest of them like oil over the surface of a plate, tension gathering. Nat rolled her shoulders twice, glancing at me. The last couple runs she'd kept pace right beside me, and once she'd grabbed my hand just as I was getting ready to launch myself over a couple of elevated trains.

Don't ask. Anyway.

Shanks threw his head back and howled. The rest of them joined in, a rising chorus of high thrillglass baying, their throats swelling and their eyes lambent. Even under late-spring sun, that cry filled my head with moonlight and plucked deep below the conscious surface. It teased and taunted and tweaked and pulled at that . . . thing.

The low, furry, clawed thing inside all of us that remembers the joy of night-hunting.

My chin was up, my mouth open, and a spear of silver ice wound through their harmony, a *svetocha*'s distinctive cry. It was uncomfortably like a sucker's glassine hunting scream, but I was helpless to stop it, and they never said a word about it.

Nat yanked on my arm, and the world turned over. It rushed underneath me, my boots touching down every so often, and my heart leapt against my rib cage like it wanted to escape. Feathers brushed every inch of my skin, and I hurled myself forward in the middle of the shifting, leaping pack of wulfen.

They closed around me even on daylight runs, arms pumping and the change rippling over them like clear heavy water, fur not quite breaking free of the surface. We poured around the edge of the Pond and the whole green length of Central Park unreeled underneath us like a treadmill's belt. As always, it was oddly silent, just the wind in my ears, stinging my eyes, all of them suddenly welded into one creature running just for the heart-exploding joy of it. If you've ever seen a cheetah going all-out, maybe you can guess what I mean.

Breath tearing in throat, I jumped and my right boot skimmed the top of a granite boulder, barely brushing the moss. My leg uncoiled, pushed me forward like a slingshot. The rest of them leapt, Evan catching a tree limb and jackknifing, launching himself into clear air. He landed with sweet natural authority and was neck-and-nose with Shanks for a few steps, but he fell back as the leggy boy veered and we burst out of the Park's green into the concrete jungle.

We ran, flashing through hot gold sun and gray exhaust-scorch shadow, and for a little while I could pretend someone else was running with us. A boy in a long black canvas coat, his green eyes alight and the change never quite breaking through his skin—because *loup-garou* use the Other for mental dominance, not for the physical morphing.

We ran, and the ghost of Graves ran with us. If tears slicked my cheeks, I could pretend they were stung free by the wind. We hit the Brooklyn Battery toll tunnel and poured through in merry violation of several laws, relying on sheer outrageousness to keep people from really *looking* as we blurred single file on the skinny walkway next to honking traffic. Nat right behind me, matching me stride for stride, every once in a while sending up her own peculiar cry that trailed off on a soprano note like crystal just before shattering. Cars whizzing slowly behind us, the glare of a summer day gone as some of the boys even veered out into traffic, playing tag-me with the cars whose drivers would only catch a glimpse or a flash of bright eyes or tossing hair. Brakes squealed, but we were already free of the tunnel, lunging up into sunlight, and the touch flamed inside my head.

We broke south as soon as we hit the entrance, and Stuvy's tangle flashed by in random bullets of impression—a dry cleaner's, a boarded-up nightclub, a row of brownstones flowing as we tore down the street. My mother's locket bobbed against my chest, a warm forgiving touch. The song of wind in my ears and the world unreeling under me shut away every nasty thought, every pain except the stitch threatening in my side and the sweet thrill of my heart working so fast it might explode with delight.

He almost made Coney Island. I almost had him, too, but he jagged right when we were half a block behind him, running all-out but not realizing he was boxed yet. Shanks leapt past me, clearing a bicycle rack and barely touching the street as he uncoiled, going airborne again. My breath came in high harsh rasps, my entire body sang, Gran's owl gave a soft cry. The rest of them closed around me like a warm coat, and Shanks brought him down in Calvert Vaux Park with an ebullient whoop that was equal parts wulf and boy. They went rolling in dusty grass on the outskirts of an overgrown baseball diamond, a cloud of gold puffing up around them, and we all put on the brakes, skidding to a stop.

Beer for everyone, then. My sides heaved. Half of us bent over, gasping for breath. And when I looked around at all the faces, glowing with excitement and sweat and the poreless healthy shine of wulfen, it was a shock right below my breastbone when Graves's green gaze didn't meet mine. Nat flung her arm over my shoulders and Alex leaned against my other side, the prohibition against touching gone for a few brief seconds as everyone collapsed together in a heap.

But I wasn't wulfen. I was still lonely.

Well, I'd had a half hour of not thinking about him. I guess it had to be enough.

* * *

The pizza parlor looked faintly familiar, even though I could swear I'd never been in there before. It was on the fringes of Augie's old neighborhood, a dingy hole in the Brooklyn brick wall where the fat balding proprietor cracked bottles of Corona without demur for the boys. Nat and I stuck to club soda, because she didn't like pop and neither of us liked beer.

Beer makes you, in her words, "muy, muy *flat*ulent-o, kiddo." And we would both crack up.

I leaned over the air hockey table, my fingers still greasy from the three slices of pepperoni-plus I'd bolted, and popped the puck back at her. The aspect was warm oil over my skin, my teeth tingled, and the bloodhunger was a rough spot at the back of my palate no matter how much club soda I washed it with. Nat was *fierce* when it came to air hockey, and she had a wulf's speed and reflexes. With the aspect all unreliable, I had to jump to stay ahead of her, and she still beat my ass six times out of ten.

Those other four times, though, I killed her. And right now, I was on a winning streak.

She snapped the puck back at me, lips drawn back from her teeth and her blue crystal earrings bouncing. I was already there, the touch flaming inside my head, and the puck shot back, banked, and thwopped neatly into the goal right past her guard.

Nat snarled, and I grinned. It felt completely natural.

"Oh, you bitch." Her eyes glowed, and I caught a glimpse of Shanks watching us from one of the booths. Evan jostled him and he jostled right back, still staring at Nat's back.

Or, more precisely, a little lower than her back.

"You're going *down*," she continued. "Is someone looking at me?"

I'd say he's trying to undress you visually, but that's just me. "Totally. Or at least, looking at *part* of you."

The puck spat back out, she popped it hard, leaning a little further over the table than was *strictly* necessary. With her jacket gone, creamy skin showed above in an indigo silk spaghetti-strap tank top, the shoulder holster looking just like a decoration. Muscle rippled decorously in her arms. "Great. He stares, but he won't talk."

"Are all wulf boys like that?" I slapped it back to her, the jolt going all the way up my arm. She leaned to the side, her hand flicking out, and the sound of puck meeting the mallet was the crack of a rifle shot.

She gave an eyeroll that could have won an award. "Wulf aside, *svetocha*, boys are *stupid*. Always were, always will be, world without end, amen."

"So how do you get him to act interested? Or get a little closer?" Like I didn't care about the answer. My heart cracked inside my chest, I shoved the feeling down and we spent about half a minute concentrating completely on the game. She finally slugged the puck past my defenses and straightened, grinning, as I let out a groan.

"Simple. He either steps up or he doesn't get to play." She shrugged. "What time is it?"

I twisted to check the clock over the front counter. "We've got plenty . . ." But my mother's locket chilled against my chest, and I cocked my head. The touch thrilled through me, not scraping but tingling. Still . . . "Whoops. Trouble coming."

She dropped her mallet with a clatter and scooped up her coat. "Back door. Right through there."

Shanks was on his feet. The other wulfen scattered, and I hoped they'd paid for the beer. Nat and I were through the steaming-hot kitchen in a flash, bathed in the yeasty cheesy bubbling-tomato-and-oregano smell before she pushed me out through a door that gave onto an alley. A rusting Folgers can full of cat litter and cigarette butts propped the door a little open, and she was up the fire escape in a trice, pausing only to brace her legs and lean down, offering me one hand. I leapt and grabbed, she hauled me up, and we were on the roof in time to see a boy in a thin black V-neck sweater and jeans saunter down the sidewalk in front of the pizza place.

Christophe. Blond highlights slid through his hair, and if we were seeing him, it was probably because he *wanted* us to. Letting us know that he knew, keeping tabs on me.

Nat let out a soft breath.

My heart leapt up into my throat and did its best to strangle me. Nat shrugged into her jacket and tugged on my hand; I followed her without demur. The sun was sinking lower in the sky, and we'd be back at the Schola before dusk really got settled.

Even though I was glad to get out, I also couldn't wait to go back to the only safety I had.

How was that for weird?

CHAPTER SEVEN

he Schola wakes up just slightly before dusk when the
days get longer. There's a sort of sound to the place, one you
can't quite hear with your ears. It's the sound of attention, of
awareness—and of possible violence.

I wasn't concerned about that so much, though. Right now I
was glad I'd had the pizza, and I was concerned about staying one
step ahead of Christophe. The *malaika*-shaped stick slid through the
air, almost kissing the front of my hoodie, and I leapt back like a cat
finding a snake on the road, snapping a kick at his knee. It didn't
connect, but it did force him back a half-step. I flung myself away,
falling and rolling, and came up with the stick he'd knocked out of
my hands. Whirling, had to get more speed, slashing at empty air
because he'd twisted aside. That was okay. I had enough room to
breathe now, stepping back cautiously. Every time I shifted weight,
it was to sure footing.

Arcus would be proud. *Don't lose your balance, girl!* the wulfen
teacher would always yell. Before Christophe showed back up, he'd

been the one to start teaching me how to use what little I had against a Real World opponent.

I hadn't seen Arcus in weeks now. Not since Christophe's Trial. I sometimes wondered what he was doing. Yet another question I didn't ask.

The gym was empty, collapsible wooden bleachers pushed up against the walls and the entire floor covered with mats. Shafts of dusky light peered down from high windows covered with chicken wire, dust dancing through the golden beams. I was grateful I was wearing jeans, because if I hadn't I'd've lost some skin when I'd done the sliding-on-my-knees trick to get away from him.

He hadn't mentioned me going out during the day. But he'd run me ragged through the first two *malaika* forms and now he was kicking my ass all over the gym. I got the idea the three things were related.

Christophe snarled as he dropped into first guard, sticks held firmly but not tightly. His upper lip lifted, and there was a thin trickle of blood from where I'd caught him on the face, threading down from his patrician nose. Lucky shot, maybe, but I was getting luckier all the time. The bruising and swelling might give me a slight edge, if I could just stay ahead of him long enough.

Oh, and kick his ass before he healed up. That too.

I didn't snarl back, but I did grin, a wide animal baring of teeth that had nothing of amusement to it. My mother's locket was a warm spot, tucked under my tank top. The bloodhunger teased at that special spot at the back of my throat, but it didn't reach down and grab control of me. I was too busy. If I moved fast enough, I could hold the rage off. "Hurts, huh?"

"Not enough," he barked. "More!" He darted forward, with that spooky blurring speed, and the sticks flashed. It sounded like popcorn, but with an extra crackle, wood groaning and popping as it smashed into more wood. *Malaika* have an edge, but these didn't. Instead of slashing, this was a battering game—but I would be able to pick up a crowbar or a stick or anything, really, and have a chance of fighting something off. Plus, a lot of the moves were the same, building up muscle and instinct for the *malaika*.

You have to think in circles, he was always telling me. *These circles, like a propeller, are your defense. This circle, with your feet, you move in. That way you're ready for movement in any direction.*

I drove him back across the mats, and for the first time I got the idea he wasn't holding back and being careful. Warm oil covered my skin, my teeth tingled, and I felt the dainty points of my own fangs touching my lower lip.

Svetocha don't get big fangs, oh, no. We get cute little ones. They look pretty useless, but they're damn sharp. You have to get real close to get them in something, though.

Sometimes I wondered about that.

Right now, though, I wasn't wondering. The world was slowing down, covered in clear plastic goop, and I was flying. It wasn't like running with wulfen—nothing was like that—but it kept me from thinking.

When I was fighting Christophe, I didn't have to think. I just had to move and do my best. He *knew* I was giving everything, and he never accused me of doing any less.

Even if he was expressing his displeasure, so to speak.

CRACK. One of his sticks went flying; he snatched his hand back as if I'd burned him, and I read his intent in the way his weight shifted. Flung myself forward, sticks blurring; he warded me off and had to step in the opposite direction. If I could keep him away from his left-hand stick, I might have even more of a chance.

The snarl turned into a smile. He wiped at the blood with the back of his hand, the sleeve of his black sweater smearing it. I could *smell* it, copper and cinnamon, taunting that place at the back of my palate where the bloodhunger lived. The hunger stretched inside my bones, glass nails turning as a crackling jolt of pure fury ran through me, and the sticks blurred as I moved much faster than I should have been able to. My footsteps were drumbeats against the mats; Christophe backed up, his eyes turning incandescent and the aspect folding lovingly over him. His fangs were out, his hair slicked down, and his remaining stick blurred through a figure-eight, battering away my attack.

The bleachers were coming up soon, no room for him to retreat unless he did something fancy, and if he did, I was going to have to react within a split second. I pressed him, sticks going like a high techno beat, and the world narrowed to a single point of concentration.

We weren't just sparring now. No, it had ended up like usual—with me honestly trying to hurt him. The anger was back, boiling through my bloodstream, spurred by the smell of copper.

The bloodhunger reliably pushed me into the aspect. It also frightened me. I could really hurt someone when I did this. I'd almost killed Shanks back at the reform Schola, because I'd totally lost it.

But under the glow of the aspect, Christophe just looked intent and thoughtful.

And pleased.

"*Hit* me!" he yelled. "*Hit* me, Dru!"

I damn well did my best. Drove him back almost onto the bleachers; they rattled as he leapt, his back foot kissing the wooden surface and propelling him outward. He flew over me, but I was tracking. I *knew* where he was going to land; I whirled and lunged.

Hit him twice on his way down, his body twisting to try and avoid the blows. Good solid hits, enough to crack a rib.

He landed and spun, foot flicking out. I met it squarely with my left-hand stick, the right curving down to smack him on the thigh. I could've gone for the nut shot, but it would have left me no recovery path. I might not have needed it with him curled up on the ground, but that was one of Christophe's sayings—*always leave yourself a recovery.*

Dad would have approved. But I was too busy to feel the way my heart wrung itself down at the thought. That was another reason why I didn't try to get out of sparring with Christophe, even if I was already tired from running over half the city during the afternoon when I should've been sleeping.

Because when I got going this fast, and I tried to hurt him, it made me forget—for just a few minutes a night—everything nasty and painful. Everything bad.

The aspect turned to a cloak of warm prickles instead of oil, my teeth aching and sensitive, and he spun in midair. It was one of the things human bodies aren't supposed to do, but he's *djamphir.* Physics and gravity don't mean the same things to him that they do to—

I didn't see how he hit me. One second I was kicking his ass while he was in midair, the next dynamite went off inside my head. I came to with my ears ringing and Christophe's arms around me as he knelt on the mats.

"You're getting better. No, don't try to get up." He pushed a curl out of my face. "Just lie still for a moment."

I don't know why he said that; I wasn't trying to go anywhere. I blinked, and the world rolled back up to speed. I tasted hot copper, and hoped I wasn't bleeding anywhere.

But wouldn't you know, I guess it just wasn't my night. A thin trickle of something warm slid down from my nose. Christophe swallowed hard, his Adam's apple bobbing, and the aspect slipped through his hair like dark fingers.

I stared at him, my heart beating thinly. Rapid fluttering beats, like a hummingbird's wings. His fever-hot fingers brushed my upper lip, wiping at the blood.

My blood. Full of happy stuff that drove boy *djamphir* crazy.

My arms and legs wouldn't obey me. We were alone in here, and if he went nuts over the happy stuff in my blood there was no way I could—

I shouldn't have worried.

He lifted his fingers to his mouth. Closed his eyes and licked them clean. I struggled to move, and his other hand—he had one arm underneath me, holding me up—bit down, fingers like slim iron bands.

I should have been terrified. But instead I only felt a sleepy sort of alarm. As if I was in a dream that wasn't too terribly important.

Christophe leaned down. His eyes were still tightly shut, and his lips met my cheek. They grazed the surface of my skin, lightly, and I felt the sharp points of his fangs, scraping just a little.

Then he kissed me.

Each time our mouths met, it was the same. Lightning crackled through me, and I forgot everything else. The only thing I remembered was *him*, his arms around me and the taste of him like night in the desert, spice and sand and fading heat. One of his fangs brushed mine and a jolt of pleasure slammed down my throat. The bloodhunger bloomed, and my fingers were in his hair, twisting and tangling. My arms tensed, and for a moment I quivered on the edge of action—wrenching his head back, kissing down the line of his jaw, and burying those dainty little fangs in his throat. My entire body curved, strength welling back up, and I struggled against the part of me that wanted to rip out a chunk of his flesh and *drink*.

Christophe's mouth slid free of mine, regretfully. He pulled away, despite my hands trying to keep him. I realized I was making a small sound in the back of my throat, a little mewling. "It's all right," he whispered. "Shhh, it's all right. It's just the hunger. It's not you. You have control, *kochana*."

It was nice of him to say it. Because really, I didn't think I did. My lips burned, my teeth tingled, and I shook like I was cold. But at least I didn't try to jerk forward and bite him.

I wanted to. I was stronger than the urge, though. By only a few millimeters, but it was something.

My fingers cramped. We were both bleeding, and the smell of it stroked that rough spot on my palate, right next to the little place that warned me of danger. I swallowed, but that just made it worse. Spit wasn't what that place wanted. It wanted what was beating through his veins. It was even worse because I knew how good it tasted.

I knew what it was like to drink his blood, desert spice and wind through car windows, thunderstorm looming and the accelerator pressed to the floor.

He tasted like freedom.

Christophe stroked my hair, not caring that I was pulling on his. I tried to make my fingers let go, but they wouldn't. It had to be uncomfortable, but he looked strangely peaceful. His mouth had relaxed, and his eyes were still closed. "It's all right," he repeated quietly. "Shhh, *skowroneczko moja, moja ksiezniczko*, little bird. All's well. Hush."

I rushed back into myself fully with a thud, shoving the blood-hunger back in its box. Dusk light was fading in the high windows; I *felt* it retreating like a huge staticky sound draining out of the sky.

My breath came in ragged gasps, and I was sweating. My tank top was all twisted around under my hoodie; I had no idea how *that* had happened. Plus the chain that held the locket was all twisted up too, digging into my skin.

"Very good." He sounded pleased. Kept stroking my hair. "*Very good.* You've acquired more control. Now, how do you suppose I defeated you?"

My mouth opened. Nothing but a dry husk of a cough came out. I coughed again, trying to get the taste out of my throat. It didn't work. Only time and getting calmed down would do it.

He waited while I cleared my throat several times. My fingers relaxed. It was work to make them slip out of his hair, especially when they kept wanting to grab and pull his pulse closer to my fangs.

Running with wulfen was one thing. Getting fangs was another. I struggled with myself. *Steady, Dru. Steady.*

"I had you," I finally managed to get out. "Then you cheated."

I felt like a hoser even saying it. Cheating is the name of the game when it comes to winning fights, right? You don't fight fair. You fight to *win*.

It shouldn't have been possible for him to look more pleased, but he managed it. "Well, I had to. You forced me into it."

That was high praise, from him. "Great." I didn't feel like celebrating. I felt like every bit of me had been pulled apart and put back together wrong. I was *exhausted*. Jesus, I couldn't wait to finally bloom if it would stop this sort of thing from happening. My mouth kept merrily going, though, independently of my brain. "Are you going to do that every time the hunger hits?"

Then I could have slapped my own forehead. It sounded like a cheap come-on line.

"Would you like me to?" Another one of those happy smiles, and his eyes snapped open. The blue took me by surprise, as always, and my fingers slid completely free of his hair. We were both probably a mess, but the aspect was already shrinking his bruises and turning off his bleeding. My nose had stopped bleeding, too, thank God. But I'd still need some time in the baths to get rid of the worst of it.

Yep. Couldn't *wait* to bloom. "Nah, that's okay." I felt like I could move now. Various muscles ached and twinged, and Christophe had to steady me. "Ouch. I need some aspirin."

He nodded. "And some food, probably. You were in the aspect for a bit, there. It was hard to keep ahead of you. *Svetocha* are generally very fast."

I'm fast enough to play rabbit, too. Still, his praise almost made me blush. "How many have you trained?" I tried not to look too interested. Sometimes he wouldn't talk about his personal past.

He had a funny idea of what "personal past" meant, too. Of course, he was older. Like, way way older.

It was kind of weird. Check that, it was *really* weird. Sometimes, when I remembered just how old he was, it was downright unsettling. I mean, he'd known my *mother*. And my hormones were jumping up and down all the time. And he was just so . . . so . . .

I couldn't come up with a word for what he was.

"Three. Including you, my dear." He set me on my feet and let go of me. I tried not to feel bereft. At least when he was that close, I felt like nothing nasty could get to me.

Things like that will do something funny to a girl's head, I guess. "My mother. Me. And . . . Anna?" It wasn't so much of a shot in the dark. They had to have spent *some* time together, right?

Them being an item for a while, however long ago.

"Training didn't interest *her* much." He shrugged. Even with dried blood and bruising all over his face, he looked perfectly finished. It was as if the blood was just decorating him. "But I tried as best I could. Nothing else a Kuoroi can do, when faced with a *svetocha*."

What's that supposed to mean? I spotted my sticks, flung halfway across the gym. One of them was a splinter-chewed mess. "Jeez. I'll need new ones, again. Good thing we weren't practicing with real *malaika*."

"Real *malaika* are just for forms practice for now. In six months or so, you'll be ready to spar with them." He was already striding away in search of his own weapons.

"Six *months*?" My voice bounced off the bleachers, and the fluorescents hanging overhead flickered unevenly. *But it's been weeks already, and I have to* . . . I stopped dead, looking up at the lights, brushing a curl out of my face. Even one of Nathalie's braids would lose a few strands when faced with a fight with Christophe.

He didn't even look back. "Until you're ready? Yes. Perhaps longer."

"You said I was coming along! You said I was fast! I killed that thing last night—"

"You *are* fast. But before *I* trust you in a sparring match with edged weapons, you need to be fast and *precise*. Not to mention completely in control of where your blades are at all times. One lucky shot against a young *nosferat*—with *malaika* your wulfen friend stole, by the way—is not enough to convince me." He scooped up one stick, half-turned on one booted heel, and set off for the other. "Anna never wanted to walk when she could be carried, your mother wanted to walk when she could fly, and you want to run before you can walk. It is"—another quick movement, and he had the other stick—"maddening, sometimes. First guard, Dru."

I thought we were done. But I grabbed both sticks and straightened, whirling, just in time to catch his strike.

Dirty fighting, again. He came at me like he wanted to hurt me, and I returned the favor. Maybe he had to make up for kissing me or something.

That was the thing about Christophe. I never knew which side of him I was facing in the practice room.

I managed to keep him off me for a full two minutes before I ended up sprawled on the mats. One of his sticks was right under my chin, touching delicately. If it was a *malaika*, it would cut.

"Half a year," Christophe said softly. "At least. More if you insist on playing slip-the-leash during the day; you need your rest if you expect to function well during accelerated training." His voice rose, but only slightly. "It takes *years* to learn this thoroughly, Dru, and I will not cut corners with you, even if I *allow* you a certain limited part in seek-destroy missions to soothe your Lefevre pride. Don't argue with me. Not about this."

So he knew. Of course he knew; he'd walked right into the pizza parlor. He just hadn't caught us outright. Still, with the smell of wulfen—and me—all over the building, he hadn't had to.

And *Lefevre*. My mother's name. As if my father hadn't existed at all. Of course, he'd just been human, right?

Jesus.

You're an asshole sometimes, Christophe. I knocked the stick away and bounced up to my feet. It wouldn't do any good to yell at him; he'd just wipe the floor with me some more. Instead, I stalked for the exit, dropping both of my weapons with hollow sounds.

He said nothing else. He didn't need to. My teeth tingled, my mouth burned, my eyes were full of tears. None of them escaped, they just made my vision waver.

And I still couldn't get the taste of him off my lips.

CHAPTER EIGHT

The baths in Schola locker rooms are weird, to say the least. The sunken tubs are full of a bubbling whitish fluid that clings to your skin and hardens like paraffin wax when the air hits it. It speeds up the healing processes like crazy, and when you wash it out in the shower, it just slides right down the drain like jelly, taking a lot of the hurt and inflammation with it. It even helps with the sandy-headed feeling you get after not enough sleep, running around with wulfen, and getting your ass handed to you by a supercilious *djamphir*.

When it gets in your hair, though, it takes a while to rinse out even in the showers, where the water pressure can strip your skin off.

Okay, I'll admit it. I outright love the Schola showers. I've cleaned up in too many cheap-ass hotel rooms where you barely get a dribble of tepid rust-stained fluid that might've been water once.

Another good thing here: the hot water never runs out. I was in there long enough to turn into a prune before I got the waxy stuff out of my curls. When I shut the water off, the whole locker room echoed. On the boys' side of any Schola gym, there's always plenty of tubs and showers, and I'd guess it's probably always full of noise after classes.

What, you thought I'd go in there to check it out? No thanks.

On the girls' side, there's never more than three tubs and four showers. Everything is scrubbed and bleached, and the steam in the air, rising from the roiling surfaces of the tubs, moves in shifting veils. It's as lonely as a tumbleweed town.

I grabbed a fresh white towel and wrapped it around my hair, scrubbed at the rest of me with another one. The bruises were green-yellow now, and the road rash from last night looked weeks old instead of poppin' fresh. At least I hadn't hurt myself on the daylight run.

I was standing there, looking at the scrape on my leg and trying to determine how much it had really shrunk, when I heard a soft sliding sound.

Gooseflesh roughened my skin. I wrapped the second towel around me tightly and glanced at the tubs.

There was nobody in here with me. Just the three tubs, boiling away with their peculiar burbling chuckles. The showerhead, dripping. All the mirrors were steam-fogged, and I couldn't even see the wall in front of the door. Benjamin would be on guard out in the hall, and nobody would get past him. Christophe would be along any second, cleaned up and imperturbable, to collect me for Aspect Mastery tutoring.

Of all my classes, I like that one least. I'd rather be sparring. And that says something.

I shivered. My breath turned into a white cloud, and electric nervousness ran along my skin, thrumming in my bones.

I know that feeling like an old friend. It's the kind of cold that hits right before seriously-weird happens along to say howdy.

The steam-fog began to flush pink along its cloud-edges. My mother's locket, lying against my breastbone, cooled rapidly as well. Had it done this when Dad wore it? He wasn't around to ask, and boy, was that the wrong thing to think.

Because if I did, I thought of the tapping sound a zombie's fingers made against cold glass, and my entire body wanted to curl up in a ball and hide somewhere dark and safe.

Or at least dark. I was getting to think nowhere was really, truly safe.

The pink edges to the fog did not look friendly. They looked like raw meat. I tasted a ghost of danger candy, just faint enough to make me wonder if I was imagining things.

But I know better. It don't matter if you're imagining or if something is really going on. Move first, worry about looking like an idiot later.

Dad never said that. But I knew he would approve.

I edged for my clean clothes, neatly folded on the counter next to the nearest sink. Bare feet gripping the rough-tiled floor, the towel on my hair sliding free and hitting with a small sodden sound, I took three steps, trying to look everywhere at once. My switchblade lay right on top of the black T-shirt I was going to wear next, and the honest silver loading the flat of the blade was far from the worst ally you could have at a time like this.

What the hell is going on? I took another couple steps, and more pink threaded through the steam. I lunged for my clothes, grabbed a fistful, and stumbled back as the fog turned an angry crimson and bulleted forward as if it had been *thrown*. It hit the mirror, which gave a high hard crack and shivered into pieces. I let out a blurting scream, my feet slipping, and dodged back into the shower stall. My jeans hit the tiled floor on the way, so did the shirt, but the switchblade snicked open as my shoulders hit the wall. I dropped my last towel, too — that thing was *fast*, whatever it was, and if I was clinging to modesty, I might end up seriously hurt.

Great. Now I was trapped in the shower stall in my birthday suit, and all the steam rising from the tubs was beginning to look like red ink in water, only it was bubbling and taking on a solidity I didn't like. The tub closest the door was really roiling red, the other two just faintly pink. Still, my skin roughened up into sandpaper gooseflesh.

I was just sitting in that! Bile rose in my throat. But that wouldn't do me any good. What was this thing? Bodiless for sure, at least at the moment, which meant it could be a bad spirit or a hex. But maybe it was going to coalesce, which would make it something else. I ran through the catalog of the weird I held stored in my head — everything Dad and I had ever seen, everything Gran had told me about, everything I'd dug up in moldering leather-bound books, everything I'd heard stories about while we went on our sixteen-state odyssey of the strange and dangerous.

Nothing came even *remotely* close.

The ghost of wax oranges lingered on the back of my tongue. Weird. Usually the aura was the first thing to warn me of the hinky going down, but it wasn't spiking now. I firmed my grip on the switchblade, silver glinting as I jabbed forward experimentally.

The crimson mist cringed a little, thickening. My mother's locket was icy; it bounced as I retreated again. I reached up, twisted the shower knob with my free hand — running water's a barrier to a lot of things. Couldn't hurt.

Then the smell hit me. Salt, and something rotting, the reek crawled down my throat and I retched, hot water welling in my eyes. I slashed again as the mist slid a tendril into the shower stall, and the blade passed through it, sparking. A thin spatter of red fluid hit the floor, washed away by the shower's steady spray. It smelled like something dying in a dark wet corner, and I retched again, my breath still making a cloud even though the shower was scorch-hot, needles of spray hitting my hip.

I'd seen that in the Real World before. Things that need to drain all the energy out of the air to hold themselves together, making the temperature go all wonky. Gran's advice was to "disrupt" them— find the thing pulling all the energy together and short out its connection to the snarled, tangled fabric of the fleshly. It's kind of like feeling around in a bathtub full of squirming maggots for a plug, and hoping it'd drain once you yanked it.

Okay. So here I was, naked, with my mother's locket, my switchblade, hot water, and my wits. Not to mention my Lefevre pride, dammit. Why wasn't Benjamin breaking down the door? Could he not hear what was going on? Did he think the breaking glass was a weird girl ritual or something?

Or could he not hear me at all? That was most likely. Anyway, I was on my own.

Well, wasn't that depressingly usual.

The mist pressed closer. It was so thick I couldn't see the rest of the locker room now, a solid wall of billowing crimson. The hot water was keeping it back, and I slashed again as it slid a tentacle finger into the shower stall. This time there was resistance against the blade, the silver sparked more definitely, and the tentacle actually plopped down before dissolving in the water.

Great. I switched the knife to my right hand, the blade reversed flat along my forearm, and shook out my wet, prune-wrinkled left hand. *Hit 'em where they hold themselves too tight,* Gran would say. *You can see it if you don't look.*

Believe it or not, that's not the most confusing thing she ever said to me. Not even close.

It's kind of hard to concentrate when a wall of red fog is pressing forward, trying to creep into a shower stall. I dropped back into a crouch, ribs heaving as I struggled not to hyperventilate or puke, trying to keep as much of the shower's spray as possible between me and the thing. It was billowing up, too, trying to slide under the blue-tiled upper lip of the stall.

Probably so it could get to the showerhead and Do Something Nasty to it. Don't ask me how I knew.

I tried to breathe more slowly. My heart pounded, and dark little spackles raced across my vision. *Look, Dru. Look where you shouldn't.*

It's a kind of sideways-seeing, not quite focusing on the thing you're seeking. You have to soften up your eyes and look without looking, without expecting. It's *damn* hard to do. I had two things on my side, though. Gran had been a strict teacher who believed practice made perfect. And with Dad, I was used to performing under fire—meaning, when something from the Real World was trying to get at us—all the time.

My teeth tingled. Under the running water and the weird scraping soft sounds the fog made, I heard an owl's quiet passionless cry. Little feathers brushed my wet naked skin, and my breath turned into flashing ice crystals as soon as it left my mouth. The shower water cooled perceptibly. It was stealing heat from the shower itself now, which meant it was getting stronger. And it was resolving into a writhing mass of finger-thick tentacles, some of them wickedly clawed at the tip.

My left hand jabbed forward, the hex flying like a flat blue star, not-quite-visible sparks pouring from its points. It was just like flicking a playing card, the way I learned to do down in Carmel with that hunter who went surfing every day. Dad had really liked him; he wasn't half bad. Remy Gagnon had a lot of weird tics, but he could stand at the front door, fling a playing card all the way down the hallway in his shotgun shack and hit the back door hard enough to make a cracking sound. Sometimes he even swore in bayou Cajun while he did it, especially if he'd had a bad day.

His idea of bad day? It involves sucker nests, flamethrowers, support just short of heavy artillery, and usually a lot of screaming. Or, you know, Sunday at about eleven at the health-food store, when the church crowd gets out and he's there looking for colloidal silver.

I wasn't swearing. I was screaming as the hex hit the thing, the feathers turned to scraping little wires all over my body, and the shower coughed. Water sprayed in every direction, and I heard shouting. Boy voices, oddly muffled and far away.

So someone had noticed I was getting eaten by tentacles and red fog in here. That was good. But I was *naked*.

The fog swirled. The hex struck true, tearing away a bit of it I hadn't exactly *seen*. It looked like a fist-sized blood clot, turning and splattering in midair. More warm water gushed everywhere, including in my face. My fingers snapped back, yanking the hex at the last moment like flicking a wet towel to snap someone's unsuspecting backside, and the clot was whipped smartly aside. It screamed as it tore away, like a rabbit under the claws of a hawk, and the sound drilled through my head until I thought my teeth would shatter.

My knees slipped on tile. The water was a couple inches deep and rising, and little bits of the fog-thing rained down with sickening wet thumps. Tentacles plopped free, bleeding fog and thin red fluid.

It sounded like wet hamburger being dropped onto sheet metal and smelled like the worst garbage dump in the world. I actually considered throwing up as I slumped, trembling, in the corner. The showerhead was sputtering, twisted and eaten as if it'd been sprayed with acid and blowtorched.

The little bits of fog-thing were a lot more substantial than they should have been. Ivory teeth clinked down, and tentacles I hadn't seen. I'd hit it just right, thank God.

I huddled there with the knife, shaking, and waited for whatever came next.

CHAPTER NINE

"*Drbarnak,*" **Hiro's voice** bounced oddly off the tiles. "The larval form could have been in here for up to a month, gathering strength. A parting gift from our Red Queen, perhaps?"

Red Queen. He meant Anna. It didn't seem her style, though.

"Perhaps." Christophe shifted his weight. I could see his boots as he leaned back against the door of a changing stall in the girls' locker room. They'd handed dry clothing over the top of the door while they cleaned everything up out there. I heard murmurs, someone muttering a sharp command. "Or an opportunist. Impossible to tell."

Hiro had about as many questions as I did. "How did she fight it off?"

"I don't know yet." Finely leashed impatience. I knew Christophe well enough to hear it, if not in his tone, then in the way he moved against the stall door. "She was . . . upset."

Upset? I'd been about ready to stab whoever came for me. It took

Christophe two towels and a few minutes of gentle talking to get me out of my crouch in the stall, and I refused to give up the knife.

He looked like he understood. Wrapped me in the towels, sent someone for dry clothes, and whisked me off to a changing stall to dry off and calm down.

All this, after I'd been a total ass to him. It kind of made me like him more. But it was *confusing*.

Hiro wasn't taking the understatement as a hint. "As well she should be. This makes ten attempts on her li—"

"Shut up." Christophe actually jerked away from the door, all his weight on the balls of his feet like he was going to throw a punch.

I pulled my damp hair out from the T-shirt's collar. It was hard to get dressed with my hands shaking like I had the palsy, like old Mrs. Hatfield—Gran's closest neighbor, back in the long ago. "Ten *what*?" The words echoed, a little more shrill than I intended. "Hiro? Ten what?"

"Attempts on your life, Milady. Since the unpleasantness with . . . *Milady*." True to form, he loaded up the last word with such sarcastic spite that there was no question who he was talking about. He used the same word for me and for Anna, but he actually sounded respectful when he referred to me.

I was taking notes on how he did that.

"Hiro." Christophe, all the warning in the world in that one simple word. "There's no need to—"

Oh, hell no. "I'll say there's a need." It was kind of a relief to feel something other than queasy, shaky terror. Irritation felt like I had some sort of control over the situation. "What kind of *attempts* are we talking about here?"

"The standard. Anything you might expect, given a *svetocha* to protect. Assassins, traps, one particularly inelegant attempt by a team of strictly human mercenaries—" There was a scraping sound, and Hiro stopped talking. Christophe's feet hadn't moved, but I could just see him staring down the other *djamphir*, one elegant hand closing into a fist.

I hastily buttoned up my jeans and unlocked the door. My hands had stopped shaking, but I still felt a little weird. It had taken four towels to scrub myself dry, mostly because I kept seeing traces of red on me and rubbing *hard* until my skin hurt. "Wait a second—*wait*. Jesus, Christophe. Why didn't you tell me?"

"There was no need to worry you." He gave me a once-over, blue eyes dark and thoughtful. "Most of them were of little account. And you are well-watched now."

Yeah, if you're following me even when I run with the wulfen, maybe. I guess. Something inside me was trying to tell me to calm down. It didn't sound like Dad's voice, which was probably good.

I didn't think I could stand that, even inside my own head.

Behind him, a group of older *djamphir* students were mopping up the flooded locker room. It looked like someone had set off an M80 full of red food coloring. Some of the tiles were cracked as well as discolored, and one of the tubs—the one closest the door, the one I never used—was draining. It looked like an almighty-big thing had busted out of it, breaking tile and shattering its edges, bleeding red everywhere. Another group, this one of wulfen students, had shovels and wheelbarrows and were carting Jell-O-like red tentacles out. Their faces were all set in that particular way that tells you someone's smelling something nasty. I didn't blame them. The thing reeked like old copper and something I'd only smelled in one or two places along the Gulf—when the sea itself starts to rot offshore and mist rolls in. A salty, decomposing reek that crawls into your clothes after a few hours and is damn hard to wash out even with hot water and borax.

I pinched my nose shut before I could help it. Christophe looked amused, a corner of his mouth lifting. It was better than that slightly mocking face he gave everyone else, but not by much. It wasn't the face I would consider drawing.

I'd been too busy to draw for *ages*. I missed it, too. Sometimes my fingers would itch and tingle . . . but I was afraid of whatever I would draw now, with the touch so much stronger.

I considered flinging the handful of wet towels I was carrying at him, decided it would be childish of me.

Benjamin was by the door, his dark emo-boy fringe—it was a popular style this year—plastered to his pale forehead. He looked okay, but anger radiated from him in colorless waves and he was splattered with the red stuff. It was all over his jeans and T-shirt. The aspect slipped through him, ruffling his wet hair and making his fangs come out and recede. They gleamed, and when he saw I was looking he straightened, self-consciously.

"I'd say this is something I should be worried about." I started rolling up the towels together, both to hide how I was shaking again and to stop myself from actually throwing them. "So I've been bopping along all this time, not knowing? And people . . . things . . . whatever, have been trying to *kill* me? And you haven't *told* me?"

Christophe brushed it aside, one elegant hand waving like I shouldn't bother him with this. His watch, a chunky silver thing that looked like a Rolex, glittered. That was new—he'd never worn anything even close to jewelry before. And he hadn't had it during sparring. "You have other things to worry about. Dealing with assassins is *my* job. It's *traditional*."

A little voice inside my head was trying to tell me to calm down. "What's my job, then? Being happily oblivious to things trying to kill me? Why are they even . . ." I didn't have to go any further. I knew.

Sergej. He wanted me dead. Christophe said he was scared of me. That was a laugh—king of the vampires, or the closest thing to a king they had anymore, scared of *me.*

Because of what I was, or what I'd be when I finished blooming.

But I'd been thinking about it lately. A *lot.* The Real World was bigger and badder than I'd ever guessed, and I was thinking maybe it wasn't just the vampires who would want me dead. Especially after Dad and I went on a sixteen-state odyssey of getting rid of things that go bump in the night after Gran died.

Dad was bound to have made some enemies other than the king of the vampires, right? Which meant they were my enemies now. And here I was, just going along fat dumb and happy, danger lurking around every corner. If I would've known, I would've been more cautious, for Christ's sake.

Like, *hide under my bed and cower* kind of cautious. The idea had a certain appeal right now.

"We don't just hunt the *nosferat.*" Hiro, as usual, didn't sound like I was being stupid. He just sounded . . . thoughtful. His face was set, and I could almost see the aspect crackling around his edges, just waiting to break loose. "Although they have apparently spread word of your existence. The attempts we're experiencing now are proof."

Well, wasn't that just peachy-keen terrific. "*Dad* kept me a secret for sixteen years." I couldn't help it, I was yelling by now. I jabbed an accusing finger at Christophe. "Then *you* show up, and all of a sudden everyone knows about me. Great job, Chris. Thanks. *Marvelous* work."

It wasn't fair, because I knew he'd had zero to do with my father's death *or* Sergej finding out about me. But neither was it fair for him to beat on me with the sticks and look all smug. *None* of this was fair.

I *hated* being left in the dark. I hated all of this.

Christophe tilted his head slightly, studying me. Hiro took a half step back, and I could've sworn he looked like he was enjoying himself. His face settled into its usual impassivity when he noticed I was staring at him, short spiky black hair beaded with drops of moisture and his gray silk beginning to droop ever so slightly from the humidity.

I dropped the towels. They hit with a wet plop that would have been funny if it hadn't made me want to throw up. It wasn't any fun yelling at Christophe; all he did was *look* at me that way. Like it was kind of interesting that I was losing my shit, but in the end, not very important.

That just made it worse.

Finally, after a long pause that made me feel like I was five years old and throwing a tantrum, Christophe folded his arms. His absolutely perfect face was set and white, and even though the aspect wasn't on him I swear I saw his eyes glow.

He spoke through gritted teeth, each word a dagger. "I am sorry to have displeased you, Dru."

There's a certain way of apologizing that isn't an apology. It's more like a slap to the face. You hear a lot of that below the Mason-Dixon, especially if you hang out with the girls.

Christophe, however, could have given even the parlor princesses down there some lessons.

"That's even worse!" I exploded. "You could at least *mean it* when you say you're sorry!"

His eyes flared. "When have I not?" Sharply now, a teacher taking a student to task. At least I'd rattled him. That was something.

That's the thing about irrational, boiling rage, especially right after you've been hunching naked in a shower, afraid for your life. Nothing anyone says will make it better. "You *never* say you're really sorry!" I didn't even care that I was shouting at him in front of a bunch of boys. "Ever!"

A muscle flicked in Christophe's cheek. That was all.

I let out a short, frustrated scream and stamped past him. It was hard to do in bare feet, and I had to splash through puddles full of ick to get to the door. At least everyone else got out of my way. The twitching bits in the wheelbarrows were enough to make me glad I hadn't eaten lunch yet.

Benjamin's mouth had fallen open. He looked at me like I'd grown another head or something. But he didn't say a damn word, just hurried away from the wall and fell into step behind me as I made my grand exit, barefoot and looking totally ridiculous.

CHAPTER TEN

"**S**ure we knew.**"** Benjamin set his tray down. "Christophe said to let you adjust, to not worry you. It seemed like a good idea when he said it. Plus, it's trad, you know. The Kouroi do the protecting. It's our *job*."

The cafeteria was empty since it wasn't quite lunchtime. But that's one of the good things about being at a Schola—when you show up in the caf, there's *always* food. Some of the teachers keep pretty irregular hours. And *you* try being around hungry werwulfen for very long. I guarantee you'll see the wisdom of having munchies on tap.

"This is *so* not cool." My feet were cold, but that was the least of my problems. I glared at my own tray—heavy varnished wood instead of the plastic kind they'd had at the reform Schola. "When was I going to be let in on it?"

Benjamin dropped down in the chair next to me. "I guess when you let us in on your habit of sneaking out during the day instead of having us tag along all invisible-like." But he was looking down at his plate. "Or when something happened we couldn't hide. Like today. How did you fight that thing off, anyway? I didn't hear a thing—that was what clued me in. It was too silent. I couldn't even hear the water running."

I shivered. *Great. And I thought we were so clever, getting out for a breath of fresh air.* All of a sudden the cellophane-wrapped sandwich on my tray didn't look so appetizing, so I cracked open the blueberry yogurt smoothie and took a long drink. It went down in a slimy rush, and I thanked God it wasn't strawberry. That would have been Too Much. "I found the spot where it was anchored to the world and hexed it right out. My grandmother . . ." I couldn't even begin to explain. *Djamphir* combat sorceries are different than what Gran taught me, and you don't even start dealing with them until your fourth year of schooling.

Great. One more thing to feel happy about. Not.

"You're lucky. *Drbarnak*—those things—are nasty." He arranged his knife and fork with prissy exactitude, picked up his fork, and spun some spaghetti around the tines. The pasta writhed against itself as if alive, drenched in marinara.

I didn't want to think about it. And if he wasn't going to say anything else about the daylight runs, I wasn't going to, either. I know a peace offering when I see one. "Lucky." I tried not to laugh, half-burped, and made a weird strangled noise. "Yeah. Listen, Benjamin . . ."

"Huh?" He forked up a cartload of pasta, slurped it down. His gaze kept moving, roving over every surface in the cafeteria. He'd chosen a spot where he could see the entrances, a wall behind us, and locked doors on either side.

Knowing why he'd done that didn't make it better. It was exactly where Dad would have chosen to sit, too. Civilians don't think like that.

I want to get out. I want to get away. "Nothing."

For a boy with such a prissy way of laying out his fork, he certainly ate like a bandit. He swallowed a load of spaghetti large enough to be floating the Hudson on its own barge. "Christophe won't get mad at you, you know. You can do pretty much whatever you want. He's, uh. You know. He's just like that. He's old-fashioned."

"Old-fashioned." I picked at the cellophane. What kind of sandwich was this? I didn't even remember.

"Yeah. He thinks we should protect . . . You know, you shouldn't be bothered with stuff while you're training."

"Stuff like people trying to kill me?" I'd put a banana on my tray, too. That, at least, didn't remind me of anything trying to kill me. *Could* you kill someone with a banana? It didn't seem possible. Maybe a possessed banana. I'd seen possessed pets before, but not possessed fruit. But I'll bet it's out there somewhere. "Or *other* stuff?"

He coughed a little, twirled more spaghetti. "Come on, Dru. Once Reynard decides about someone, he's loyal. I never believed all those rumors about him working for his father."

"Yeah. He's some angel, all right." I set the banana back down. My stomach had closed up. Now not only was I hungry and unable to eat, but I also felt like an idiot for screaming at the one person I should've been able to trust. Hadn't he proved as much, over and over again?

He'd always arrived just in the nick of time. And there were the times he did things like . . .

Like holding the knifepoint against his own chest and telling me not to hesitate. Like forcing me to drink his blood after Anna shot me and I lay dying.

Like kissing me so hard I felt it in my toes.

So that's it, huh? He swaps spit with you and all of a sudden you're not into Goth Boy anymore? How do you know how you feel now? Graves is somewhere out there, he's probably being tortured, *and he's betting on you finding him. Here you are playing footsies with Christophe. You told him you didn't even* like *Christophe that way!*

Oh, God. Now I was going to start thinking about *that*, too, and getting even more tangled up. I pushed my chair back with a long linoleum-scrape sound. "I'm going to my room. No, stay here and eat your spaghetti."

Benjamin was already halfway to his feet. "I'm supposed to—"

"Leon's right over there." I pointed at the hall where I could *feel* a *djamphir* lurking. The touch told me who it was, too, like picking out where in America you were from the quality of the radio static. "I'm getting better at spotting you guys."

Benjamin relaxed a little. Lowered himself back down slowly, with one quick longing glance at his plate. He was pretty much always hungry. The other *djamphir* on his crew were the same way, almost wulflike in their urge to chow down at every possible opportunity. "You sure you don't want me to—"

"I'm sure. I just want to go up and lock my door." *And cry. Or try to cry. Funny how I don't seem to have any tears left. Just this lump in my throat and a serious case of water blindness.*

He didn't look convinced, but he did take another mouthful of spaghetti. I felt his eyes on me all the way across the cafeteria's empty expanse, each table sitting neatly with chairs around it, like a hen brooding over chicks.

The hall I'd pointed at looked empty, sure. Heavy hunter-green velvet drapes, marble busts, dark wood wainscoting—and a little patch of wall a few doors down that shouted *don't look at me*.

"I can see you, Leon. So cut it out." I didn't even bother to glance at him as I swept past.

He caught up with me easily, swiping his lank mousy hair back from his forehead. Of all Benjamin's crew, he was the only one who wasn't classically handsome. He would've been cute, if he hadn't fought it so hard. "Getting better, *fräulein*. Soon I might have to start trying."

"Blow me." I was really feeling savage. It's hard to get a satisfying snit on when you're barefoot.

"No way. Christophe would have a fit." He gave his sarcastic little laugh, and I lengthened my stride a little. Heat rose in my cheeks. "Oh, I see. Trouble in paradise?"

He was *so* not going to analyze me. "Didn't I just tell you to blow me?"

"What's gotten into you?" He sighed. "Other than getting attacked by tentacles during your shower, that is. Or is it something else? Something missing? Something perhaps tall, and not so hairy, with green eyes?"

I rounded on him, my fists itching and my teeth tingling. Leon stepped back, his hands raised.

There was no sardonic smile. He looked deadly serious, and if you've ever seen a lank-haired, average-looking *djamphir* look serious, you know it's not comforting. Especially if you've seen him in action. Christophe treated him almost like an equal, which was thought-provoking in its own way. "Easy, *svetocha*. I'm not blind or stupid. I am, however, a very good guesser."

"They can't find him." The words burst out of me. "They can't *find* him, and I don't even know if they're really looking. They can't even find Anna, and she's not likely to keep a low profile. They *have* to know where Sergej is, or at least have a good guess. But Christophe says it'll take months to get me ready. *Months*. The same thing he said a month ago."

Leon nodded, his hands dropping. Said nothing, just waited for me to finish.

I appreciated it. But he wasn't who I wanted to be talking to.

I wanted Graves. I wanted my Goth Boy in his long black coat, with his goddamn cigarettes and his sarcastic little asides and his green eyes and the way he made me feel like I could handle this shit. I wanted to hear him breathing in the middle of the night, from his sleeping bag. I wanted to see him in the morning while he teased me about always being late. *Girl can't ever get out the door on time, don't worry Dru, first one's free,* and all the little things he did. Like pecking me on the cheek before walking off to class.

What's that saying? *You don't know what you got until it's gone?* Yeah. Sure. I hadn't even known what we had while he was around.

I swallowed, hard. "He could be Broken. Or dead." I stared at Leon's narrow chest. *And it's my fault.*

"Then we need to be sure you won't join him." Leon didn't shrug, but his tone was dismissive.

"Sure, he's just a *loup-garou*, right? One step up from a wulfen, but still a second-class citizen." I pushed back my damp hair, twisting it up. It would come unraveled as soon as I took two steps, but I twisted it into a bun. Tighter and tighter, slippery against my fingers. The more I twisted it, the better I liked the almost-pain. "I know the score, *Leontus*. I'm getting some shoes and I'm going to visit Ash."

He shrugged. "Visiting the Broken won't make you feel better. And don't you have an appointment with Taft for Aspect Mastery?"

"What's the point? I'm not fricking bloomed yet, Christophe's going to come looking for me and we're going to have another fight, he's not even going to let me out of my room without a guard, I'll bet they're not even looking for Graves, and all of this is *fucking useless!*"

Yelling. Again. Like it would solve anything.

He cocked his head, going still in that way older *djamphir* have. That's sometimes how you can tell the old ones—the way they go immobile, like a cat with one paw in the air, considering something. It's like they forget their bodies are there while their attention turns inward. When he was still like this, you could see where he'd be handsome if he would get a different haircut and stop with the wall-flower act. Even Benjamin seemed to sometimes forget Leon was around, until he opened his mouth and delivered a sarcastic little bite.

I liked that about him.

When he finished thinking, his chin dropped a millimeter and he looked at me. "There's a simple enough way to find out if they're truly looking for him, Dru."

I couldn't help myself. I looked over my shoulder, nervously. Checking to make sure nobody else was in the hall. Benjamin couldn't hear us on the other side of the caf, and he would be more interested in his spaghetti anyway.

Leon gave a little half-snort of almost-laughter. "Don't worry, I'm one of the few Reynard trusts on my own around you. Well, are you interested?"

I let go of my hair, wet curls slithering through my fingers. My stomach settled, like a fish giving up the fight and drowning on dry land. "I'm all ears."

"Formally charge me, as a member of your Guard, with finding out." A humorless smile—his lips never relaxed; they stayed blood-less-thin all the time. It kind of looked like he was constantly sucking on something astringent. "A private commission, from a *svetocha* to a Kouroi who has sworn obedience. If *you* trust me that far."

My mouth snapped shut. I thought it over hard, eyeing him.

"Great. Perfect. How do I do *that?*"

His mouth twitched. He rolled his shoulders back in their sockets, once, precisely. His jeans looked battered and his sneakers weren't much better—it was a wonder Benjamin didn't fuss over *him* about his clothes. Or Nathalie. "Consider it done. Give me a week to find out. Can you wait that long?"

Normally, I'd've jumped on it. But I stood there for a few more seconds, considering him.

"Very good," he said finally. "You're beginning to weigh people instead of judging them solely on instinct. That's a relief."

Wonders never ceased. "You're not just going to turn around and tell Christophe all about this, are you?" *Because he seems to know everything I do anyway.*

He actually looked *amused.* At least, the corners of his eyes crinkled slightly. "I'd be in more trouble than you could imagine if he knew I'd even suggested it. I'll consider it a formal commission, then. Come on, let's get you some princess slippers so you can go consort with your faithful dog."

I fell into step beside him. Was it relief I was feeling? That lightness under my heart, right next to the empty hole that had opened up when I figured out Dad wasn't coming back? "Every time I think I like you, Leon, you say something like that."

"It wouldn't do to get too fond of me, Milady." He shook his hair back down over his face. "Those you get too fond of seem to have a dreadful time of it."

"Fuck you too," I muttered, and that shut him up. It was funny, though.

I was still feeling relieved.

CHAPTER ELEVEN

The heavy, barred iron door was pitted with rust, but still solid. Down here the halls were stone, no paneling to soften them up. No velvet draperies, no marble busts, no bookcases or lockers. Every school has industrial places, where they don't bother even slapping on a coat of paint. Usually that's the best place to slip around if you don't want to be seen.

But I was down here for another reason.

The door was locked, the key hanging on a nail. I had to go on tiptoes to grab it. It was high enough that a wulfen in changeform could reach it easily. Which was thought-provoking, really.

Leon stepped back. A low, throbbing growl rattled the entire huge iron thing, but I was in no mood for it. "Stop that," I snapped, and the growl petered out. "You know it's me. Jeez."

"He's reacting to me." Leon retreated further and leaned against the wall a good fifteen feet away. He closed his eyes and, to all appearances, settled into a light doze.

I wasn't fooled, but I did appreciate the privacy.

I pushed the door open. It groaned, despite me oiling the hinges the first night we'd brought him down here. It was way too heavy to do anything else.

At least he'd stopped throwing himself against the walls every night. And he'd recovered from taking on three vampires at once. It had been touch and go there for a while, but he'd made it.

I could feel good about that, even though I hadn't had anything to do with it, right? It had been all Dibs, patching him up and fighting for his life.

Ash greeted me with a low whine, his narrow head dropping. The pale streak running along his left temple glowed in the light coming in from the hall's fluorescents. The crusted seepage along his jaw, where I'd shot him with one of Dad's silver-grain bullets, was slowly healing. Nobody was sure if the silver still buried in his flesh and bone was interfering with Sergej's control of him—*his master's call*, Christophe would say, grimly. If his body expelled the silver and I was in the room with him . . .

. . . well, they called him the Broken for a reason. Broken to the will of the king of the vampires. I was looking at something Graves might become, only he wouldn't get all hairy, unable to change back into a boy.

Nobody could tell me quite what would happen. Not even Nat, and she was probably the only person I could bring myself to say anything about this to. I hadn't yet, though. I was working up to it.

I even had the note in my bedroom, locked away in a vanity drawer, Sergej's spidery handwriting in scratchy, rusty-red ink. *Since you have taken my Broken, I will break another.*

The room was actually a cell. There was a long narrow metal shelf that served as a bed, and he hadn't shredded the last blanket I'd brought down. The bowl his nightly meal had come in was licked clean and shoved in a corner, and that was an improvement too. There was a toilet bowl, but I didn't look at that. Instead, I stamped across the cell to the shelf bed, picked up the plaid blanket, and shook it out. Folded it in quick swipes. "You've stopped tearing them up. That's great."

Ash settled back on his haunches. Almost eight feet of pretty-unstoppable werwulf regarded me with his head cocked to one side. He looked for all the world like a golden retriever wanting to play but afraid to ask.

"All sorts of fun. First I get beat up, then I get attacked by the Spaghetti Monster. Only not so nice, and it's not so much fun to fight off loads of spaghetti when you're naked in the shower. You ever had that happen to you? Probably not." I dropped down on the bed, holding the heavy blanket awkwardly. I'd done a sloppy job folding it; the edges were all messy. Gran wouldn't approve.

Maybe I could even introduce a mattress now. Big fun down here, between the Broken and me. Both of us useless. At least, he was useless to Sergej. Or so we hoped.

Ash was pretty useful when it came to saving my bacon, though.

The Broken werwulf settled down further. If he'd had stand-up ears, they would have drooped.

"We're a good team, you know." I didn't look directly at him. I know enough about stray dogs not to do that. He inched closer, moving with slow supple grace. "We kicked a sucker's ass last night, didn't we?"

He made a low whining noise. Cocked his head. He was really good at telling when I was upset. Funny, he was about the only boy who reliably could. Or who knew to keep his yap shut when I was.

Of course, the fact that his jaw wasn't made for talking in changeform probably had something to do with it.

It was about between midnight and one, almost lunchtime for the rest of the Schola. If I was where I was supposed to be, I'd be sitting on a stool in an empty classroom, trying to make the aspect show up on command while the tutor lectured me. Christophe would show up, too, and add his two cents.

Abruptly, my skin itched. It was night out there. The Schola had a lot of green space. I couldn't wait for another daylight run, even if the *djamphir* did tag along all invisible. Now I could see if I could catch them doing it, and figuring out how to be invisible . . . well, that would be a skill worth having, wouldn't it.

When I bloomed, Shanks had promised me that I could be the rabbit one day. I was looking forward to it. It's an honor to be chosen to run. Dibs had been plied with pizza and beer, the hero of the day.

Ash had moved forward. His ruined cheek rubbed against my knee. He whined again, and rubbed some more.

I put my hand down, blindly. My fingers met the curve of his skull. The hair rasped, amazingly vital, against my skin. I petted him, scratched behind his ears—set low, the curves of cartilage hidden in fur.

The trembling in him relaxed. His fur rippled, waves passing through it like wind through high corn.

Sometimes, when I did this, patches of white skin showed. So fragile, unlined, something soft under all that fur and wildness. It looked like those bits of skin never saw the sun.

"I wish I knew how old you are." I scratched and soothed, smoothing the fur, but avoided touching the patches of bare skin when they showed up. It just . . . it didn't seem right. "You knew Christophe, right?"

The whine turned into a low growl. I tapped the top of his narrow head. "Stop that. I was just asking."

The growl modulated, like he was trying to talk. It sounded like he was trying to say my name. *Roooooo* . . . A long pause. *Grooooooo.*

"It's okay." I sat up straight, opened my eyes, and soothed him. "Really. It was just a question. Hey, I know. Let's go for a walk, huh? Walk? You like the idea?"

Jesus Christ, Dru. He could use your guts for garters anytime he felt like it, but you treat him like he's a lapdog. Not very smart.

I couldn't help myself. Not when he was leaning up against my leg like a hound on a cold night and orange gleams swirled through his irises under heavy lids.

He didn't look too jazzed at the idea of going for a walk, but I slid to the edge of the shelf bed, bumping at him. "Maybe you're ready. We could walk around, huh? Even just down to the end of the corridor and—"

"Bad idea," Christophe said from the door.

I actually jumped, forcing my free hand down from the reassuring lump of the locket. Ash tensed, but his head didn't leave my knee.

Christophe didn't look angry. He just stood there, leaning against the doorjamb, his arms folded. Never in a million years could I ever look that graceful just standing still. Plenty of the other *djamphir* couldn't either. He looked like the entire world was nothing more than a picture frame to set him off right, but not in an *I'm so pretty* way. More like in an art-print sort of way, the kind you'd find hanging in an expensive coffeehouse somewhere on the West Coast.

Ash blinked, very deliberately. First the right eye, then the left. The specks and swirls of orange in his eyes had run together into a steady glow.

I curled my fingers in the thick ruff of hair at the back of the wulf's neck. Nobody except Graves had ever stood in the door when

I visited Ash, and things had been all right then. Or at least, less messed up than they were now.

"You've never come down here before." I was glad I'd stopped to put some shoes on. There's nothing like staring at a boy you've both kissed and yelled at on the same night to make you feel grateful for having all your armor on.

"There was no need. And Ash and I have . . . history." A small, tight smile. "Also, there is an emergency Council meeting. Your presence is requested."

He said it like it meant *required*. I guess it kind of was. "This is about the shower, isn't it."

"Only tangentially. There's information." The pause was significant, but his expression didn't change. "About Anna."

Ash's tension turned into sound. The subvocal growl was so low I felt it in my bones, and the blanket fell off the bed. He rolled his head back, looking at me, and his eyes were orange lamps.

"Leash the dog, Milady." Christophe had stiffened perceptibly, and the aspect folded softly over him. His hair slicked down, darkening, and now *his* eyes were glowing, too. Cold, cold blue. "You seem to be the only thing keeping him calm."

"Oh, please. I weigh a quarter of what he does in changeform. Like I'm going to stop him if he goes for you." All the same, I hoped he didn't. Of all the things that would just cap off the worst night I'd had in a while—and that's saying something—it would be Christophe and Ash going at it in a cell. With me in it.

"If he comes for me, you'll lose your Broken." He managed to make it sound like a quiet statement of fact. "He *is* yours, now. Silver doesn't account for this." Christophe straightened and took one deliberate step over the threshold. Heel to toe, rolling through, so that he had his balance at every moment.

He was expecting Ash to do something.

The Broken werwulf went very still. He was staring at me, not at Christophe.

"I want to take him for a walk." I didn't mean *right this moment,* but I also didn't want to be put off again. I stole another glance at Christophe's face. My fingers ached in Ash's fur, my fist clenched tight and sweating. The Broken still watched me, and his lip lifted silently. Sharp teeth, very white. And a lot of them.

"Not tonight, Dru. Please." And how was it that Christophe could just *ask* me sometimes? If he did that more often, I wouldn't get so frustrated.

My chin rose, stubbornly. *That's a look like a mule,* Gran's voice said in my memory, and missing her rose hard and fast in my throat. "Then when?"

"Tomorrow night. We'll leave *malaika* practice. You've been going at it harder than I've ever seen a student work. I think you need a holiday."

"Then it'll take even longer. We aren't ever supposed to relax, Christophe. *You relax, and the night will hunt you down.* Wasn't that what you said?"

"What I say to you during practice doesn't need to be repeated. It's my job to push you, Dru. I have to be twice as hard as anything you'll find out there. I've trained hundreds of Kouroi. Some of them are dead. I wonder, if I'd been more ruthless, pushed them harder, if they'd still be alive."

But he wasn't thinking about them, I'd bet. From the look on his face, I'd bet he was thinking of someone else. Someone with my hair, only sleek ringlets instead of frizz, and a heart-shaped face.

My mother. He'd trained her, too.

"And you want me to take a vacation." Yes, I was being pissy.

But he always had the goddamn answers. It was comforting, until it wasn't.

Dad would've just told me to go do my katas and quit bitching about my bootstraps. I would've even done it.

Wouldn't I? How would Dad have dealt with all this? He hadn't even told me the most basic things about myself. About who or what I was, who he was, who Mom had been . . . but I hadn't needed to know, had I? I'd known everything there was to know when I was his helper. His little girl.

Daddy's little princess. Who had emptied a clip into the shambling corpse that used to be her father.

Of all the things that will fuck you up in the head, that had to be in a class all its own.

Christophe didn't move. "I hope for the best, but I train you for the worst." He let out a sigh. "The Council awaits your pleasure, Dru."

"They can go on without me." If I kept this up, that tone of painful patience would crack. I hadn't managed to make him lose his shit yet, but I kept trying. I could almost *feel* him taking his temper in both hands, as Gran would've said.

His eyes were just as glowy as Ash's, bright piercing blue. "No. They can't. You're the only *svetocha* we have. You are the head of the Order, even if most of your duties are ceremonial at this point. And information on Anna could lead to . . . other information. That you have expressed a great deal of interest in."

He never really referred to Graves by name. It was kind of insulting.

I patted Ash's head with my free hand, smoothing down the hair. He was still as stone, his teeth bared, watching me. It didn't scare me as much as it should have. Stray curls fell in my face. I wished my hair was down all the way; it would hide my expression. "They liked it better with Anna running things. At least she knew what the hell to do all the time."

"She was just as profoundly uncertain as you when she first arrived." Choosing his words so, so very carefully. And he was tense, his shoulders stiffening.

"And I'll bet you helped her get right over that, didn't you. You're so *helpful*." Yes. I was being a total bitch, okay? I just couldn't stop myself.

He'd gone just as still as Ash. "I did what duty required."

"Is that what you're doing here, too? What duty requires?"

He actually sighed at me. "No. Right now I'm understanding your anger and loneliness as best I can, as I overlook your daytime games."

My chin set stubbornly. "You don't know what it's like to be cooped up in here all the time."

"Which is why I let you go during the day, and only follow at a distance. For your safety."

"*Let* me go. Like I'm a prisoner."

"Why don't we address what is truly troubling you, *kochana*?"

Oh, there was no way I wanted to do that. "Sometimes," I addressed the wall opposite me, not looking at either of them, "I could *really* hate you, Christophe."

"You act out with me because it's safe."

Oh, goddammit. What do you do when someone says something like that? I snuck another glance at him, and all the tension had gone out of his shoulders. The aspect had left, too. He just stood there, as if I wasn't holding on to a pile of kickass werwulf, as if we were alone in this narrow cell. His hands dangled, loose and empty, and he was staring right at me.

At my face. Where every little thing I was feeling was probably written in neon capitals. And underlined.

"Of all the words I could pick to describe you . . ." I was about to say, *safe isn't one of them*. But that would be a lie, wouldn't it. He wasn't the kind of safe I felt when Graves was sleeping in the same room, where I knew I would wake up and things would be all right.

No, Christophe was the kind of safe that had teeth. Where you know that the bad things are outside the door, but none of them are as bad as the thing inside standing guard over you. He was like a roller-coaster ride, or a twister. Not comforting at all.

Except it *is* kind of comforting when the twister's on your side.

"Which one would you choose?" He was still staring.

I patted Ash's head. "I guess *obnoxious* would be a good one. Move it, kid."

The Broken werwulf obediently stepped aside. He edged back, trying to slip between me and Christophe without being too obvious about it. I reached out, snagged his ruff, and pulled gently. "Over here. Don't think I don't see that."

He was stiff and resistant, but I finally got him on my other side. I spread the blanket out on the shelf bed. "I'll be back. Have a good night, okay? And don't worry. You're showing more skin than ever. You'll change back. I know you will."

Yeah. Right. But Christophe didn't say anything, and Ash gave me one long extraordinary look. Like he understood, and he believed me. And like he wanted to say something, but he couldn't. His jaw crackled as he opened his mouth, showing all his teeth in a yawn. A sound came out from the bottom of the well of his throat, and I could swear to God, *again*, that he was trying to say my name.

CHAPTER TWELVE

The Council were all standing when I came in the door. They usually did that.

I got the urge to glance behind myself every time, to see what they were looking at. Christophe, who had opened the door, glanced in, and told me it was safe with a short nod, stepped in after me. That was enough to get me moving. It was either that or be herded.

The chair at the head of the table didn't get any more comfortable. When I dropped down, they still remained standing.

I guess Anna had trained them well. "Well, let's get this over with." I tried not to sound tired and bad-tempered.

As usual, the first to sit was Bruce. He lowered himself down in the seat to my left, his sharp dark face set. That was the signal for the rest of them. Slim blond Ezra had his usual cigar, but it was unlit. Mostly because I wrinkled my nose every time he fired the damn things up. He was in his usual jeans, starched-white dress shirt, and black suit jacket. It should have looked *Miami Vice* corny, but it didn't. The fact that he'd hit the drift late and looked about twenty-five helped.

Alton's dreadlocks moved like a live thing as he sat, slowly. He wore a cheery red and yellow rugby shirt, and his usual smile, shocking white against his ebony skin, was missing. I was so used to Alton's sunny good temper, it was kind of a nasty surprise. Of all of them, I suppose he was the most cheerful.

Right next to him, Augustine's chair scraped as he dropped down. He didn't look too happy, either.

Kir and Marcus were off the Council because they'd helped Anna play her little games. Marcus hadn't done it knowingly, but he still refused to come back and be a part of the meetings. Christophe was okay with that; I wasn't so sure. Kir, on the other hand, had been packed off to teach in a satellite Schola.

Probably a reform one, too. Like the one he'd helped send me to.

That left two spots open. One was Christophe's, of course. They'd asked him, and he made a big deal out of asking my permission and generally driving home that they'd accused him of being a traitor before all that. I guess he was bitter about the whole thing. It wasn't like I blamed him, but if he kept rubbing it in, we were going to have more shouting matches in this windowless room.

Big fun.

For the other seat, I'd suggested Augustine, and been surprised when he showed up at the next meeting, scrubbed and looking miserable as a kid on School Picture Day. He was Dad's friend and fellow hunter, from the old days. Blond hair slicked back, his uniform of white tank top and red flannel clean as if I'd washed it myself that month I spent in his Brooklyn apartment, waiting for Dad to come back.

On my left-hand side, there was an empty chair. Christophe rarely sat down. Sometimes he prowled the Council room as if looking for an exit, sometimes he stood beside and slightly behind my seat. Tonight it was behind-the-chair. He hadn't said a word since I'd closed Ash's door.

Three chairs down—because he wouldn't even sit next to Christophe—Hiro perched, ramrod straight. His coppery fingers rested on the glossy tabletop, and his mouth was a straight line. In front of him was an expensive-looking, cream-colored envelope.

My mouth dried up. I stared at it.

Since you have taken my Broken, I shall break another. But Christophe had said this was about Anna, hadn't he?

Hiro, of course, knew exactly what I was thinking. "It is a communication from the traitor."

He wouldn't even call her *Anna.* It was always "the traitor" or the sarcastic *Milady,* and the gleam in his dark eyes when he said it made me want to back up a couple steps. I was always glad he never looked at *me* like that.

I waited, but nobody said anything else. "And?" The single word fell like a rock into a quiet pond.

Hiro shifted, as if uncomfortable. "It is . . . addressed to you, Milady."

"Okay." I leaned forward, held my hand out. But it was Christophe who took two steps down the table, leaned across Hiro, and scooped the envelope up. He actually sniffed it, too, bringing it just under his patrician nose and inhaling deeply.

"No trace of *nosferat.*" But his face was set, his jaw an iron line. That expression was the one that made my heart do a little scared leap inside my chest.

If he ever looked at me like that, I'd find a wall to put my back to.

Pronto. "Well, hand it over. I'm sure pretty much everyone here has read it except for me." But I was wrong about that. Christophe laid it gently in my outstretched palm, and it was still sealed. *Dru Anderson* was written on the front in block letters, curiously childlike printing in fountain pen, the edges of the letters bleeding faint blue.

"How was this delivered?" Christophe wanted to know.

Ezra shifted in his chair, toying with the cigar. He looked like he *really* wanted to light it. "A drop box in Newark, an old one. Nothing else in it, and the teams retrieving drop items are on alert. We don't know what other information she's passed to the *nosferat*. No tracks, no scent."

"Probably one of her Guard delivered it." Hiro's lip curled. "I would not have suspected them of professionalism."

"We trained them and made them loyal to her." Bruce's faintly English accent made the words crisp. "She did the rest. They're not to blame."

That was enough to get Hiro going on an old argument. "The retainers are not to blame, certainly. It will not make their punishment any less—"

"Here we go again," August muttered. "Just open it, Dru-girl. Let's see what she's got up her sleeve." Everyone looked at him. He sat bolt upright, and he still looked profoundly uncomfortable. But it was nice having him here.

"Let's argue once we actually know what it says, all right?" They all shut up, and I tore at the thick paper. Christophe wouldn't have handed it over if there was anything on it likely to be triggered, but I still used just my fingertips. A ghost of spice clung to it—Anna's peculiar flower scent, like carnations on the verge of going bad. It made me think of curly red ringlets and her delicate little fangs, the high-heeled boots with the tiny buttons marching all the way down, the silk dresses and the high gloss. She'd pretty much always looked like a model, or an illustration in some fantasy magazine.

Except for when she was trying to kill me. Then her face had contorted and flushed, and she'd had an assault rifle spewing fire while she screamed. Not a nice picture.

I sighed, yanked the folded sheet of matching paper out of the savaged envelope, and flicked it open. That same childlike block printing, neat little sentences.

You think you know everything, but you don't. If you want to rescue your friend, come visit me. Alone.

It was signed with a huge, florid calligraphy $\mathcal{A}$.

There was another sheet of paper—cheap copy stock, a satellite photo you could pull off the Internet. One building was circled with thick red Sharpie. I took it in, noticed an address typed at the bottom.

Gee. Subtle.

Christophe leaned over my shoulder. "Trap. Not even worth the paper it's printed on."

I stared at the address, marking it in my memory. There was something else in the envelope. I tweezed it out, delicately.

A silver earring, just the post part, no back. The skull and cross-bones swung as I held it up, and my heart twisted like a sponge in a merciless, bony hand. I made a tiny little sound, like I'd been punched.

"What the hell's that?" Augustine leapt to his feet.

Christophe's hand jerked forward, but I snatched the earring away. Folded it in both my hands, as if I was praying. The silver was cold, but it warmed quickly. My mother's locket was warm against my breastbone, too.

I let out another tiny sound. I couldn't get enough air in.

"No." Christophe grabbed my shoulder. His fingers dug in, and I could feel the prickle of claws through my hoodie. "*No, Dru. Don't even think about it.*"

I brought my hands up to my mouth. Inhaled, smelled nothing but the faint fading tang of Ash's vital, springy fur. Opened my palms a little, saw the earring's gleam.

"It's his." That small, quiet voice couldn't be mine. It burned my throat, squeezing its way out. "It's Graves's earring. He had it when I met him."

In the American History classroom, in the Dakotas. Before he'd gotten bit. Before everything.

"Oh, *fuck.*" Augustine dropped back down in his chair. Of all of them, he'd been the only one to move. Bruce and Ezra watched me, a line between Bruce's dark eyebrows and Ezra's cigar finally laid on the table instead of in his nervous, slender fingers.

Hiro, on the other hand, was watching Christophe. Very closely.

I swallowed hard. "You can let go of me, Chris." I didn't even sound like myself. The very small, very calm voice was almost lost in the static filling my head.

"Not until I'm certain you won't do anything silly." He leaned down, and his fingers eased a little but didn't let go. "Let me see."

I shook my head. Clasped my palms together. Laced my fingers as if he was trying to pry them apart.

He was not going to take that for an answer, though. "Dru. *Kochana.* Let me see."

I shook my head again. Wished he would shut up. The static was getting louder, and if I could just calm down a little, the touch might tell me something. If they would just all be quiet for a few seconds so I could shake the roaring inside my skull away.

"Let me—" Christophe's other hand flashed forward, caught at my clenched fists. His skin was warm, but his fingers hurt, digging in with more than human strength.

"No. *No!*" I actually screamed, jerking away as far as I could. His fingers bit down again, and I felt bone creaking. *My* bones, the little ones in my hand and the ball of my shoulder.

Hiro's chair scraped along the floor. The scraping became noise, a lot of it, and Christophe's hand was ripped away from my shoulder. Someone was yelling. Confusion, my chair hit hard and bumping the table like a balky carnival ride. The earring dug into my palms, and I tried to clear my head. But there was too much noise—a deep thrumming snarl, and the sound of fist meeting flesh.

I opened my eyes. The world rushed in, full of smeared color, and I leapt out of my chair.

A thin amber tide of spilled coffee covered the floor. Christophe faced Hiro next to the table near the wall, the silver samovar on its side and chugging out a waterfall of more hot coffee. Bruce had hold of Hiro, while Augustine had grabbed Christophe's arm. The aspect rushed and crackled over all of them like a forest fire.

Ezra was suddenly right next to me, appearing out of thin air with a little whispering sound.

I *hate* that. I let out a thin little shriek, which managed to distract everyone. Ezra caught the back of my hoodie, bracing me as I almost went over, and Christophe's eyes flashed.

"Settle *down!*" Augustine shoved Christophe back against the table, and Bruce had all he could do holding Hiro back. Hiro leaned forward, his fangs out and the thrumming coming from his slim chest.

Djamphir don't growl like wulfen. But when they make that sort of humming noise, they mean business. It's more like a subsonic vibration than anything else, and it sounds like it can rattle china right out of the cupboard.

"You should probably calm them down." Ezra made sure I was on my feet and stepped away. He lifted a silver Zippo, flicked it open, and scooped up his cigar.

Great. Thanks, that helps a lot. I found my voice. "Stop. Stop it." Made sure the earring was safe in my left hand and stepped forward.

Normally, putting yourself between two crazy-angry *djamphir* isn't the smartest thing to do. But I braced myself and slid between them, stepping in the tide of coffee. It sploshed against my sneakers. "*Stop.* Both of you. Stop it."

Christophe inhaled sharply as I edged between them, cutting off his view of Hiro. "Dru—"

"I need you guys to simmer down." I aimed for a businesslike tone, but just got a shaky almost-squeak. "Anna would like it if you both killed each other, wouldn't she? You're playing *right* into her hands. Or someone else's."

I didn't have to say whose.

Hiro's face contorted once, his eyes glowing dark amber. His fangs had scraped his lower lip, and a thin trickle of blood ran down his chin. I swallowed, hard, and hoped the bloodhunger wouldn't hit. If *I* started going crazy now, there was no telling what could happen. My shoulder throbbed—I was going to have a bruise there.

It would match the rest of me. This was turning out to be one sucky-ass night.

Hiro stared at me. I stared back, trying to plead with him silently. I don't know what he saw, but his face changed and the aspect slid away. He straightened slowly. His hand came up, and he wiped at his chin. Bruce didn't relax, though, locking his other arm, braced in case he lunged.

I nodded. Turned, splashing even more in the tide of spilled coffee. That was going to be a bitch to get cleaned up, and it might stain the hardwood. Not my problem right now, though. "Christophe."

He didn't look calm. Blue eyes fixed on Hiro, pale and cold and glowing, his fangs out and Augustine straining to hold him back. Augie's foot slid a little in the coffee, and Christophe half-lunged forward. August shoved him back, but his hold was slipping.

I did the only thing I could think of. It wasn't the *best* thing, mind you, but I think he deserved it.

I slapped Christophe.

Chapter Thirteen

t was a good hard crack, too, unwinding from my hip. The sound bounced off the walls, and Bruce let out a curse that would have made Dad proud.

The blow actually knocked Christophe's chin to the side. Some sense came back into those mad blue eyes, and now he was looking at me instead of Hiro. Anger and readiness leaked slowly out of his body, but Augustine didn't relax. If anything, he tensed *more*, like he was afraid Christophe was going to go postal on me.

Of all the things I was worried about right at the second, that wasn't one of them. Which was oddly comforting.

A queer little smile touched Christophe's lips. "Go ahead," he whispered, as if it was just the two of us in the room. "Go ahead, *kochana*. Hit me again. I'll let you."

A chill walked down my back. He'd said something like that to my mother, a long time ago. I'd dreamed it, or seen it, or something.

Who did he think he was talking to *now*?

"Settle down." Now I sounded more like myself. The earring dug into my palm. "I like Hiro. Leave him alone."

Christophe's shoulders dropped. His fangs retreated slowly, and it was so quiet I heard the crackle of his jaw structure shifting. His hair, slicked down under the aspect, ruffled a little like he'd run his fingers back through it. "My apologies."

"Yeah, well, I won't make you apologize to him. Even though you *should*." I nodded at August. "He's okay now. Aren't you, Christophe? I can belt you again if you need it."

The mark of my hand flushed briefly on his cheek, already fading. Blond streaks threaded back through his hair. A small movement went though him, like an animal settling into itself. "Save it for sparring practice."

"Yeah." I slid the earring, carefully, into the little coin pocket on my hip. "Sounds good. Now will you guys sit down and behave? It's been a hideous day— or night, or whatever—and I'm tired."

August slowly let go of Christophe, a finger at a time. The air was tight and hurtful, tense and nervous. The touch throbbed inside my head like a bad tooth, soaking up all the rage and hurt. It felt the way a house does right after a huge vicious fight but before someone starts cleaning up the broken stuff—thick, a little lonely, and a whole lot unsettled.

I waited until Christophe straightened. He tugged on his sweater sleeves, as if he was used to wearing a suit. I had a mad Technicolor flash of him pulling down snow-white cuffs, adjusting the fit of a black jacket with tails, and had to blink to clear it. Behind me, Hiro and Bruce were silent, but I could feel their readiness. It was just like those bars Dad used to take me into, the ones I'd find on instinct that would lead us to the Real World. I'd sit and sip my Coke, and he'd take care of business. A couple of times things had gotten hazy, and it had felt like this. Like a thunderstorm just about to let loose.

Once, and only once, Dad had drawn a gun and we'd left without what we came for.

I pushed the memory away. "Will you simmer on down? Both of you?" There. That was just the right tone. Polite but firm.

Christophe inclined his head. The blond was back in his hair, thick streaks and highlights. "Of course."

I turned back to Hiro. Who was already stepping back, shaking off Bruce's steadying hand. The blood on his chin had disappeared, but I could still smell it. The inside of my mouth was dry, and my throat ached. The bloodhunger turned over uneasily inside my bones and, thankfully, retreated.

Hiro bowed slightly, inclining from the waist. I couldn't help myself—every time he did that, I bowed back. He always looked pleased when I did, and you know, when in Rome, right? If it kept him happy, okay. I felt like an idiot doing it, but I'd feel like an idiot for *not* doing it, too. Might as well be polite.

"Forgive me." Hiro stepped back, mincingly. Headed for his seat, with stiff shoulders and his usual graceful glide. "I thought he meant you harm."

Oh, great. That's really smoothing the waters there, Hiro. I didn't blame him . . . but still. The urge to say *Christophe would never hurt me* rose to my lips, but I swallowed it. "Well, um. Never mind about that. Let's just sit down and discuss this."

"What is there to discuss?" Christophe stalked away behind me. Now he was going to pace like a caged tiger. "You are not to even *think* of risking yourself anywhere near that location. We should send teams to look it over and pick up any traces. Two combat units and two sweep teams, as well as a tracker."

"Steady on, Reynard." Bruce let out a heavy sigh. "It's a trap for whoever goes near it."

Christophe rounded on him. "This could be her first mistake. And better we send Kuoroi than my *kochana* gets it in her head to take a look. Anna wants her *dead*. I will not let—"

"*Christophe!*" I actually yelled, grabbing the back of my chair like I was going to pick it up and swing it. He was working himself up but good, and once he did that, good luck calming him down.

He stopped dead, staring at me. And chalk one up for the surprise-o-meter, because he actually looked haunted. Shoulders hunched, spots of fevered color high up on his cheekbones, and his hair messed up. Had he been running his hands back through it? That was *really* unlike him. Or maybe it was the aspect, but that was weird, too.

"Sit. Down." I pointed at the chair to the left of mine. "Now."

It was kind of gratifying, the way he immediately stalked around the end of the table. Hiro stiffened as Christophe drew near, but Chris just kept going, pulled out the chair, and dropped down. Laid his hands flat on the table, palms down and slightly cupped, fingers held close together. Like he wanted to curl them into fists, but didn't dare.

Bruce coughed slightly. The sound fell dead into tense, thick air.

"Now. Let's get this straight." I folded my arms. It felt good to be standing. Like I was in charge. I don't get that feeling very often. "If I'm not going near this place, then nobody else is either."

Ezra's jaw dropped. Cigar smoke threaded out from his nose. Augustine muttered something I was sure was a gutter-Polish curse word. Hiro actually slumped down into his chair, sagging.

"That's a very bad—" Bruce began carefully.

I ran right over the top of him. "So that's decided. I'll take Ash, and Shanks. And Hiro. Christophe will get teams together to cover us, and he'll monitor from outside."

There was a faint skritching sound. Christophe's fingers flexed, and his claws dug into the glossy tabletop. "No." Just the single word, his jaw set stubbornly. His eyes half–lidded, burning blue. Bruce slowly rose from his chair again, like a tired jack-in-the-box.

My knees felt mooshy, but I kept right on going. "She didn't kill me last time, when she had the advantage of surprise." I congratulated myself for saying it so calmly. "This time we're forewarned and forearmed. With both Hiro and Christophe there, not to mention Shanks and Ash, nothing's going to get to me. Not even suckers." *Not even Anna.*

"Milady." Hiro had lost a great deal of his color under his caramel tone. He looked pretty ghastly. "Please, reconsider."

"You're all telling me I'm the head of the Order." Very logical, once I thought about it. I only wondered why I hadn't played this card before. "Right? I'm the head; what I say goes. Well, this is what we're doing. Anna wants me there? Fine. Alone? Not a chance." I took a deep breath, bracing myself. "If she wants another crack at me, maybe we can make this a trap for *her*. And then she'll tell us where Graves is, and we'll pick him up." *If he's still . . . No, don't think that. We're going to rescue him.*

No matter what.

"No," Christophe repeated. He was looking pretty sick as well. He and Hiro with the empty chair between them made quite a pair. Bruce stood behind *his* chair, clutching it like he was expecting the floor to sink. He was chalky too. Ezra's mouth was still open, his cigar fuming. The thing stank, but at least it and the spilled coffee covered up the copper tang of blood. August rubbed at his face, like he was tired.

"You really think she'll show up if you just send a bunch of boys?" I shook my head. My hair was drying out a little, but it was still damp enough to make me shudder a little. "No way. I played bait last night, I'll play bait on this, too."

"Dru . . ." Christophe, changing it up a little with the one-syllable words.

"That's what we're doing. Make the arrangements. I don't want to be caught by surprise like I was last night." It wasn't very nice, but I wasn't *feeling* very nice right at the moment. As a matter of fact, I was feeling like a huge raving bitch.

And I didn't care.

I made my hands let go of the carved chair back. "I'll want a progress report tomorrow night, as soon as I'm up. Bruce, you can bring it to me before classes start."

I chose to walk down the side that had Bruce and Ezra, because I didn't think I'd get past Christophe without something else happening. I made it almost to the door before there was a splintering crack from the table.

"Dru." Christophe's voice, very soft. "We should discuss this."

I waved one hand over my shoulder. "Nope. Don't think so. See you later."

I yanked the door open and made my escape before they could figure out who was supposed to follow me around *now*. Once I hit the hall outside the second set of doors, I was running.

I didn't look back.

Chapter Fourteen

flipped every single lock on the door, settled the bar in its brackets with shaking hands, and turned around. Put my back against the door and let out a long, quivering breath. The wards flexed and trembled, bright blue, sliding soundless through the walls.

That was not fun. So not fun.

It was only four-thirty in the morning. Just about time to start winding down. Nathalie would be along soon, or she'd go to the room where I was supposed to be studying to pick me up. I felt bad about leaving her hanging, but Jesus.

I needed some time alone in the worst way. They didn't leave me alone much except to sleep. It got a little . . . overwhelming, having someone *on* me all damn night and day. Always someone watching, some danger, something I hadn't thought of, having to keep my face composed and my thoughts to myself all the time. I was used to Dad giving me some *space*, at least. And at the other Schola, well, I could feel them watching, but I didn't *see* them much. It was different now.

Everything was.

My mother's room looked different, too, with the lights off and the breathless dark of early morning covering its skylights. Like a stage set, the white bed floating ghostlike and the books all closed, shadowed doors. The bathroom glimmered, and the wide white window seat looked like the edge of a bleached skull.

I shuffled across the room. My sneakers were going to smell like coffee until I could wash them, so I dropped down on the floor next to the white bed and stripped them off, flung them in the general direction of the closet, and grabbed the pair sitting next to the small nightstand. I got a good look at the empty space underneath the bed and had a sudden, disturbing thought.

Is that my mother's mattress? Oh, God.

The dizziness came, sweeping over me in a dark sparkling wave. I folded my knees, rested my forehead against the hardwood, and tried to control my breathing. The shallow gasps I was hearing were from *me*, I realized, and the reality of the past few hours hit me like a sucker punch.

I rolled over on my back, digging in my change pocket. The earring was warm, and I tweezed it delicately out. My stomach hurt; I was making little noises in between the gasps.

The bed was neatly made, but I crawfished up to it and *reached*. Nathalie made it tight enough to bounce a quarter off of—Dad would have approved—and I had no idea how she did it with the coat in there all the time.

I wormed my hand between the top and bottom sheets, pulling everything askew. My fingers touched rough heavy canvas, and I yanked and pulled until I'd got the length of black material free. With the earring in my sweating fist, I hugged the balled-up lump the coat made and buried my face in it. Willed the shaking to stop and the touch to show me something, anything. To give me some hope.

Nothing. I was too miserable, trying too hard, for the touch to do more than give me a throbbing headache. The sobs quieted; I rocked back and forth, holding the balled-up coat. I knew I was getting tears on it. I hoped I wasn't also smearing snot.

If Graves just would have *listened*. If he would've come with me after Anna and I had our last real run-in. If he'd just been . . .

But that was wrong, wasn't it. I hadn't been able to find the words to make him stay. I hadn't been able to make my stupid mouth work. It was my fault Sergej had him now. And Anna? What game was she playing? How had she gotten his earring, and had it hurt him when it was taken out?

Oh, God.

There was no blood on it, at least. I blinked the tears away and held the earring up, a hard gleam in the dimness. Just a little dangling thing, silver if the guy that sold it to Graves had told the truth, the skull's grin mocking me.

The shakes and gasps retreated, little by little. I got up, aching all over like an old woman, and made it into the bathroom.

The diamond studs Christophe had made me wear the other night still glittered in my ears. I undid the one in my left ear, tested its golden back on Graves's earring. It fit just fine, and I slid it in. I didn't even bother to clean it. What was the point?

It was a little heavier than the stud. I shook my head a little, testing. It would sway like this, each time Graves turned his head sharply. It tapped my cheek just above my jaw, a little lower than it would hit on him.

All at once I felt better. Numb, yeah. Cried out. But still, better. Like I had a handle on something.

I washed my face, blew my nose, and shrugged into his coat. The mending I'd done with navy thread—Nat hadn't found black thread, but it was good enough—was pretty good. Gran would have sniffed at the job I'd done on some of the rips, but jagged claw-ripped seams aren't any good without a machine to help. The sleeve had been kind of a bitch to reattach, but I'd done it over a few nights. All in all, it was a pretty fair patch-up job.

The coat was absurdly big on me, since I was slighter than even the average teenage male, and he'd been tall.

Not been. Is. Graves is tall. I took a deep breath, did not look at myself in the mirror. My hair hid the earring just fine, and the tumbling curls were dry by now. It was a moment's work to throw my hair into a ponytail, then I shut the bathroom light off and crossed to the window.

The white satin window seat, wide as a single bed, creaked slightly. I knelt awkwardly and yanked at the window, pushing it up. Cool air, laden with the scent of spring, flooded past me. It was getting nicely green down in the gardens and out on the lawns. The smell of cut grass was probably the polo field. I'm told *djamphir* play polo, mostly to teach them to control horses. It's a tradition. Werwulfen play soccer and basketball. I wanted to catch a game one of these days. I'm not big on organized sports, but seeing a bunch of wulfen play hoops sounded like a good time.

"I hate it here," I whispered. "I want to go home."

That was what my mother would have said. She never could stand being cooped up. It was one of the few things Dad would ever say about her.

God, I understood.

I didn't really have a home, did I? Dad and I traveled. It was what we *did*. No place was home, unless it was maybe the old blue truck with him driving and me naggervating. Or Gran's house, all closed up in Appalachia, everything under dustcovers and the key right where it should be. We only went back once after she died, to set everything to rights so it could be closed up.

Other than that, there was nothing. No place was safe. I didn't have anywhere to go. I could've kept Graves and me on the run for a while, before the suckers hunted us down. Long enough to figure out something else, right? He was smart, he could have helped.

If I'd been smart enough, quick enough, to *explain*. Instead, he'd thought I was covering something up. Just like *his* mom.

It was kind of ironic, actually. Both of us paying for things other people did, over and over again.

I braced my hands on the windowsill. Doing this without Nat was going to be a little freaky. I hadn't realized how, well, *used* to her I'd gotten. She was just that kind of person, easy to spend time with.

Benjamin told me that some *svetocha* had made a game of slipping away from their guards and escorts. At the time, I'd thought it was a stupid idea. Escape from your only protection when there were vampires trying to kill you? At least I'd always had the sense to go during daylight, and never very far without Nat.

But some kinds of protection are more like smothering. Suffocation kills you more slowly than evisceration. The end result is the same. You get to where you'll run almost any risk to escape, if only for a few minutes.

I made sure my sneakers were tied securely, braced my palms on the ledge again. Peered out and down.

It was a different thing to be doing this at night, too.

At least I didn't sense anyone outside my door. I could bet they were out in the hall, though. Probably Benjamin, and most probably Christophe. Just waiting for me to come out and argue.

I didn't give myself time to get nervous. There was a ledge running around the building here, just below the window. I crab-walked my foot out, then twisted so I was crouched with my back toward the drop. Graves's coat hung like black wings, and for a second I felt like I was inside his skin, tilting my head the way he would have.

Just do it, just like you've done it before. And don't make any noise.

I jumped.

CHAPTER FIFTEEN

I **dropped three floors** and landed like a whisper, the aspect snapping over my skin like a rubber band again. That was one of the first things Christophe had taught me. If I'd been raised *djamphir*, I probably could have been doing some of this stuff all along. And nobody had thought to teach me what was, to them, such a basic skill.

There was that, at least. Christophe didn't take anything for granted when it came to training me. He started with stuff even *djamphir* babies knew.

Stop thinking about him, Dru.

The balcony here gave onto a number of classrooms and a long wood-floored room with mirrors along the side. I'd've thought it was for ballet, but the lines painted on the floor were weird. I wanted to ask, but I also didn't want anyone to know I was using it like a freeway. The windows were all locked, but on one of them, the lock was broken.

Don't ask—I'll just say that it's really easy to hex a lock. Gran always went on and on about how you need to be careful with that because people need their privacy and everything. But I figure Gran would've been the first one to tell me that having an escape route all picked out from my room would be a good idea.

Thinking of Gran here at the Schola made me smile. A goofy grin, I could tell just from the way it felt against the bones of my face. It was also painful, but in a sweet way.

Except that it led to me thinking about Dad, and that freezing day when his corpse had come looking for me. A shiver went through me, and I shoved the memory away as hard as I could. With an almost-physical jerk that made the coat swish a little.

I padded through the long, dark room. The mirrors were dusty, and it always smelled stuffy, like nobody had been breathing in here for a long time. I twisted my ponytail up as I walked, digging another elastic out of my pocket to keep it in a sloppy bun. Nathalie was just going to have a fit over brushing it out later.

I wished she was right beside me, kind of. It would've been nice. It would've been even nicer if Graves was right next to me, slinking along quietly, that sarcastic little smile on his face and . . .

God, will you just stop it? Sticking the knife in.

The double doors were quiet when I put my hand against them. I extended the fingers of the touch, didn't feel anyone breathing outside. Still clear. No little static-laden pools of *don't look here* that would have meant a teacher or one of the guys meant to watch me. Graves's coat brushed my ankles. I could kind of see why he wore it everywhere. It was armor between me and the world. Like a snail's shell. There were plenty of pockets, too. I didn't want to stash anything in here—it felt like putting stuff in someone else's purse, you know? You just *don't*.

But I could see where a kid who liked to be prepared for

anything would find it comforting. I might even invest in one of these coats if—*when*—we got him back.

Except we might not. It's been weeks, you can't track him, and going out there to get him isn't a good idea. Everyone keeps telling you that.

I was getting to the point where I wasn't sure how much of what everyone was telling me was in Graves's best interest. Or mine.

The hall outside was dark. Marble busts glowered across the hall at each other, perched on their carved pedestals. I waited a little bit, breathing softly and making sure. Then I slipped out and headed for the stairs at the end.

From there, it would be a short crisscross and a dash across one of the quads, and I could hook around and find the little copse of trees where I'd lost Graves's trail last time. With his earring and his coat, I stood a better chance of seeing something. Getting some kind of clue.

It couldn't hurt. And seriously, if I had to stay up in that room and just pace until Nathalie came to check on me, I'd go nuts. Out here, with Graves's coat making that familiar whispering sound, I could pretend I was Goth Boy, stretching my legs to imitate his loping, gangly stride. It was just one step from the pretending to the seeing, and if I was patient enough, it would happen.

If it didn't, well, I'd just keep trying. At least it was something I could *do*.

What was that? A noise, behind me?

I shot a nervous glance over my shoulder. The hall was deserted, the marble busts absolutely still between falls of dusty velvet. Still, something was off. Anxiety tightened my stomach into a squirming ball. It was ruining my concentration.

I sped up a little, but that didn't help either. I took another glance over my shoulder. Nothing in the hall but dim dusty shadows.

When I turned back around, Christophe was suddenly *there*.

I actually flinched and let out a strangled shriek. I backpedaled furiously, almost tripping on the coat's long hem. He moved in on me with spooky darting speed. *Herding* me, just the way I hated. I ended up with my back against the wood paneling right next to a long curtain of faded red velvet. He'd backed me right up into the wall.

He kept coming until he was nose to nose with me. A warm draft of apple-pie scent touched my face, and his eyes glowed bright blue in the dark.

"Jesus!" All my breath jolted away, leaving me starving for air. I felt like I'd been caught sneaking out my bedroom window.

Kind of funny, because I *had*.

Christophe studied me. I wasn't used to anyone getting this close, *or* staring into my eyes like they wanted to read the wrinkles on my brain. Plus, he was probably not happy with me. I didn't need the touch to tell me that.

I slid to my left, instinctively, wanting to get away, but his hand darted forward and spread on the wall next to my shoulder. His other hand did the same, and now I was practically in his arms.

Wait, isn't he mad at me? I froze, trying to think of what to do next. No good. Body buzzing like a lightning rod. Brain vapor-locked.

"I think we should talk." The aspect slid through him briefly, his fangs peeking out from under his top lip, halting, and retreating.

"Um," was my totally profound response. "Uh, Christophe—" Jesus. Did he have to follow me *everywhere*?

"Have I been in *any* way unclear?" Quietly, as if he was asking me for a cup of coffee.

Huh? "Uh, what? Look, Christophe, I—"

He leaned in even further, and his nose touched my hair. He inhaled, deeply, and the flush that went through was so incredibly hot I was amazed my clothes didn't start smoking. The apple-pie smell wrapped around me, and I wondered if it came from him drinking human blood.

My own teeth tingled at the thought, right down to their roots. The bloodhunger turned over inside my bones, uneasy.

Oh, God.

When he spoke, warm breath tickled my hair and touched my ear. "Have I been in any way unclear about my feelings?"

What the hell? I could barely get enough air in. Graves's coat was way too big, but it was suddenly feeling heavy and uncomfortable. "I, um. I . . . Christophe, what?"

"*Skowroneczko moja.*" His right hand slid up the outside of my shoulder, along Graves's coat, and he was touching my hair as well as breathing in my ear. All the blood sort of rushed to my head and made a sound like pulsing static. "I won't push, and I don't pry. All I ask is a little attention. A little consideration."

My brain seized up. Attention? He was around all the time. Who else did I pay attention to? "What?"

He inhaled again. He was *smelling* my hair. Jeez.

Oh, wow. This was a lot more intense than kissing him. That just kind of . . . happened, you know? I could say that I just let him do it, it wasn't really me.

This was something else. Because he smelled good, male and spice and that golden apple scent all mixed in, and the bloodhunger half–woke at the back of my throat. It didn't send glass shivers through me, and it didn't make me want to drink. It made my skin feel too small, and it made me move restlessly. Not to get away, though.

I didn't precisely want to get away.

It was so different from anything else I've ever done. I mean, catching a quick makeout session with a middling-cute boy in the band room was one thing, because I knew I'd be gone in a couple weeks anyway. I didn't get involved across sixteen states, but I did *experiment*, okay?

Graves's coat made a sound against the wall as I moved, fetching up against Christophe's other arm.

Graves . . . he'd kept backing up when it was time to get a little closer, so to speak. If he'd been all over me like this, I'd've . . .

What? What would I have done? It was so hard to think with Christophe so close. Especially when he leaned all the way in, pressing himself against me.

It was . . . nice. It was like the whole world had been shut out, and there was just him. Like he was a wall between me and everything that had happened since the night Dad hadn't come home. I could relax, be open fingers instead of a closed-up fist. I could let a little of myself go, because he was there.

"I don't mean to be cruel," Christophe murmured. "I just want you prepared. I want you *safe*. Is that so hard to understand?"

He didn't sound angry, thank God. For the umpteenth time that night, I was shaking. It wasn't fear, though. It was relief so deep and wide I wasn't sure I could stand up. My knees had gone noodle-gooshy and I found out my hands had crept up around his neck, fingers lacing together like I was afraid he was going to get away. Vanish, somehow, like everything and everyone else that had made me feel safe.

Everything tangled up inside me, and I let out a long sigh. My breath touched his neck, and he shivered. Like it was pleasant. My teeth tingled more fiercely, my jaw shifting, and the fangs were sharp aching points.

I inhaled sharply, and that was a mistake. Because I could smell the fluid in his veins, copper and spice, heat lightning and the smell of the desert when you drive with the windows down after dark and you're not stopping anytime soon.

The hunger woke up the rest of the way. I turned stiff as a board against the wall, fighting off the urge to push my chin forward, mouth opening, and go for the pulse I could suddenly hear.

"Go ahead." Christophe's head tilted back slightly. The shaking had invaded him, too. Like there was an earthquake, and the only people noticing it were us. "I trust you. You're all I have, Dru."

What? "Chr-chr—" I was trying to say his name, but my tongue was clumsy around the fangs. They pricked, sharply, and I tasted my own blood. It stroked the hunger, red crawling up over the darkness behind my eyelids, and my hands untangled enough to shove violently at him. He stumbled back a step, and I clapped my right hand over my mouth like I was trying to stop myself from puking.

He grabbed my shoulders. "It's all right. Shhh, it's all right." He said something else, too, but too low and confused for me to hear it.

I tried to back up through the wall. He held me still, and my stomach cramped in on itself. I shook my head, holding my mouth closed, trying not to *smell* him. Not because it was offensive, but because he smelled so goddamn good.

Or the blood did. I couldn't tell them apart now. What if that apple-pie smell was him smelling like a *snack*, for God's sake? Like a Hostess apple pie, just waiting for me to tear the wrapping off and take a bite?

My knees gave way. I slid down the wall, and he came with me. Graves's coat tangled up my feet, and if Christophe hadn't been holding on to me, I would have ended up sprawled instead of sitting on the floor.

"Now." He sounded completely calm. "Where are you going? Let me guess. Anywhere you can, to get away."

Not really. I kept my hand clapped tight over my mouth. He crouched on his heels like it was as comfortable as breathing, leaned forward a little. His fingers tweezed at the heavy material of the coat, on the right where it was shredded by something's claws and I'd carefully stitched it together.

"Or," he said, quietly, "you're looking for someone."

The bloodhunger retreated, snarling, step by step. After a little while, I could peel my hand away from my mouth. My teeth tingled, but they were only bluntly human. "Christophe—" I sounded like all the air had been punched out of me.

"He'll be alive." Christophe's hands dangled, loose and expressive. Even that looked graceful and planned. "But he won't be unchanged. Sergej will use him as bait to catch you. You're the real prize."

The name sent a twinge of pain through my head. I wasn't sure if it was the word itself, or the load of hate and contempt Christophe's voice carried every time he said it.

And there was something bothering me lately. My mouth started working again, thank God. "Why won't he just go after Anna? She's easier to get to, isn't she? What with sending him information all the time and stuff."

"You're the bigger threat, Dru." As if talking to an idiot. "He's already corrupted Anna. You? You've not only fought him off, but you're incorruptible. He lives to *twist* things, *kochana*. You wouldn't understand."

Great. What? "Okay, sure. Look, Christophe—"

He reached up. I almost flinched, but he only tucked a fallen curl behind my ear. His fingertips brushed my cheek. Warm skin, soft and forgiving. But my shoulder hurt, the bruise throbbing. His fingertips slid down, touched under my chin, and I found out I was staring at his chest before he pushed gently and I was forced to look up at his shadowed face.

"Will you at least consider me an option?" A bitter little half-smile, and his shoulders hunched slightly. "I don't know how much more open I can be. About how I . . ."

Oh, my God. The tangle of feelings inside me snarled even further. "I like you." There, it was out. It was said. Had I been lying to Graves, or to myself? "I really do. You're . . . different."

I could have kicked myself. "Different"? That was all I could come up with?

Now there was a ghost of amusement in his expression. One half of his mouth curled up, a quiet, companionable almost-grin. "Is that the word you'd choose?"

I grabbed my courage with both hands, so to speak. "Yeah. One of them, anyway."

A single nod. Then he went still, in that way older *djamphir* have. "What happened between you and the *loup-garou?*"

Oh, for God's sake. But then I realized he probably wasn't asking about the state of the union, so to speak. He was asking about something else. Or at least, I was only going to answer him as if he was asking about something else. "You mean, that day? He, uh, he found me. After Anna and I had a . . . a fight. She had the gym cleared and came to do something, I don't know." I leaned back against the wall, because Christophe's attention was so focused. It was like having a laser drilling right through me. All this time, and he was the only person who *really* looked at me.

Even Nat sometimes didn't see me. She saw a *svetocha*, that was all. Something I had to live up to. Something I had no *idea* of how to live up to, when I was just regular me.

Just Dru.

I swallowed hard, continued. "I got busted up a bit. Graves . . . he wanted to know who'd done it. I didn't want to say." *I couldn't get the words out. I was stupid.* "He got mad. Stamped off."

Another single nod, breaking his eerie stillness. "Leaving you unprotected."

Defending Graves was like defending Dad. The urge was immediate, overwhelming, and instinctive. "I didn't—"

He made a sharp slashing movement with one hand. "I know you'll hear no word against him. But no matter how angry he was, leaving you alone should *not* have been an option."

Meaning, probably, *I wouldn't do that.* But Christophe had left me alone before, hadn't he? Or let me *think* he wasn't hanging around.

I slumped against the wall. "Can we get off this subject?"

He shrugged. I waited for him to say something else, but he just rose, fluidly, and held out a hand. I took it —there was no reason not to—and he hauled me up as if I weighed less than a feather. The leashed strength was frightening. Especially since I'd seen him use it.

When I had my balance, I tried to pull my hand back. His fingers tightened, briefly, before he let go. Just to make sure I knew he was *choosing* to turn me loose, I guess.

Or just because he didn't want to let go.

"Dru." He was looking away now, up the deserted, shadowed hall.

The busts gleamed as they watched with blank eyes, each one a *djamphir* famous in the Real World for something or another, but not to be found in any ordinary history books. I suddenly wondered if they minded. Brought myself back to reality with a twitch. "What?"

He kept staring away. "I don't mistake you for your mother. She was the closest I had to . . . a friend. A real friend. She taught me much." He stopped, inhaled sharply as if the words pained him, and dropped his chin a little. "But I didn't have trouble sleeping or eating when I thought of her in danger. I didn't feel my heart tear itself out of my chest when she looked sad. I did not ever fear for her the way I fear for you." The aspect settled over him in a wave, and I could see it rising from him like heat shimmers from pavement on a scorcher of a day. "I don't blame you if it's not . . . enough. I'm tainted, I know as much. Just . . . let me stay near you. Please."

What could I say to that? Especially since *my* heart gave a huge painful leap. Somehow I crossed the space between us, and when I put my arms around him, he hugged me back. I didn't smell his blood now. I just smelled *him*, that maddening apple-pie-and-male blend that yanked everything inside me sideways. It helped that when I laid my head on his chest I could hear his heartbeat going like a clock. Tick-tock, tock-tick, each beat strong and steady.

Right then it didn't matter that he was like a twister, or that he was infuriating when it came to sparring, or that my shoulder still hurt. What mattered was the way he slumped against me, sighing a little, and the way I finally felt like I was . . . home. It mattered that he always came back for me, and it mattered that he'd said those things to me.

Nobody had ever said anything like that to me, ever.

That was the first time I ever really kissed him. As in, the first time *I* kissed him without waiting for him to try for me.

And it was great.

CHAPTER SIXTEEN

t was the middle of the day, the long sleepy time when sunshine comes down like golden honey, and someone was shaking me awake. I wanted to roll over and stick my head under the pillow. The thought—*it's not time for school, leeme lone*—was familiar because it'd hit me every morning when the alarm went off, no matter where in the country we were.

"Milady." Nathalie, whispering fiercely. "Dru, please, wake *up*."

I sat straight up, almost cracking my forehead against hers because she was bending down. She jerked back gracefully, and I got a good lungful of her perfume. She wore a strange musky blend from a little blue bottle, and it suited her. Right now, though, it had a weird coppery edge.

I know that smell. Fear.

"Christophe?" It was the first word out of my mouth. I blinked, rubbed at my eyes. "What the hell?"

"He's gone. Benjamin is down the hall. It's Ash." Her dark eyes were wide, and her sleek hair was mussed. Just a little. "We'll take you to him, Shanks and me. But hurry up. Please."

I scrambled up out of the white bed. I'd fallen asleep in

Christophe's arms, still wearing Graves's coat. Sometime during the night I'd shucked the coat and my jeans and crawled under the covers. I was hoping I'd done it while I was alone.

I grabbed for my jeans, but Nathalie was quicker. She hooked them up off the floor and shook her head. "Clean clothes. You never know. It's not *that* urgent."

"Benjy could come along any moment," Shanks hissed from the door. He was in a gray T-shirt and comfortably ripped-around-the-knee jeans, but his dark hair stood up wildly in all directions. It was such a change from his usual emo-boy fringe I began to get a bad feeling. "He *always* checks when there's a wulf on guard. Don't trust us."

Nat snorted. "She has time to get clean underwear on, Robbie. Jeez."

I seconded that emotion, and I was damn glad I still had a T-shirt and panties on. I mean, it was just Shanks, but still.

"You're such a *girl*." He tensed, leaning toward the door and cocking his head as if he heard something.

"What's going on with Ash?" I moved as quietly as I could toward the dresser.

"Best you come see." Nathalie glided past me and in seconds had T-shirt, panties, and jeans in her capable hands. Today she was in a purple V-neck and a black scarf, and her jeans looked faintly tinged with purple, too. She even had purple Uggs, and they didn't look ridiculous like they would if I was in them. "Hurry."

I did. Three minutes later we were heading down the hall for the stairs, away from the end where Benjamin's closed door glowered. I didn't ask why we were slipping away like this. If Shanks thought there was a good reason, there was a good reason.

But where was Christophe?

We were on the stairs before I could ask. "Where's Christophe?"

"Gone." Shanks shrugged, hopping down the stairs two at a time. "He left before dawn. Most of the Council went with him. Think Leon went, too. Left me and Benjamin and the twins to stand watch over you. Then Ash started . . . well."

"What's going on with him?" I got no answer. "Nat?"

"You'll have to see for yourself." She brought up the rear, her footsteps silent. I was the only one making any noise, and not a lot of it. "He's not dying, if that's what you're worrying about. At least, I don't *think* he is."

"Great." I rubbed at my eyes, getting rid of sleep crusties. "And you don't want Benjamin to know, because . . . ?" I could probably guess.

Shanks snorted. "Instinct. Christophe and the others left in a hurry. Something about a daylight run, gathering intel."

I stopped dead. Nat bumped into me, got me going again. I hate being herded, but she managed to do it without irritating me. "A daylight run? Intel?"

"Yeah. A compromised site or something. Pretty hush-hush." Shanks tossed me a look over his shoulder. "What do you think?"

I think they're going after Anna. "Jesus." A sick feeling began right under my breastbone. "I think I shouldn't have said *tomorrow*."

"Care to share? Just askin'."

"Anna sent a note. And . . . something of Graves's." I brushed my hair back, wishing I'd thought to grab a ponytail elastic. I realized in the middle of the motion that I didn't want to show the earring, and let the curls fall back down.

"Shit." Shanks didn't speed up, but he did put his head down.

I am just going to kill Christophe. I concentrated on not tripping down the stairs. He'd been so *nice* last night, holding me, not saying much. Just being there, until I finally fell asleep. And I'd been grateful.

I was pretty prepared to find Ash howling and battering at the walls of his room. The plain concrete-and-stone hall was silent, though.

Silent as the grave.

I wished I hadn't thought that, swallowed hard. "Is he—"

There was a sound from inside the cell. A scraping crackle, as if he was trying the change again. My heart sped up, a high hard hummingbird beating against my ribs.

Nat handed me a thick brown elastic. "I heard it when I checked him, about ten minutes ago. Take a look."

"You've been checking him?" I got my hair pulled sloppily back and stepped up to the door.

"Of course I have." She said it like, *Are you stupid?* I decided not to ask.

The observation slit gave off a gleam—daylight, from a small, thickly barred window high on the opposite wall. I went up on tiptoes, grabbed the edge of the slit, and hauled myself up to take a look.

There wasn't much to see. Ash lay on the floor, shaking like he was having a seizure. Fur roiled, his spine arched, and he clawed at the stone floor. There were deep slices crisscrossing it—he'd been scratching for a while. The patches of white skin were growing. Each time the fur crawled back up to reclaim him, it was beaten back.

I dropped back down, lunged for the key. Shanks grabbed at it, but he was too slow, for once. "Wait a second—"

"He's changing back!" I yelled, fumbling with the key. "This is *great*, he's actually changing back!"

"We don't know that yet. He could *hurt* you, Dru, he ain't rational right now!"

"He's *never* been exactly rational." I shoved the key into the hole, twisted it. The lock gave with a slight groan. I wrenched the door open, just as I realized I couldn't hear the crackling anymore.

Oh please, no. I peered into the dimly lit cell, pushed the door a little wider, and slipped inside. It was too late to back out now, so I made it across the cell to where he lay, ready to jump back if he started looking like he was going to claw at me. Thick silence swallowed everything inside the cell, and I half-bent, my fingers out, meaning to touch him.

He lay on the floor, the fur still reaching up in ropes and twists. His body was rigid, his eyes rolling and glowing glassy orange. Like they were on fire, molten something poured into his sockets.

Ash's mouth opened, and he screamed.

It was a long, despairing cry, and it chilled me right down to the core. It blew my hair back, and the touch sparked into life inside my head. A cascade of horrific images, dead bodies and hot blood and despair, roared through my skull.

I dropped to my knees, the sudden impact jolting up through my thighs and jarring every bone in my body. It was *agony*, bones twisting and every inch of flesh crawling with jellied fire. It burned and it clung, but even worse than the burning and the breaking bone was the soft evil creeping inside my head, its clawed fingers digging at the very core of what made me, *me*.

It only lasted a few seconds, but those seconds were a lifetime. Something in me twisted, *pulling*. As if I had hold of an invisible rope and all Gran's careful training from the time I was a toddler had hardened the invisible muscles I was using to pull. I hauled, a cry to match Ash's rising out of me, and for a moment we were screaming in unison. I was on my knees, body tilted all the way back, my hands out and knotted into fists like I was pulling on something. It wasn't a rope now; it was chains wrapped around my wrists. Cold metal chains that *burned*, and the force on the other end was a riptide of deep black hate.

I'd seen that black before in a sucker's eyes. In a cold lifeless house in a snowstorm, where Sergej had expected to trap Christophe and got me instead. Slim handsome Sergej, with his teenage face and his honey-brown curls and those black eyes, their hourglass pupils tarns for wild creatures to sink and die in.

I *pulled*. My knees slipped, I was yanked forward, and suddenly something grabbed me from the other side. For a moment I was horribly *stretched*; the thing on the other end of the chains had sunk its claws into me and was pulling me just like taffy. Someone else was yelling, and Ash's howl broke on a high throat-cut gurgle as he ran out of breath. So did mine, and for a long horrible moment I couldn't see anything but a deep velvet blackness starred with amazing little points of color. My lungs seized up, I couldn't breathe, the thing pulling on Ash was going to win—every ounce of stubbornness I had crawled up inside me and I gave it one last lunging, tearing, hideously silent effort.

Something tore inside me. A veil made of wet paper, ripped right in half.

There was a wet crunching noise and a *pop!* The smell of wet salt showered over me, and the pressure retreated. I fell over backward onto Shanks, my elbow sinking into something soft, and he let out an actual squeal. My head rang like a gong and my arms felt like someone had tried to tear them off. I blinked, and for a second the hazy thought *I shoulda stayed in bed* occurred to me, like the world's slowest genius moment.

My breath whooped back in again. I was too grateful for my lungs working to care that I was making coughing, gagging sounds.

Someone let out a small, sobbing noise. My head hurt viciously, and I smelled copper.

Blood. The hunger yawned inside me, opening its red eyes. Tugged on my veins, but faintly.

I got the retching under control. Lay there for a second. I couldn't tell if my eyes were open or closed. "Ohshit," I whispered, hoarse and rasping. "Nat?"

"Right here." From the door, a shocked whisper.

"Shanks?" I had to know. I blinked the blood out of my eyes. Was that why my head hurt so bad? The torn thing inside me quivered, too. What had I just done?

Shanks moaned, stirring. "You broke my *nuts*."

So that was what my elbow had hit. "Sorry." My voice cracked. My throat was sore, too, and the bloodhunger rasped unhappily at the back of my throat. I knew I was lying on him, but I couldn't get up the gumption to move.

"Mother Moon," Nat whispered. I'd never heard her sound actually shocked before. It was a revelation. "Oh, Mother *Moon*."

"And Father Fucking Sky, she broke my *nuts*." Shanks curled up; I slid bonelessly down to the stone floor. The claw marks were sharp and fresh, one of them scratching against my wrist as I lay there. It took all the energy I had left to turn my head. My vision cleared. The blackness retreated, bit by bit, like a movie's first scene opening up.

The long pale shape curled in on itself like Shanks. A muscled back, three jagged scars swiping down across the skin. He was fish-belly white, with a shock of dark hair. It looked like it hadn't been cut for a while. He shuddered, naked on cold stone, and when his head moved, I saw the streak of white at his temple. It reached all the way back like a skunk stripe now, and the white hairs had a silvery cast.

Like moonlight.

"Holy shit," I breathed.

Muscle moved under that too-white skin as he shook. He coughed, a terrible wet retching sound, and I realized he was crying.

That somehow gave me the strength to move. I rolled, awkwardly, one of my sneaker soles skritching against the floor. Managed to make it to hands and knees. That was as far as I could get. I was shaking like I'd just run five miles without letup. My bladder was near to bursting, and I wished I'd taken the time to brush my teeth. Blood slicked the left side of my face, hot and maddening, I licked my lips and wished I hadn't because I could *taste* it, a flood of red and jumbled images of my own face swirling through me.

Dammit. The torn-open spot inside of me quivered again, like it wasn't quite sure what to do with itself. I had a hazy idea it was going to start hurting pretty soon, but I was too tired to care.

"Ash," I croaked. "Ash."

He twitched. The sobbing was like a toddler's, messy and huge.

I couldn't get up. So I crawled.

"*Dru!* You're bleeding—" Nat scrambled away from the door. Shanks let out another yelp; I heard her fall. She landed on him as well. He was really winning the lottery today.

"OwwwWWWW!" Shanks yelled again, and I reached Ash.

His skin was so soft. I grabbed his shoulder, and he curled even tighter around himself, hugging his knees. I couldn't get my arm under him, but I threw my left one over and hugged as hard as I could. He lay shivering, and the sobs were pouring out of him hard enough to hurt my ribs, but I held on. Graves's earring, in my left ear, lay against my cheek. It was ice-cold, and so was my mother's locket, but both rapidly warmed as I hugged him, breathing into his hair. He smelled like outside at midnight, one of those clear-cold nights with a full moon where ice makes every edge stand out razor sharp. Under that was the tang of boy, and dirt. He smelled a little . . . unwashed.

But he was *human*. He was boy-shaped again. I didn't know what it meant, unless it meant something fantastic. All this time he'd been trying to change back, and he finally did it.

"Dru?" Nathalie sounded scared half to death. "Milady?"

"Everything's going to be fine," I croaked through my rasping, bloodhunger-dry throat. "Everything's going to be *just* fine."

I even believed it for a little while.

CHAPTER SEVENTEEN

"**There were reclamation** teams in the twenties." Shanks eased gingerly down on the satin window seat. "Casualties were high, prolly 'cause the *djamphir* wouldn't lend support. It was just us. We thought that with enough food and quiet, we could maybe bring 'em back."

"Did it work?" I held the ice pack to the left side of my forehead. I didn't even know what had opened up the gash on my head, just above my eyebrow. Midafternoon sun fell through the skylights, and I heard Nat's murmur from the bathroom. She and Dibs were trying to coax a wild-eyed Ash into getting his blood pressure taken. Dibs insisted, right after he insisted on disinfecting the slice on my head and butterfly-bandaging it, then clapping the ice pack on.

Dibs does *not* mess around when it comes to patching people up. It's weird, because the rest of the time he can barely stammer out a hello without blushing.

I wished I knew what had opened up the cut on my head, though.

And I really wished I could heal faster than human right *now*, instead of when I bloomed.

Benjamin leaned against the door, his arms folded. "You should *not* have gone down there without me," he muttered again, glaring out from under his dark emo fringe. As usual, he looked too handsome to be real. Pretty much all *djamphir* boys do, except Leon. "Reynard is going to kill me."

The torn-open spot inside me still felt empty. But I could deal. I shook my head, managed to focus again. "So we don't tell him." I turned my attention back to Shanks. "Did it work?"

The long dark wulfen shrugged. He was pale under his tan, and he looked like moving hurt. Apparently both Nat and I had nailed him pretty good. "Not anytime I ever heard of. Dad doesn't talk about it much, except when he gets mad and he thinks the cubs are in bed."

"I can't hide this from Reynard." Benjamin was talking like Shanks wasn't even here. I guess coming out of his door to find Nat dragging me and Shanks, and Dibs dragging a newly-boy Broken into my room, blood all over me and my hands shaking, had not put him in a good mood. "He'll *kill* me."

I pushed the ice pack more firmly against my forehead. "He didn't tell me the whole Council was going out this morning. Fair's fair." Looked back over at Shanks in the window, who had hunched his shoulders and was staring at me. "But there had to have been something, right? Some method? Or maybe we just lucked out. I don't even know what we did."

"What *you* did." Shanks was having none of this "we" business. "*You* did that."

"I don't even know how." I could guess, though. At least some. That pressure on the other end of the chain—that had probably been Sergej. His will.

His master's call. I shivered. Had Ash been feeling that pull the whole damn time? Fighting it off?

No wonder he'd gone nuts every night. I would've, too.

Right now I had an uneasy idea that that cut on my head was Sergej's doing, at whatever distance. *That* was nastily thought-provoking, not to mention nightmarish. I could've lost an eye or something. Plus, I'd hurt something inside me by pulling so hard. I wished everyone would shut up for a bit so I could probe at the big raw empty thing inside my head, figure out what was going on. It wasn't like the time Christophe drank my blood, where the touch had fled me and the entire world had looked two-dimensional. This was more like . . . some covering I hadn't even known was hanging over me had been ripped away just like a scab, and I was raw underneath it. The touch still echoed inside my head, but faint and far away, like it was in a much bigger room than it was used to.

Like before it had been showing me the inside of a bedroom, but now it was echoing inside a cathedral.

"Hey! *Hey!*" Nathalie almost yelled. "Calm down!"

I was off the bed in a heartbeat. Benjamin let out a blurting sound, but I got to the bathroom door before him, despite my legs shaking like they wanted to walk off in the opposite direction.

Ash was, of all things, crouching on the toilet, clutching the heavy blanket from his room around his shoulders. The red and yellow plaid cloth looked too bright to be real. Dibs was holding the blood-pressure cuff, and Nathalie was standing on the bath mat. There wasn't room for anything else.

And *they* looked different, too. Like I was seeing them for the first time, every hair and tiny line, even the weave of Nat's T-shirt and the fine thin threads of gold in Dibs's hair. I could've counted all the hairs on his head, given enough time.

Ash's mad, dark gaze locked on me. He was so white he was almost transparent. It was corpse pallor, and it did nothing for him. His hair hung down in greasy strings, and if not for the scarring running up the left side of his jaw, he probably would have been handsome in a raffish sort of way.

Now that he was human again, you could see just where the bullet's silver grain had plowed into his flesh. Looked like I'd hit him off-center, but at least the skin wasn't weeping a raw clear fluid anymore. There were just pockmarks and white stars of scarring, which probably meant the silver had been pushed free and the allergic reaction had stopped. Unless there was still silver buried in his jawbone. That was a real possibility.

It must've hurt like hell. I felt bad about it, even if he'd just bit Graves and would have killed us both at the time. Because he'd been under Sergej's control.

But he wasn't now. Or at least, I was belting he wasn't. *Hoping he wasn't.*

Dibs blew out a frustrated breath. "I don't think he understands." He gave me what passed for a Significant Glance in his book, which meant he looked at my face for a whole half second before dropping his gaze. He didn't blush, though. "We need to get him cleaned up and dressed. And feed him. The change takes energy, and if he has another session he could relapse."

"Okay." I could almost feel my tired, cotton-fogged brain click over to working. Everything else could wait while there were immediate problems in front of me. Maybe in a little while I could lay back down and go to sleep. That sounded *awesomely* good. "Nat, you think you could scare up some food? I'll get Benjamin to find him some clothes. Or wait . . . some of Graves's stuff is around. Dibs, just relax. Ash?"

He cocked his head, still watching me. Something about him reminded me of a feral cat, trapped and just waiting to see how everything would go down. His mouth opened, but no sound came out. The streak in his hair glowed, sun through the skylights drenching the entire white-tiled bathroom. Maybe it was the light making everything look so hyper-real.

"On it." Nat squeezed past Dibs—who would have folded in on himself to make himself smaller if he could—and slipped past me.

"Be careful." Benjamin now, fussing from behind me. "He's dangerous, Milady."

I snorted. Laid the ice pack down on the old-fashioned sink's rim. "If he didn't hurt me then, I don't think he's likely to now. See if you can find some of Graves's clothes, or anything that'll fit him, huh? Please, Benjamin." I didn't have to work to sound weary. The torn place inside me was beginning to hurt, like the novocaine on a tooth wearing off. "Let's just take this one step at a time."

"You should really keep icing that—" Dibs piped up.

"It's iced enough." I eased into the bathroom. Ash stared at me. "Hey. Bet you're pretty weirded out. It must feel strange to be smaller now, and not so furry." The edges of the words slurred. My mouth wouldn't work quite right.

"Dru." Benjamin sounded queerly breathless, and he was suddenly at the bathroom door. "Milady—"

The bone-rattling growl that came out of Ash surprised everyone. Dibs squeaked, flattening himself against the tiled wall and a towel rack. Ash's lip lifted, showing white teeth. A tinge of orange ran through his dark irises.

"Now stop that." I tried to sound firm, but I only sounded tired enough to lay down and pass out. "He just wants to help. Cut it out."

The growl cut off midway. The orange died in his eyes. Ash cocked his head. His lips moved soundlessly, as if he was trying to speak. The scarring made one half of his mouth a grotesque smile.

"It'll help if you sit down." I slid past Dibs, who tried flattening himself even further. I was close enough now to reach up and touch the blanket around Ash, wrapping it more securely. He was bareass underneath it, and I didn't want to look. I'd be embarrassed, if I wasn't so goddamn exhausted. My head was really starting to pound now, too, and that empty torn place was sending little daggers of sharp bright white through me. Especially my joints. I felt like I had what Gran always called "the rheumatiz." "Look, we're trying to help you. It's all going to be okay."

His lips moved again. I waited. His shoulders came up, and a hiss of air escaped him. It mutated into a word, one I knew.

"*Sssssssvedosha.*" His chin dipped. He nodded at me, his greasy hair falling over his face.

"That's me. Your friendly neighborhood girl *djamphir.*" It felt odd to say it out loud. I made sure the blanket was wrapped nice and tight, and guided him down to sit on the toilet. Wished I could sit instead, told myself not to be such a wuss. "I'm Dru. You're Ash, right? Can you say that? Can you say your name?"

"Shhhhh." Frustration turned his mouth into a downward curve. "Osh. *Osh.*"

My heart squeezed painfully down on itself, adding to all the other pain. But I put on a bright face. "Yep. Ash. Now look, Dibs has to take your blood pressure. I don't know why, but he's got a good reason." I pulled the blanket aside, making sure it was bunched up securely at his waist but loosening it at his shoulder. "All right? Give me your arm."

He did. He kept staring at me while Dibs messed around with

the stethoscope and the blood-pressure cuff. Ash's mouth worked silently, but at least we knew he could talk now. The light was starting to get glaring, and the inside of my head felt scoured clean. I swayed a little bit, but made my knees stiffen up each time.

"I don't think he'll regress," Dibs finally said. He glanced at me, stopped, looked again. "Dru?"

"So he's okay? He's going to be okay?" I couldn't believe it. For *months* I'd been looking forward to this. Now he was crouched on the toilet, thin and white and blinking furiously like a newborn. It had actually happened. Score one for the good guys, and all that. "Really okay?"

"He's shifted back. That's all I can say." Dibs was looking at me now, steady and worried. "You don't look so good. Let's sit you down."

It was a great plan, except for the most obvious flaw in it. My mouth felt funny, loose and awkward like it wasn't really part of me. "There's no place to sit."

That was all I remember saying, because the white glare took over inside my head and I keeled right over. I'd've hit my head on the sink if Dibs hadn't caught me, and the next few minutes are kind of confused. I could hear myself from a very long way away, saying *I'm okay, I'm okay*, over and over again, in a breathless funny little whisper. Benjamin, almost screaming. Ash growling. Dibs, his voice breaking as he cried out, miserably.

I came to about a minute later with my head in Dibs's lap, lying over the bathroom threshold. He looked scared to death, his eyes wide and his mouth wetly open like a little kid's during a horror movie. My teeth were chattering, and for a moment I couldn't figure out why.

Then it occurred to me: I was cold. So cold. My body was leaden; I couldn't even lift my arms. The torn-open spot inside me was getting bigger, and I suddenly understood it was a *mouth*, and it was going to swallow me whole. *What the—*

"Do you smell that?" Dibs whispered, and for a mad second I was thinking I'd puked or something when I passed out. But the taste in my mouth was blood, not acid bile. The copper in it whispered to me, and a shiver went through the center of my bones. I caught a breath of spice, but it wasn't Christophe and it wasn't Anna. It was the heavy aroma of cinnamon buns boiled down to its essence, and it was bubbling up from my skin in waves.

"I think I pulled something," I whispered. Everything slurred inside my mouth, and the reality of what I'd done caught up with me.

Ash was human again. He was going to be okay. Great. Except something inside me was torn up now.

"No shit." Dibs clicked over into "bandage it up" mode. "You need food and rest, I don't—"

"He's going to kill me," Benjamin muttered darkly. "Just *kill* me."

And right on cue, someone hammered at the door.

CHAPTER EIGHTEEN

Leon's eyebrows nested in his hairline. He'd just swept the door open and stalked in, pretty as you please. Seen in full sun, his hair became a mass of fine golden threads over a well of rich fine brown, not mouse-colored at all. "What the *hell*—" he began, and caught sight of Ash crouching by my feet, still cocooned in a blanket and the bathroom's white-tile glare. "*Gott im Himmel.* That's the Broken."

Ash's ruined lip lifted, but he didn't snarl. He just went very still, looking up at Leon, muscles slowly tensing. Orange flashed in his eyes.

"What's going—" Benjamin had his hand halfway to his shoulder holster.

"Milady." Leon folded his arms, looking down at me. "I have executed your commission. Shall I report now, or when we have privacy?"

I lay there blinking for a few seconds. Nothing made any sense. "Um."

"I rather think *privacy* would be a good thing. But it's also something you'll want to hear soon." A significant pause. "*Very* soon."

I am lying on the floor, Leon. Obviously this has not been a good day. "Uh-huh," I managed.

"You have to smell that." Dibs bent over me, his thumb peeling my right eyelid up. I wanted to shove his hand away—it was my *eye*, dammit—but I couldn't muster up the moxie to move. "Right? Tell me I'm not the only one."

"Oh yes. She's cresting and will bloom soon, the primary changes have started." Leon stared down at me. A curious expression drifted over his face, part bitterness, part something I couldn't define. "What happened?"

Oh, so *now* he wanted to know what happened. "Ash," I whispered, and the world turned into shutterclicks of light as my eyelids fluttered.

The werwulf boy crouching at my feet made a low, unhappy sound.

"Help me get her on the bed," Dibs said, and the shutterclicks turned into a dozy bruised darkness.

* * *

I was pretty out of it for most of that day, and even now I can't tell what I really saw and what was . . . well, fever dreams. Or nightmares, as my body struggled to cope.

The visions were odd—brightly colored fragments, each with their own static buzz around them, like and unlike what Gran called "true-seein's." Clear, so clear. Technicolor bright and sharp-crisp. They had weight. The touch echoed inside my head, showing me maybe-was, is, and will-be, like it was suddenly in a space much too big for it, spinning like a mad carnival ride through time.

Christophe, leaning against a tree in a shadowed clearing. His eyes turned blowtorch-blue as he watched, and the expression on his face was chilling. Because under the set grim look of a guy watching something distasteful, there was faint, scary amusement. He watched as the struggle took place, and when it was over, his smile was a ghost of itself.

"Just get it out of my sight," he said, and their narrow white hands lifted the other boy, his long dark coat flapping as he struggled uselessly.

Blackness, cutting between the scenes like a knife blade.

The naked boy crouched in the stone cell, his fingertips resting against the weeping wall. He coughed, his ribs heaving, and the faint shine on his skin told me he was sweating in the damp. That wasn't a good sign. He turned his head, sharply, as if he heard something, and I saw the flash of paleness at his temple.

His eyes fired green, and Graves sniffed suspiciously. That set off another round of coughing; he spat something into a corner of the cell. I lunged forward, trying to reach him.

Another knife blade, this one loaded with static. Chop.

The white bedroom was full of golden afternoon light, and there was a body on the bed, a mess of curled hair. Dibs paced, nervously watching the Broken. The mirror watched it all, a blind eye. I was inside the reflection, screaming and pounding my fists on its slick clearness, as Nathalie leaned over the too-still body and glanced up at Ash.

Who crouched next to the bed, staring at me inside the mirror with orange-flecked eyes, like he could hear me.

Chop.

Christophe knelt motionless at the head of the stairs, staring unblinking down a filthy, dusty hall. Beside him, Benjamin also crouched, his mouth moving. Explaining something. But instead, I looked at Christophe's hands. They hung, flexing and releasing, like he was wishing he had someone's neck in them. And I began to feel . . . odd. Not afraid, but like I was missing something.

Chop. More maybe-was and will-be, pouring into my head like they intended to stretch out my skull. Gran's face, wise and wrinkled; Dad spinning in a field of daisies while I shrieked with laughter, his big capable hands under my arms and the entire world rotating around us; Graves lighting a cigarette; Benjamin slumping against an alley wall and slowly going white as blood slid out of the hole in his shoulder; Augustine's face a rictus of horror as he screamed, his arms stretched out; my mother's face brighter than the sun, laughing as she tickled me . . .

One last image, slowing down and cramming its way into my overloaded head. It *hurt,* shoving its way past a confused jumble of memories and physical misery. My heart labored under the strain, climbing uphill in steady beats.

The long concrete hall stretched away into infinity. I saw him, walking in his particular way, each boot landing softly as he edged along, and the scream caught in my throat. Because it was my father, and he was heading for that door covered in chipped paint under the glare of the fluorescents, and he was going to die. I knew this and I couldn't warn him, static fuzzing through the image and my teeth tingling as my jaw changed, crackling—

—and Christophe grabbed my father's shoulder and dragged him back, away from the slowly opening door. The sound went through me, a hollow boom as the door hit the wall and concrete dust puffed out.

BANG.

"Bang," someone whispered, and hot breath touched my cheek.

I shot straight up, clawing at the air and screaming. Ash went over backward in a flurry of pale limbs. Nat, dozing on the chair she'd pulled up, shrieked and jumped to her feet. The bathroom door flew open and Dibs leapt out, wild-eyed, his little black medi-bag in one hand and his narrow chest furred with wiry golden hair. He was stark naked, and most of him was wringing–wet. Lather stood up in his hair, and I heard the shower running as I gasped, trying to make my lungs work. The room looked strange, every angle askew and the light somehow *wrong*.

I choked on glassy air. Nathalie leaned over and whomped me on the back. The blow stung, but somehow, it worked. I sucked in sweet air, blinking as the touch turned around and settled inside my skull, nestling like a feathersoft bird.

A really *big* bird.

"Jesus," I husked. "What the . . ." The light was all weird, and after a moment I realized why. It was dusk-gold, not the glare of noon, lying over the room like honey, which meant I'd been out for a while.

Leon looked up from the window seat. "They'll return soon. We need a plan."

Nat rolled her eyes. "Oh, yeah, sure. A plan. How exactly is a *plan* going to help *this* situation? Get back in the shower, Dibs."

I blushed scarlet. So did Dibs. He also squeaked and ducked back into the bathroom, banging the door shut. Nat let out a sigh my Granmama might've envied.

Wow. Now I knew a lot more than I ever wanted to about him.

I scrubbed at my forehead weakly. "Jesus." I couldn't come up with anything better to say. "What's going on?"

"You need food. It's not hot, but the calories will do you good." Nat stretched, turning the movement into a graceful, coordinated rise from her chair.

Somehow she'd gotten Ash into a pair of slightly–too–big khakis and a sleeveless denim button-down. Muscle moved under white skin as he peeked up over the edge of the bed at me. Orange sparks drifted through his dark irises, the pupil flaring and shrinking as he examined me. "Bang," he said sagely, and nodded. Greasy strings of dark hair fell in his face.

"Milady." Leon slid off the window seat. "Dru. I bring tidings, if you can stay awake long enough to hear them."

My mouth tasted like old dried-up copper and I hurt all over. The pain settled in deep, not like a bruise or a burn but instead as if the center of my bones had been stripped out and filled up with a grinding low-level ache. I rubbed at my grainy eyes. I'd lost pretty much a whole day, and wouldn't you know, I felt like I could just lie down and sleep for another two.

"Here." Nat came back from the door, carrying a plate one-handed. "Not a word until she eats something."

"This is important, Skyrunner." But Leon subsided when she shot him a look that could have broken a window. A flare of yellow went through her irises, and I actually found myself really, really glad Nat was on my side.

I reached for diplomacy. "I think I can eat and listen at the same time." My stomach actually rumbled, and when she gave me the plate, I saw a pile of ham sandwiches on wheat toast. The lettuce and tomato looked a bit soggy, but my stomach spoke up again and I grabbed the first half-sandwich on top. "What the hell, Leon?"

"You gave me a *commission*." His chin jutted.

"Sure I did." I glanced at Nathalie. "Thanks." Back at him. He was looking like a sulky third-grader. Jeez. "Spit it out."

That was the exact moment what he was saying caught up with me. He was telling me he'd found something out.

About Graves.

Leon spread his hands a little, a curious little helpless motion.

I took a huge bite of sandwich, chewed, and my stomach started singing hosannas. It was work not to talk with my mouth full. "Oh, you mean . . . Well, whatever you've got, Nat can hear it. She's my friend."

For some reason, that made Nat stand a little straighter. She folded her arms, and her earrings—purple metal hoops with little silver rings hanging at the bottom—swung a little.

"Are you sure?" He held up both hands when *I* glared at him, too. "I'm not impugning your duenna, Milady. There are some things it's safer for a wulfen not to hear."

"Oh, dear me." Nathalie sank back down in the chair and examined her Uggs. The sarcasm could've started dripping off her and staining the floor. "Is it conspiracy, treachery, murder, or open warfare? I'll have to choose my lipstick accordingly."

Ash still peeked up over the edge of the bed at me, and I grabbed another sandwich half and held it out to him. He studied it, studied me, then grabbed it so fast his hand blurred. He disappeared, hunching down next to the bed.

Leon's face twisted itself up slightly. "I don't know what to call it at this point." He folded his arms, shook his lank, fine hair down. "Except *unsavory*."

"Excuse me? I'm sitting right here." I tore off another huge bite of sandwich. Have you ever been so hungry even cardboard would be oh-my-God *fantastic*? That's how it was.

"I'm not quite sure how you'll react, either." He stared at a spot about two feet above my head. "It concerns Reynard."

I swallowed a huge load of toast, cheddar cheese, ham, and tomato. It tasted like manna, or like Gran's cooking. All it needed was some fresh milk. "What about him?" The food hit my stomach with a thump I was surprised wasn't audible. Then I started to get a very bad feeling. "Wait. What does this have to do with—"

He dug under his jacket, and Nat tensed perceptibly. Leon glanced at her, making another odd little face like he was amused, then pulled out a sleek silver thing. "I decided to start at the beginning, with the moment your *loup-garou* disappeared. There must have been a security feed for that sector, I thought. So I went looking for it. Found out the raw footage had been yanked, but there are always backups. I called in a favor and had a friend of mine go digging until he found a ghost-shell image of the time in question. He brought it out and reconstructed it—but in the middle of the reconstruction he got transferred to Oklahoma. I'm not at all sure those two events aren't related, but that's beside the point." Leon opened up the silver rectangle. It was a screen on top and a touch pad on the bottom, a cute little thing. He pressed a button on the side, showed me what had to be the world's smallest DVD on a little tray sliding into the bottom half. "So I took it to another friend, this time outside the Schola, and called in another favor. He finished, and I went on my merry way. Take a look."

He handed it over. I stopped stuffing my face long enough to press the play button, tilting the screen so the glare didn't hit it. The bathroom door opened again. Dibs, rinsed off and dried, wearing (thank God) a pair of jeans and a blue T-shirt silk-screened with an elephant, peered out.

He was still blushing fiercely, deep crimson staining his cheeks. I didn't blame him.

"What you're seeing is security footage outside that gym exit," Leon continued. "Your *loup-garou* should be coming out right about . . . now."

And there it was. A slice of wall, the camera angled to show the gym door, two paths, and the baseball diamond and bleachers in the distance. The door blasted open so hard little things popped off, a slam I could almost hear as it flew wide and hit the concrete wall. Graves stalked out.

He stamped, coat flapping silently. Veered away from the baseball field, passed behind the bleachers. Crouched and sprang, his hands jetting out, grabbed the top railing of the bleachers, and cleared it in a swoop of graceful authority no human body would have been able to pull off. My heart lodged in my throat, but I took another bite anyway. Had to swallow twice to get the chewed food down.

There he was on the bleachers. He crouched, and it was difficult to make it out at that distance on the small screen, but maybe his shoulders were shaking.

Oh, God. Is he crying?

"Now watch," Leon said, leaning forward with his gaze fixed on my face. Like he could tell exactly what I was seeing by my expression.

I took another bite, my eyebrows drawn together, and almost choked.

Graves straightened and leapt off the bleachers, running with fluid grace. He was gone in an instant, but there was something else.

A shadow came from the other side of the baseball diamond. A streak of something that resolved into another boy-shape as it paused behind the bleachers, tipping its head. Sleek hair, a dark sweater, and sharp handsome grace.

Djamphir grace.

"What the *fuck?*" I breathed. Lifted the sandwich to my mouth again.

It was Christophe. I'd know that body language *anywhere*.

Christophe paused for just a moment, then loped in the same direction Graves had gone. He passed off-camera toward the little copse I'd found a scrap of Graves's coat in, determination evident in his stride.

The touch twitched inside my head. A scene painted itself in quick swipes, like a motion-capture sketch, black and white. I'd do it with as dark a graphite as I could find, then go over it with black pen to make the shadows even deeper.

Christophe, leaning against a tree in a shadowed clearing. His eyes turned blowtorch-blue as he watched, and the expression on his face was chilling. Because under the set grim look of a guy watching something distasteful, there was faint, scary amusement. He watched as the struggle took place, and when it was over, his smile was a ghost of itself.

"Just get it out of my sight," he said, and their narrow white hands lifted the other boy, his long dark coat flapping as he struggled uselessly.

I shook my head, sharply, trying to dislodge the thought. The clip ended in a fuzz of static. "What?"

"Does Reynard have a grudge against your *loup-garou?*" Leon's tone held exactly *no* mockery, and that was odd to hear. "I ask because . . . well, he hasn't mentioned being the last to see the wulfling, has he?"

"They said Shanks was the last one to see him," Dibs whispered. He'd grabbed the door frame, his curls dark with water and heavy on his forehead. "But . . . Christophe was?"

"Shanks saw him exiting from *inside* the gym; he stayed to make sure Milady was protected. He couldn't see outside." Leon neatly subtracted the silver thing from my fingers. "There's more, Dru. Are you sure you can stand to hear it?"

I stared at him, my hand in midair holding a sandwich half. "I . . . Just what are we talking about here?"

But I had a sneaking suspicion that I knew.

Just keep waiting, Dru. If I'd heard anything, you would know. How many times had Christophe repeated it?

"*Someone* erased that security feed. Someone on the Council, no less, transferred my friend when they caught wind of his poking around for the raw footage. I decided to go very carefully, and it's good that I did. Because—" His fingers flicked again. Hell of a magic trick—a white envelope appeared in his hand, just like magic. "I found out where he's being held, too. And how do you think I did that?"

I lowered my hand. Nat moved restlessly, Dibs held on to the door like it was keeping him from drowning, and Ash peered up over the edge of the bed again.

"Bang," the not-so-Broken wulf said, gravely and expectantly.

I handed him the fresh sandwich half, and he ducked down again. My fingers tingled, and rushing noise filled my skull.

Like wingbeats, feathers frantically brushing air.

"Tell me." Dry-lipped, I whispered the words.

"By following Reynard until I found one of his lairs. He's a tricky fox indeed. But once I found his latest den, I found papers. Some of his *private* papers. These were among them." He offered me the envelope. "Only take it if you're certain you want to know. Milady."

"Dru?" Nathalie moved again, like she didn't want me to go any further. "Eat. Whatever happens, you need your strength to face it. Leave this for after you've eaten."

If I do that, Nat, I'm not going to be brave enough to open it up. I reached up. My nerveless fingers closed on the paper. "Is this a copy or the original?"

"I didn't see a copy machine around." Leon shrugged. "He'll know someone was in there. He has a sharp nose; he may even know it was me. In that event, you're the only person who can possibly shield me from his vengeance."

Yeah, like he listens to me at all. "Wait." My head ached, the rushing noise threatening to spill free of my ears and go walking. A crackling ran through me, like the static was somehow being transmitted from my bones outward. Leon shook his head a little, a curious look falling over his sharp face. "Just hold on a second. Let me think."

"You're radiating." Nat handed me another sandwich half. Even her eyeliner was purple, and it glittered in the honey-gold light. "Please. Eat more; you'll need it."

I lifted it mechanically to my lips, put it down again. Stared at the envelope in my right hand. "You're saying Christophe was there when something happened to Graves. And that he knows where Graves is and . . ."

"I don't know if they left this morning to free the *loup-garou*." Leon showed his teeth. "I doubt it. The entire Council, gone to rescue a wulfen, even a prince among the furred? No offense." Here he glanced at Nat again.

Her mouth was a thin grim line, and her eyes flared yellow. "None taken."

"He promised he'd tell me." My right hand curled up into a fist. "He *promised*."

"No doubt he would, when he judged the time right." Leon folded his arms again. The glow of dusk through the window deepened, the sun's last hurrah before it sank. "The Council will more than likely return at dusk, Milady. When they do, I'd ask that you allow me to stay in your presence. If Reynard finds out I've been in his papers . . . well, as I've said, you're the only person in the Order who can stop him from making me extraordinarily uncomfortable."

"I don't understand," Dibs croaked. "Why would he . . . I mean, *Graves*. He's one of us. Why would Christophe do that?"

"For the oldest reason in the book, Dibsie." Nat sounded tired. She was looking right at me. "How maddening, for a *djamphir* to get edged out by a wulf."

"Nothing ever changes." Leon's mouth pulled down bitterly. "You'd do well to remember that, Skyrunner."

"Some things change." She watched me, steadily. "You're proof of that, aren't you. *Leontus*."

I honestly couldn't tell what the fuck. It went right over my head. "Wait. You're saying Christophe would . . . would give Graves to . . ." The only possible explanation took shape inside my head. "Give him to Sergej." The name burned my lips, and Ash shivered. "Because . . . of me?"

"Maybe not necessarily." Leon shifted his weight slightly. He had the look of someone smelling something unpleasant who couldn't move away. That slightly set, slightly disgusted expression, mouth tight and eyebrows level—you can see it on plane trips or bus rides all the time. Usually when someone's sitting next to someone else who doesn't have the same hygiene standards. "Maybe he gave the *loup-garou* to Anna, who—"

I shook my head. Curls fell in my face. "But Anna . . . she *hated* Chris. You were there, you saw as much!"

He shrugged, the sharp points of his shoulders coming up, dropping. I had a mad thought of offering *him* a sandwich. Leon spread his hands, a helpless gesture. "He could have played her for a fool, too. Let her think she was striking at you. It has a certain symmetry."

"But Anna had just finished . . ." The enormity of it walloped me sideways. I held the envelope up, sweating fingers crushing the paper. It was thick, stuffed full. "He couldn't have. She'd just . . . I'd just finished having a fight with her. She wasn't about to go meeting up with him. She didn't even know he was around."

Leon let his hands drop. "If you say so, Milady. In any case, you have a decision to make."

I set the plate aside on the rucked-up covers. Nat twitched. I ripped the envelope open, and the sound of tearing paper was like my heart breaking. I *felt* it, a sharp tearing in my chest, and a steady slow leaking.

Leon actually took two steps back, his boots soundless on the hardwood.

Ash's head popped up again. He studied me for a moment, then actually climbed up on the bed while I slid the six sheets out and opened them up. A whiff of apple pie rose, and my stomach closed around the lump of rock that had been food a little while ago.

I won't push, and I don't pry. All I ask is a little attention.

I opened up the sheaf of paper. Have you ever wanted to wash your mouth out with bleach? I wanted to scrub every part of me that had ever flushed each time Christophe got close to me. I spread the sheets of paper out, crackling, and stared at them.

"Jesus," I whispered. Everything blurred. It wasn't just dusk slipping across the sky, creeping in through the skylights. It was hot water in my eyes. My chest ached. I blinked furiously, and a hot drop fell on my hand, spattering. I was shaking.

Pictures. A list of locations, crossed off. One circled. More pictures on copy paper, showing different angles. A mansion; the address was out in Queens. A folded city map, beat up and scuffed like it had been carried in a pocket for a long time. Notations in a thin calligraphic script, I'd seen Christophe's handwriting on Council paperwork.

This looked similar.

"No." It didn't even sound like my voice. Ash reached across me, snagged another sandwich, and settled back on his haunches. At least someone would get the benefit of all that food. "Oh, *hell* no."

Everything clicked together inside my head, and my face settled against itself. It felt frozen, and heavy, and just a little bit like Dad's face must have felt when he was wearing his stare-down look.

"What are you going to do?" Leon took another two steps back. Like he was getting ready for an explosion.

I looked up. Dibs stared at me, deathly pale. We watched each other for a few seconds, the blond wulf and me.

He already looked hopeless. And I was just about to make it worse.

"Get out," I whispered.

He stared at me like I was speaking a foreign language. I hoped like hell he couldn't read my face. At least the skin lay stiff and mask-like against my bones; maybe it would help keep what I was planning a secret.

I slid off the bed. Swayed for a moment, and Nat reached forward as if she was going to help me. My hand flashed out, and I slapped hers away. The sound of the slap was like the last piece of my heart shivering into pieces.

Dibs let out a small, soft, hurt sound. Leon was watching me very carefully, his odd-colored eyes narrowed.

I found my voice again. "Get out. All of you, *out*."

"Milady—" Nat had gone white, and I didn't want to see the flash of pain in her wide blue eyes, no trace of yellow glow left in the irises. I didn't want to see the way she'd grabbed her hand, either, as if she'd touched a hot stove.

Or as if I'd hurt her, with just my puny human strength.

So I half-turned and pointed at Ash. "I said *get out*. And take him with you." My hands turned into fists, and I dropped them.

Ash looked at me gravely, his scarred boyface set and pale. His head was cocked just a little, and the way his hair fell in his scar-jawed face hurt me suddenly. Would Graves end up like this?

Broken?

Oh, hell no. Everything that had shattered came together inside me again, sharp edges sliding together like puzzle pieces.

"Dru—" Leon, now. He stepped forward, but I rounded on him.

"I am *svetocha*," I said quietly. "And I want you all to get *out* of my goddamn bedroom. Right. Goddamn. Now."

The words rocked him back on his heels. Dibs let out a squeak and bolted for the door, fumbled with the locks, flung it open, and was gone. I pointed at Ash. "You. Down."

He hopped fluidly off the bed and crouched, hands and feet on the floor.

"Take him, Nathalie. Ash, go with Nat. Don't give her any trouble." Who was the girl issuing orders in this crisp, cold voice? It couldn't be me. My face was frozen, and the ice was starting to work down to the rest of me. I had to get them out of here. Because once dusk hit and Christophe got back, good luck doing any of what I had planned.

"Milady—" Leon attempted, again. Maybe he thought he was going to calm me down.

That was *so* not happening. The entire room flexed around me, a sudden drenching wash of spice exhaling from my skin, and an odd crackle ran along the surface of my skin.

"Get. The. Fuck. OUT!" The last word was a yell, and Nat actually jumped out of her chair. She reached down, her fingers slipping through Ash's greasy hair, and the two of them were suddenly at the door. Ash looked back, but Nat jerked on his hair like it was a leash, and he piled out into the hall with her.

Leon and I faced each other. His shoulders were up, but high flags of color stood out on his cheeks, and he wore an odd, set little smile that was more like a grimace of pain.

"What are you going to—" he began, but I took two steps toward him. My hands were knotted up so tight they made little creaking sounds, and I felt little prickles in my palm that weren't just fingernails. My wrists ached, twin fiery bracelets. The aspect slid over me, oil-hot and soothing, and for once I didn't care that my teeth were tingling and he could almost certainly see the little fangs dimpling my lower lip.

I held his gaze, and his pained expression grew deeper, like silt building in the bottom of a clear pond.

I didn't care. "Get. Out. Or I will hit you."

He backed up, watching me like you'd watch an angry rattler. For a single second I felt a flash of guilt. Nat and Dibs would probably never forgive me for losing my shit; I'd probably scared the hell out of both of them. Hurt their feelings big-time. And Leon?

Who cares what they think? The cold was all the way inside me now, determination taking shape. *It's not important. The important thing is getting that door locked and getting your gear.*

Leon backed out the door. His hand flashed out, caught the knob, and drew it closed behind him. It closed with a definite *snick*, and before I knew it I was across the room, locking every single lock. I settled the iron bar in its brackets and saw the thread-thin lines of blue warding sizzling as they ran through the physical fabric of the walls and spun together in a complicated Celtic knot in the middle of the door. They were getting brighter, trembling on the edge of the visible, and that made it official. The touch was stronger. *I* was stronger.

Something was happening to me, building inside me. Some

change, like the tide shifting. Whatever it was, I didn't care. If it was the blooming, finally, great.

It would make it easier to kick some ass.

I stood there for a couple seconds, my eyes suspiciously prickling.

I won't push, and I don't pry . . . All I ask is a little attention, Dru.

Christophe had laid right there on the bed. Held me while I cried. Kissed me, and all the while he knew where Graves was. He *knew*. And he hid it from me.

From me, and *because* of me.

Jesus.

I swallowed the stone in my throat. Forced the hot prickles in my eyes away. My fangs pressed out, insistent and achingly tender. The bloodhunger quivered at the back of my throat, and that made me conscious of what, exactly, I was feeling. There was a whole complicated tangle, but the biggest dog in the pile was clear, cold anger.

Not anger

Rage.

I turned around and surveyed my room. I had my emergency bag, and there were my mother's *malaika* hanging in a harness, on their peg next to the vanity. Dusk was gathering in the window, and Christophe and the Council would likely be back any moment now.

Get going, Dru.

I got going.

Chapter Nineteen

Getting off the Schola grounds without Nat was child's play with the aspect so thick on me. It ran over my skin in intensifying waves, no longer warm but just on the verge of hot, like a good strong shower. I didn't have the benefit of one of Nat's braids. The curls occasionally slipping free of the sloppy ponytail were veined with gold, long and loose and silky.

For once, my hair was behaving in a pinch. But I couldn't even care.

It was dusk, time for the changing over of the guards roaming the Schola grounds, and I'm sure that helped. I moved when I didn't hear anyone, froze and faded into the walls or bushes when I did, and when I got to the wall I hopped up on top of it like it was a stepping stool. No Nat around to give me ten fingers, but with the aspect, I didn't need it.

Poor Nat.

Once I got off the grounds it was time to worry about transportation. Ran into a problem there—with the *malaika* harness on, I couldn't take a cab. Could I slide by on the subway?

I thought about it, and I decided if I could take on a sucker in a moving subway car, I was probably able to handle some cops. At the very least I could get *away*, and that was good enough.

When you've run with werwulfen, a human can't hope to catch you.

Still, it was probably best to stay below the radar. A cop would babble into a walkie-talkie, and if anyone was listening to cop chatter on a scanner they might catch wind of me. I couldn't afford that right now; I couldn't afford to let anyone know where I was until I *wanted* them to know. So I walked, and I tried to stay out of sight as much as possible. It was amazingly easy, with the aspect tingling every time someone glanced at me and instinct moving under my skin, telling me in clear radio bursts when to move and when to stop and wait.

I walked the whole way to my first stop. I barely noticed the scenery, because the rage inside me made the twilight crowds smell like . . . Well, let's just say the problem of keeping my mouth shut had never been so simple or complex all at the same time.

Night had fallen fully by the time I turned a Brooklyn corner and saw the suddenly–familiar) street brick apartment houses marching all the way down and the black bags of trash piled all along the curb. It looked just the same as it had years ago, and a moment of homesickness crawled up my throat, displacing the rage for a second.

The little bodega on the corner looked the same, too. Red and yellow, packs of gum and cartons of cigarettes stacked neatly, crowding around a man with a shiny bald head and a red plaid shirt instead of the spare white-haired woman with a breath of weird on her who used to be in the window when I'd been here with Augie. The pizza place I'd been at with Nat and the wulfen just a short while ago wasn't far from here, either. It was nice to find my navigation-fu was still strong.

I ducked into the alley, took a deep breath, and stared at the blank brick walls. Trash drifted in corners, the Dumpsters were over-flowing, and the reek almost choked me before I shut it away. Which was easy to do, with the aspect so close to the surface.

The fire escape was no problem, and I even managed to do it quietly. The entire apartment building thrummed with sounds of habitation—everyone was home from work, and sleeping or doing whatever it is people do in apartments at night. I reached the roof and hopped down, taking my bearings even before my sneakers hit the weird, gritty surface.

A cool spring breeze skimmed across the rooftop, other build-ings clustering around bouncing the wind in odd directions. It lifted one of my curls, brushed it against my cheek, and I caught a fading, flaring drift of familiar scent. The touch woke up inside my head again, a sudden vivid mental image of Augustine slipping across this same rooftop, his yellow hair combed back and his jacket open, slid-ing a gun back into its holster. Moving too swift and sure to be any-thing but *djamphir*.

I found myself silently stepping across the roof, too, until I reached the weird three-sided gap between buildings. Augie's kitchen window only looked out on blank brick in this triangle of forgotten city space, and he'd made me look out the window so I could see the hand- and footholds. It was ridiculously easy to climb down and jimmy the window open—I knew just where to press.

Oh, ewww. Augie, yuck. Something *smelled*. Like rotting food, and a particular sharpish undertone. I almost got hung up in the window, the twin hilts of the *malaika* awkward while I was crouch-ing, but then I slid inside and hopped down from the counter.

His kitchen was an unholy mess. I've seen vampire destruction before, but each time it's . . . well, incredible. The cabinet doors were busted, the fridge blown open like someone had stuffed dynamite in it, and the smell of rotting exhaled from both there and the kitchen garbage, which had been upended. The dishes were all broken.

Jesus. I wrinkled my nose, peeked out into the living room. His plasma TV was busted all to hell, the couch was shredded, but the wall with the front door was curiously unharmed. Had they come in through the window? Had he been attacked after I called him from the Dakotas? He hadn't said anything about his apartment being busted.

The cache was in the bedroom, which wasn't damaged much. The narrow single bed I'd slept on was ripped up, the antique dresser sledgehammered to bits and vomiting up clothes, and the closet door reduced to matchsticks. Fortunately I could get one of the wrecked closet doors aside, and I pulled out some of Augie's familiar plaid shirts and found bare carpet. I pressed in the right place; there was a *click!* and a square of carpeted floor rose.

It hadn't been rifled. Thank God.

Silver-grain ammo and a spare gun — a serviceable 9mm, basic Schola armory issue.

Thought-provoking, but it was gear and I took it.

I took that and a clip-on holster, emptied the blue bag full of cash, and stowed it in my emergency bag — a canvas messenger number I'd managed to sew a false bottom into in between training these past weeks. Most of the cash went under the flap, but I did up a few rolls for stashing in pockets and in the top of the bag, too, my fingers moving with habitual ease.

I took as much ammo as I could carry without clinking, stuffing clips into the pockets of Graves's long dark coat, too. There was a spare Medikit in there too, a homemade one that held penicillin and other stuff as well as a stack of hypodermic needles in shockfoam.

"Oh, Augie," I whispered.

It's bad manners to clean out another hunter's cache, but I didn't have a choice.

A sudden ringing made me jump. My heart leapt like a fish pulled from water, and one of my fangs pricked my lower lip. I tasted the copper sweetness of my own blood before swallowing, hard, and taking a deep breath.

It was the phone.

I went back to the cache. I took another city map and a couple glass ampoules of what had to be holy water. Hey, better safe than sorry. The phone shrilled four times, then I heard a click and a whir.

It was just like Augustine not to have voice mail. He had a great plasma TV and only watched black-and-white movies on it, too.

"*Leave a message.*" A thin growl, Augie sounding scary as possible. A long static-laden pause, and a beep.

I jumped again when he spoke.

"Dru, *kochana*, if you are there, pick up the phone."

Christophe. I clipped the holster on with shaking hands. How much time did I have? God*damn* him being so smart. How would he guess?

"Dru. Pick up. You're in terrible danger." He sounded frantic, and I could hear a murmur behind him. A faint thopping, like a helicopter.

Oh, this is so not even funny. I loaded the gun, chambered a round. The sound was very loud in the hush. How had Augie's neighbors not heard vampires in here? But maybe that's the big city for you. Nobody in anyone else's business, everyone taking care of himself, and devil take the hindmost.

"Whatever you think, whatever you've been told . . . Dru, please. *Please*. Pick up. Let me explain."

Explain? Oh, yeah. Sure. "Not fucking likely, Christophe," I muttered. Here I was like an idiot, talking to an answering machine that couldn't even hear me. I slid the gun into the holster, checked the cache one more time. The touch tingled faintly inside my head.

"Please, Dru. *Please*. Pick up. Pick up the phone, *kochana, milna, skowroneczko moja*, little bird, *please—*"

The machine beeped and cut him off. I let out a shaky exhale, checked my watch. I had a whole night to keep everyone off my trail, find the mansion in Queens, and lay low until dawn. But first I had to get out of here.

I didn't want to use the front door, and I didn't want to use the roof again. You should never ever use the same exit as entrance path, especially if you're visiting what is almost certainly what Dad would call a "compromised location." His other term for it started with "cluster" and ended up rhyming with "duck."

So it was up on the bed, sliding the window open—it looked down onto the street, and I'd spent so many mornings that whole month Dad was gone laying on the bed and craning to get a glimpse of the sky—while the phone rang again.

I checked the street—clear. Knocked the screen out with one well-placed kick.

"*Dru!*" Christophe was yelling into the phone now. "*Dru, please, please pick up!*"

Time to go. I launched myself feetfirst through the window as the ghost of wax-orange danger candy filled my mouth.

CHAPTER TWENTY

ran until the danger candy faded completely and I was just left with the copper taste of adrenaline. Then I hopped on the subway— no reason not to, now; they could start chasing me now that I was prepared—and rode toward Times Square until the crowd got thick. It was closer to the Schola Prima than I liked, but there was plenty of crowd cover and it was the last place they'd look for me.

Or so I hoped.

I surfaced, found an all-night diner, and ordered coffee and a club sandwich, keeping a watch out the window at the crowd flowing by while I bolted the food and looked over the printouts and maps.

I picked out the neighborhood on both Augie's and Christophe's maps, looked at likely ways in and out. I tried to consider the whole thing like Dad would. Angles of attack, the getaway—I'd have to find a car. Or something.

Worry about that when you get on-site. Can't do nothin' here, and if you steal a car now and take it there you're askin for trouble. Calm and easy, Dru-girl, just like I taught you.

Had Dad ever guessed what he was training me *for*? Or did he just not think much about it one way or the other? Yet another pile of questions I'd never get an answer to.

I found myself reaching up to touch Graves's earring, fingering the skull, running the edge of a crossed bone under my thumbnail. *Don't worry, I'm on my way. I'm coming.*

But then I worried, too, while I downed the last of the coffee and neatened everything up, stuffing it back in my bag with the ammo. What if they'd moved him? How old was the intel? If the place was crawling with vampires . . . Well, I was fast enough to kill one of them, wasn't I?

But more than one? And Sergej, too?

You need a better plan, Dru.

One started to take shape as I paid the bill and hit the streets. I kept moving, and it evolved inside my aching head. Here I was, two *malaika* strapped to my back and a long black coat wandering around, and nobody paid any attention. True, it was night in the city, and there were weirder things than me on the street. .

Most of them were even human.

Some of it could have been the touch throbbing inside my head, keeping me moving. I heard soft wingbeats through the crowd noise and sometimes caught a glimpse of the owl. Perched on a blinking *Girls Girls Girls* sign, circling at the end of a street, floating down to land on the hood of a parked car. I even caught it filling itself out like a charcoal sketch with quick strokes, leading me in a wandering zigzag pattern that kept me away from trouble, and also away from the green quiet of Central Park, vaguely north and east for a little while.

All this time I'd thought it was Gran's owl. But now I felt the beat of its heart and the wind through its feathers, and I knew it was a part of me. Just like I'd known in the gym facing Anna. When the owl had hit her animal aspect, the tortoiseshell cat crouched at her feet, with the sick crunch of continents colliding.

So I'm an owl, Christophe is a fox, and Anna's a cat. And Graves is loup-garou. *Funny.*

Only it wasn't.

Sometimes flashes of that night come back to me, mostly when I'm trying to fall asleep and I get that weird sense of falling. I'll jolt awake, expecting to be on the pavement again, sliding past groups of hard-faced young men on corners or melding with a flow of tired adults flooding down subway steps, seeing my reflection—pale cheeks, hair pulled back, the twin hilts of the *malaika* poking up over my slim shoulders, the coat flapping around my ankles. I hung around the edges of the Pier raves for a long time, moving in aimless circles as trance and electronica throbbed through the air, then sometime after three I slid through the quiet of Battery Park like a ghost and started working my way north and east, cutting around the Schola Prima's slice of Manhattan like it had plague. Risky to stay this close, but again, the last place they'd look for me.

I ate a couple more times, too. It was like I couldn't get full, and I was always finding those carts that sell pretzels or chicken satay or burritos, especially near Midtown. I wasn't worried about money; I was worried about the huge hole under my ribs that just kept getting bigger. When I turned onto deserted streets I could hear a little crackling, like static. It was coming from under my skin, and I wasn't sure if I should be worried.

I moved with the crowds through the arteries of the city. Safety in numbers, and I liked the hustle and bustle. Even in the dead of night, something was happening somewhere. This is why the Real World hunts mostly in cities. I mean, there's rural Real World, too, but it's a different flavor. The nastier, sharper-edged stuff lives in the urban jungle.

The worst hours were between three and five in the morning while I was walking with vague intention, the long slow hush before dawn. I wandered around, pretending Dad was picking my plan apart, making it as good and solid as I could and hoping I'd covered everything.

Back at the Schola it would be time to tuck Ash in and retreat to my room, let Nat brush my hair, and look forward to Christophe knocking on the door. I got antsy, working my way across the river toward Queens, and stopping every once in a while as the ghost of waxed oranges slid across my tongue. That was another thing to worry about—the aura wasn't as strong. Everything else was, but the danger candy was only a ghost of itself, and I couldn't think it was because I was safer.

I found a working phone booth about twelve blocks from the mansion. It was harder than it sounds—now that there's cell phones, the pay ones are going out of style in a big way.

Dad groused about that sometimes. It wasn't any harder to get an untraceable cell phone, but there was still the problem of triangulating from the towers that receive the call. Not really any worse than a pay phone, but Dad was old-school.

My heart made a funny ripping motion inside my chest, but I was too busy to worry about the pain. Story of my life. If I ever slowed down all the crap piling up would make me cry for a week, probably.

I plugged in quarters—I had plenty of those, though I'd given the rest of my change away—and dialed. Normally I keep numbers in my Yoda notebook, not my head. But this one I'd fallen asleep reciting for a while because it was my personal drop line for the Order, the number that would light up their switchboard like a distress flare.

Which meant that the call would be traced. After all night keeping to the shadows and hoping nobody would catch me, I was about to say *here I am, come get me.*

I listened to it ring, cleared my throat, and tried to look everywhere at once. The street was a nice one, this particular convenience store across the street from Flushing Park's bruised green in good shape and the lines in the parking lot freshly painted. All the trash was picked up, and it didn't smell like old-man urine, which meant this was a Relatively Nice Part of Town.

I guess when you're near a graveyard, nice is relative.

Two rings. Three. Four. It picked up, and there was a series of clicks. Then, silence while they started tracing my location.

"Goddammit," I said to the listening quiet. "Say something."

"Dru." Augustine sounded incredibly weary. "What the hell you doing?"

What do you think? "Rescuing Graves. Christophe knows where. Have him bring backup. I'm going in at first light, which is—" I checked the sky. "Very soon. The more they distract whoever's holding my Goth Boy, the safer I'll be."

"Dru-girl, sweetheart, listen to me. Something's going on. You're in trouble, and—"

"Damn right I'm in trouble, August. I've been going along trusting Christophe, and all he does is lie to me. I'm *done.* If the Order wants anything out of me, they'll do what I tell them, starting *right now.* And what I'm telling them to do is to get Christophe to admit he knew where Graves is. And to come and help me rescue him. Otherwise they're going to be out one more *svetocha.*" I wet my lips with a quick nervous flick of my tongue, watching the street. The sky was turning gray in the east; I could *feel* dawn approaching as if a thousand little tiny threads were pulling against my flesh. The crackling under my skin was intense, almost to the point of pain.

"Please, Dru. Please just listen—" Now Augie was pleading with me, the way he never had when I lived with him. Of course, I'd been young then. He hadn't had to plead; he'd just told me what to do and I did it.

Screw that. I was about to start misbehaving in a big way.

"I ain't listening to *jackshit*," I informed him, every inch of me alert. For the first time, I heard the ghost of Dad's slow sleepy accent in my voice. "I listened for a long time and got nothing but *lied to*, Augustine. You go tell them. Or maybe they're listening and they already know." I recited the address, reeling it off like I was right in front of it. "I'm going on in, and I'm getting Graves. If you guys want to come play, fine. If not, then kiss your *svetocha* goodbye."

I hung up. Hung on to the phone, shaking. My legs were rubbery. I lifted my hand and heard the crackle again. Little things moved in my wrist, popping and sliding. The bones were shifting. Kind of like a wulfen's when they go into changeform, but with a queerly musical tinkle to it. Like bells.

Holy shit. I swallowed hard. I had a plan, and I had to stick to it.

I stepped out of the booth's three-quarter enclosure and sniffed. Smelled nothing but car exhaust, wet green from the trees and lawns, and the dirty smell of a city. People jammed together like rats, except out in this piece of town the holes were nicer. Still, out here the mansion would have smaller homes pressing against its walled grounds, trying to get in. Property values out here were probably enough to give people heart attacks.

I sniffed again. There was a faint breath of rotting.

Nosferat. There were suckers in the neighborhood.

There was a thin thread of cinnamon, too, weaving under all the other smells and tying them together. Not tinted with apples, like

Christophe, or carnation-flowery, like Anna. This was like big gooey cinnamon buns, and it reminded me of my mother's warm perfume.

That was the wrong thing to think. Because it made the night much bigger and darker, pressing between the streetlights and against the store's fluorescent glare. Even though dawn was coming, it was still awful dark.

A snap-ruffle of muffled wingbeats, and the owl coasted in. It landed on the gas station's sign, mantled once, and looked at me. Blinked one yellow eye, then the other. Its talons skritched a little, a small sound under the drone of faraway traffic, the murmur of the city, and the thrumming at the very edge of my consciousness.

The touch slid free of my head. Uneasy static, a thunderstorm approaching. I tasted wax oranges, but only faintly. A brief glass-needle spike of pain through my head, and I was back in myself, staring up at the owl like it was going to tell me something.

Well, I wouldn't be surprised if it did. But still.

I reached up to touch the skull-and-crossbones earring. My mother's locket was a chip of ice against my breastbone, safe and snug under my T-shirt and hoodie. Graves's coat flapped around my ankles in the uneasy breeze. Goose bumps spread over me. The air itself was electric.

Come on, Dru. Time to do the throwin' down, not just the starin' down.

I headed for the edge of the parking lot. The owl called softly, but when I glanced up it had taken off, a soft explosion of feathers.

I stepped out of the light and into the darkness before dawn. Twelve blocks to the mansion they were holding Graves in, if they hadn't moved him.

Then it was showtime.

CHAPTER TWENTY-ONE

Things went okay enough for the first few minutes. I dropped down on the other side of the high brick wall and didn't immediately glance up to see what Dad was doing. I'd almost forgotten what it felt like to be out at night, sneaking around somewhere the Real World was rubbing through the fabric of the everyday.

No. I hadn't forgotten. I'd just forgotten what it felt like to do this with Dad, him taking point and me doing backup and sweep–behind. The comfort of knowing that I just had to wait for orders and let training do the rest.

A thin film of rotten, waxed oranges slid over my tongue. I swallowed hard, the aspect smoothing down over me in deep waves of sensation. Christophe had marked this entrance in red pencil on the satellite photos, along with a couple other routes.

Always planning ahead. Had he thought I'd never find out?

The thing was, I still flushed hotly, thinking of him. Thinking of his hands in my hair and the lightning that went through me whenever—

My grandmother's owl hooted softly, sharply. Consciousness of danger prickled under the surface of my skin. The shifting in my bones retreated, silence filling my flesh.

I faded back into the shrubbery lining the wall. My breathing came soft through a wide-open mouth, my right hand reaching up and curling around a *malaika*'s warm wooden hilt. I felt a pair of *nosferat* pass, a drift of bad drain-smell and hatred sending glass pins through my temples.

That's the thing about suckers. They *hate* so much. I don't understand it. It's not like they have a monopoly on hate—human beings have a big chunk of the market, and other Real World stuff has its slices of the pie too—but a sucker's hate is so intense, and it clouds around them like dust around that kid in the old Peanuts cartoons. The one who was always filthy.

I didn't blink, I didn't move. The aspect made it easier, and I suddenly understood how the older *djamphir* fell into that spooky immobility. It was so easy, a stillness enfolding the entire body like a cradling bath, the world moving past on a slow river. My concentration turned fierce and one-pointed, and all Gran's training seemed like kid games.

Two more suckers, patrolling. They smelled male, and peppery with excitement. The touch whispered in my head, averting their notice. Gran's owl called again, but neither of them noticed. One made a low aside in some consonant-filled foreign language, their shapes blurred like ink on wet paper, and the other one laughed before they vanished with a tiny, nasty chattering little sound.

Man, I hate that. I hate it when djamphir *do it, too.*

I studied the house a little more. It was a big sprawling brick monstrosity, looking for all the world like a square red-brown fungus had suddenly got drunk, smoked crack, and decided to stack itself up to impersonate a mansion. It was *dark*, a dark the coming morning probably wouldn't penetrate very far. I didn't have to think about where I'd seen this sort of miasma before.

It had been back in the Dakotas, under a snowy sky with Graves in the truck right next to me. Going to meet Sergej.

Christophe had saved us then. Or, more precisely, saved *me*. Like he was always doing.

Like I was counting on him to do now.

A complex, tangled wash of feeling slid over me like the aspect. I was counting on him an awful lot here. .

Just as I thought it, I heard the *thwap-thrum* of a helicopter. It got louder and louder, and the fungal mansion took a breath. Like a lion smiling right before it gets up.

Let's hope this goes well, Dru.

I slid out of the bushes, thin danger candy waxing and waning on my tongue. Creeping along, each foot placed silently, my right hand still awkwardly up, clasping the *malaika*'s oddly warm, satin-smooth hilt. The path marked with red pencil took advantage of every bit of cover, and about halfway to the house I paused, something nagging inside my head.

You're in terrible danger, Dru.

Well, duh. But Graves was also, and he was in this house. Who knew what they were doing to him? I had a chance now to—

"*Svetosssssssssssssha . . .*" It was a hiss, off to my right. A cold, lipless, hate-filled voice. "*Little svetosssssssha, come out and play.*"

All hell broke loose.

A high scream cut short on a gurgle came from the other side of the mansion, and the night was suddenly full of noise and motion. Geysers of dirt exploded up, black scarecrow forms leaping free and bits of grass flying. I tugged sideways on the *malaika* hilt, a motion

I'd practiced so many times with Christophe it was now natural, like loading a gun. My left hand flashed up, closed around wood, but I wasn't ready when the first sucker leapt for me, its narrow teenage face contorted. His hair stood up in dead-black spikes, rubbing against each other with little squealing sounds, and I had my right-hand *malaika* free, the edge cleaving air with a gentle whistle lost under the chaos.

Bloodhunger lit up inside every vein in my body. I *felt* it, as if the map of my circulation had just been filled with electricity. The aspect flared, my fangs dug into my lower lip, and I slashed—

—but the curved edge just slid through empty air because the sucker dropped in midleap, clutching at his throat like he had a rock lodged in there. He curled up like a pillbug, but I was already past. I'd expected him to hit me and flung myself forward. Landed hard, sneakers digging into soft-churned earth, the left-hand *malaika* free and whirling like a propeller.

I was already in second form, Christophe's voice echoing in my head. *Knee! Keep your knee in line! Think of the whole edge, not just the point; for God's sake*, kochana, *keep your back straight!* It was like hearing Dad's barks while on the heavy bag, an unwilling comfort.

The scarecrow shadows leapt at me, and I almost panicked. Fangs glowing ivory and champing, foam spraying from their reddened lips, their hair standing up as their version of the aspect crackled through them, the suckers moved in with that unholy speed. The world slowed down, the clear plastic goop that was my own super-speed kicking in hardening on every surface, the *malaika* whirring outward in the two great defense-movements in second form, which is the beginning of the one-against-many. First form is to build your speed and precision; second through eighth form are all about being the underdog; eighth through thirteenth are the solo combat forms.

I'd barely begun on third form. But Christophe also said that mastery lay in the first two, that if you practiced only those, you would have the essence of all of them. He took me through them every night before sparring, over and over again—

Quit thinking about him and start paying attention!

I hop-skipped forward, weight precisely balanced, and the *malaika* bit preternatural, stone-hard flesh. But it wasn't the wooden swords that did all the asskicking. As a matter of fact, I might as well not have had them.

Because the scarecrow vampires seemed to hit an invisible force field. The bloodhunger flexed inside my veins each time, and the suckers crumbled, choking and gagging. One of them fell before I even hit him, clutching at his throat.

Looked like I'd finally become toxic to suckers. In a big way.

Toxic enough that Sergej can't get to me? That'd be real nice. I leapt forward again, my feet landing as if I was running with the wulfen in Central Park's dappled light and shade, my heart in my mouth and the world rolling underfoot while I popped from place to place like a girl playing hopscotch.

But if Sergej had been able to endure my mother's toxicity for long enough to hang her in the oak tree outside that yellow house—

Dad's yell snapped me to attention. *Focus on what you got in front of you, Dru!* The *malaika* whistled, I was moving so fast. Suckers fell, gasping and choking, I hit the small wooden door on the side of the house like a bomb and was through, splinters flying so fast they embedded themselves in the wall opposite. Spinning on a dime, my left-hand *malaika* flicking out like a snake's tongue.

This sucker was more durable. He was choking as the blade sheared through his right leg, and it was a good thing I'd ducked because his claws were out and whistling through where my head would've been if I hadn't been down. The touch burning inside my head like napalm in a barrel, a gush of black stinking acidic blood from the sudden shortness of his leg, I drove up with long muscles in my legs, left-hand *malaika* flicking again. His eyes were like pools of rancid oil, and the worst thing was he looked a little bit like Dibs. Golden-haired, with a soft babyface contorted in agony before my aspect flexed again and he fell, choking up a thin green-black scum.

Why couldn't this have happened earlier? But I was already moving up the hall. The walls were painted white, but there were streaks of something I didn't want to think too much about all over them. Crusted streaks, dark red and smelling of copper. It was a complex braid of smells, like in Paranormal Biology where you had to open the ampoules, sniff the blood inside, and list characteristics. *Blond, male, young, hospital. Brunette, female, middle-aged, wounded.*

Sometimes suckers like certain victim types. And also, doing the sniff test sharpens your tracking ability. With the touch burning in my head, I was never wrong.

These were shutterclicks, images of bodies carried down this hall, prey thinking it had escaped and brought down so close to freedom, a collage of nasty images slamming through my head like iron dodgeballs smacking unprotected flesh.

The floor plan was clear in my head. The door was ahead of me, looming, and I left the ground in a sidekick that would have made any superhero proud. The thought that maybe if the door was locked or barred I'd just hurt myself didn't even cross my mind, because before I got there, it exploded.

Literally *exploded*, a flash like heaven itself opening and the shock like a wave face-crashing a surfer. I tumbled, head over heels, the wall clipping my shoulder and sending me spinning. Landed hard, the *malaika* still clasped in my fists and the world ringing like a gong inside my skull. The aspect flared with heat, cushioning me from the blow, but it still rang my chimes pretty good.

Smoke. Yellow flame crawling over the walls. *What the—*

Then I was scrambling to get on my feet, because *he* appeared out of the flames. Honey-brown curls and a face stamped from an old coin, chiseled and hurtful. A thin black sweater, jeans, and his paleness with its tint of copper over the top. And his eyes, my God, his eyes now black from lid to lid and so deep. You could fall into those eyes and drown before the soft sucking blackness at the top closed over your face.

You wouldn't even struggle.

My mother's locket gave a flare of painful heat, so hot I was suddenly afraid it had melted on my sternum. I let out a soundless cry—soundless because it was *loud*, my ears still ringing and shouts, cries, the sounds of a pitched battle going on all around me.

Sergej grinned. And right before he blurred through space and I brought the *malaika* up, I thought, for one terrible second, how much his smile looked like Christophe's chilling little grimace when he wanted to scare someone.

CHAPTER TWENTY-TWO

came to in bits and pieces, lying on my back.

Dust. I smelled dust, and something like burned coffee. Dampness, the peculiar smell of something underground, like a root cellar. And spice, like carnations. *That* was a familiar odor, and I tried to place it in the darkness. I realized it was dark because my eyes were closed.

On the heels of that realization came another one. I *hurt*. It was like growing pains, a deep burning ache in the bones. The idea of moving, even to open my eyes, seemed to make it even worse. But I had to. I had to know where I was.

But . . . I couldn't see.

I blinked a couple times. It made no difference. The same thick darkness, like a blanket against my eyeballs. I let out a short sound, the gasp chopped in half because I *sensed* someone looking at me. It was the sort of feeling that will make you turn your head in a crowd, certain of being stared at, and it's right more often than not.

What the hell? Am I blind? What happened?

The last thing I remembered was Sergej's hands around my throat, my scream cut short, and the bloodhunger pulling on my veins like it wanted to rip bits of me out. Little bits of blackness had crawled up under Sergej's skin, and he had *squeezed*—

Someone let out a short sigh of frustration. "You're not blind." Female. Young. But so, so tired. "You're just changing."

Fear crawled up into my throat, grabbed me, and I flailed. There were sheets, and a blanket, and even more dust puffed up.

Someone grabbed my shoulders. Strong broad hands; I struck out wildly. He let out a yelp as my fist connected, good solid hit.

"Goddammit! Dru, quit it!"

I knew *his* voice too. It made no sense. But I sagged in his hands. All the fight went out of me, air out of a balloon.

"Graves?" I whispered.

He coughed, racking. I sniffed deeply. I couldn't see, but I could smell him. Strawberry incense, and boy. He hadn't had a shower in a while, and that was wrong, because he'd always been so clean before. But it was *him*. Even his hands were familiar, now that I knew.

"Jesus," he whispered. And that was enough. I knew him.

I'd know him *anywhere*.

I reached forward, blindly. He climbed the rest of the way up on the bed and I hugged him, hard. His arms were around me, and his fingers were in my hair. He was here and he was *real*, and it was like he'd never been away.

I let out a dry barking sob.

"Shit." He even sounded like himself. Same old Goth Boy. "How did they catch you? What happened?"

The words ran up against each other, trying to spill out faster than my mouth could move. "They—I—we were coming to rescue you. Leon, he had a—he found . . . Graves, my God, oh my God—"

"Charming." The female voice spoke up again, dry and disdainful. "Calm her down so we can get something useful out of her. We don't have much time."

I jerked like I'd been hit. "What the fu—"

"Ease up, Dru. She's not the enemy." Graves paused, and I could imagine his rueful expression. "At least, not here."

"Bullshit!" I tensed, but Graves didn't let go of me. So I didn't let go of him. "She *shot* me!"

"What?" But he didn't sound surprised. "You shot her?"

There was a long silence.

Then she sighed. "It seemed like a good idea at the time," Anna said.

* * *

First it was a filmy haze, diffuse light coming through. Then it was like a thick layer of cheesecloth over the world; I could make out shapes as I spilled out everything that had happened. I hopscotched around a bit as I got confused, backtracked, and tried to fill him in on everything at once. Graves just listened, his arms around me, and I was so happy to finally see him again—even if I wasn't really seeing him, so to speak—that I almost forgot Anna was in the room.

Almost.

I was just telling him about Anna's little note with the earring inside when she cleared her throat, a small but definite call for attention. "That wasn't me."

I flinched a little. She sounded like she was a ways away, maybe on the other side of the room. But that was no safety—I knew how scary fast *djamphir* truly were, and even though I'd toasted Anna's cheese once in a gym at the Prima, I wasn't anywhere near fighting form now.

"It sure as hell smelled like you." The bitterness I was tasting wasn't just the words. "You. You betrayed my mother. You came down to the gym to beat the shit out of me. You *shot* me. You—"

She actually *laughed*. A sour, clear little sound, like a wrongly tuned bell. "I'm not a nice person, Dru. You can take some comfort in the fact that I am, now, suffering for my sins."

Graves's voice rumbled in his chest. "Let's just figure out who to blame later. Right now we've got bigger problems."

His bare skin was against my naked arms; my hoodie was gone, but I still had my T-shirt and jeans. I had my sneakers, too; I could feel them. I wanted to ask if Graves was at least wearing underwear, decided not to. "Where *are* we?"

Anna laughed. She did really sound exhausted, not nearly as nasty as usual. "Can't you guess? *He* has us, little one, and with both of us here . . . well, the odds aren't good."

Ho. Sorgej. The name twisted inside my head like a fish made of broken glass. "You've been feeding him information. Traitor." I blinked a couple more times. Things were rapidly getting clearer, at least in my eyesight.

The rest of me was confused as all get-out. I held on to Graves, my arms aching.

I heard cloth moving, as if she'd shrugged. "And now that you're cresting through the secondary bits of the change, he'll use me as a hostage and drain you dry. Or the opposite, since I'm more danger to him than you. You won't need to kill me, Dru. He'll do it quite handily." She actually sniffed. "You should worry less about what I've done and concentrate on what we should all do to get the hell out of here."

"Word." Graves actually *agreed* with her. He didn't move, thought I might've been hurting him by clutching so hard. "As soon as we're out of here, we'll sort out everything else. But I *really* don't like it here. I'd prefer to fight it out somewhere else."

"What happened to you?" I grabbed at him again, like he might get away. "Was it Christophe? I saw something, did he—"

"He was there." Graves moved slightly, but not away. He moved closer to me; I could almost *see* the bitter little face he pulled. "That night. But all he did was . . . we just had words, him and me. That's all. I went out for a run to calm myself down, and the instant I was off the Schola property, they snatched me."

"Wait. What?" Cold disbelief warred with uneasy relief inside me. I couldn't tell which would win, but at least the light got a little brighter. Graves was a shadow now, his hair standing up wildly and making his head into a monster-shape.

"He was there. Had a couple other *djamphir* with him—some I didn't know, and that kid Leon. Said he wanted to know what my intentions were, if I thought I could do any good hanging around you all the time, stuff like that. I almost hauled off and coldcocked him. They had to hold me back. They dragged me away, and—"

"Wait. Leon was there?" The world actually rocked out from under me, and I grabbed at Graves again. He took a sharp breath, stroked my hair. "He was . . . oh, my God."

"Ah." Anna breathed out, a long exhalation of comprehension. "Now *that* makes sense."

Says you. "What? What makes sense?"

For once, Anna didn't sound like she was enjoying herself by spreading bad news. "Leontus had a *svetocha* once. He was bonded, and . . . well, an *ephialtes* killed her. I suppose they thought he would guard you all the more fiercely; I could have told them the very sight of you would make him far more dangerous than he usually is."

Bonded? Well, I could guess what *that* meant. The rest of it, though . . . "Why?" If I'd been able to stand up, I would've hopped from foot to foot impatiently. Nobody ever gave me answers fast enough. "Why would he . . . Jesus."

And I wasn't sure I could trust Anna's answers, either. The list of things I could trust was shrinking rapidly.

Anna gave a chilling little half-snorting laugh, and I could just tell she was tossing her head. "Because the *ephialtes* who killed his lady Eleanor was none other than one of Sergej's many traitors, trained by his oh-so-helpful son." More fabric moving. "It's close to dawn."

Not Leon. I'd actually *liked* him, too. And he'd been so helpful and all.

I held on to Graves. *Well, Jesus, Dru. Now get yourself out of this one.*

CHAPTER TWENTY-THREE

A **couple of minutes** later, nausea hit me hard. I swallowed against it, blinked. The world came slowly into focus as the seasick feeling retreated, colors sharpening and outlines no longer fuzzy. It was as if a film had been peeled away from my eyeballs, and I looked up.

Graves was a mess. His dark hair stood up curling-wild, dirty and greasy, the undyed roots so full of crud it looked just like the dyed-black bits. Bruises, new and red-purple and older blue and even older yellow-green, spread over his face and down his bare chest. You could barely see the even caramel of his skin tone, he was so bruised all over. He was scrawny-thin, and there were weals and little cuts all over his torso. He had a pair of jeans, but they were flayed around the knees and dark with gunk. He had sneakers, oddly clean but terribly worn, the laces broken and reknotted.

We looked at each other. I let out a hurt little sound. "Oh. You look *awful*."

"Yeah." He shrugged, green eyes burning. Same green eyes, their depths oddly shadowed now, same half-pained curl of his lips passing for a smile. It was like seeing him for the first time, the landscape of his face shifted just a few millimeters so that instead of just looking like a really handsome half-Asian boy he looked . . . well, more like a wulfen. The eerie almost-similarity of bone structure I shared with Christophe and Benjamin and all of them was shared between Graves and Shanks and Dibs and even Nat.

"I'm sorry." The words spilled out. "I didn't know. They told me they were looking for you. They . . . if I'd known, if I'd—"

He moved a little, restless but careful. "If you'd known, you would've run off the Schola grounds and got caught too. *He's* been watching you pretty close, Dru. I'm okay; I'm just wishing you hadn't got caught. I . . ." He swallowed, hard, and I realized I was probably grinding on his bruises bigtime. "It got me through, knowing they'd take care of you. Two days ago—I *think*, time gets funny—they dragged me up here and put me with *her*. It's been interesting."

"Hardly. He's such a *loyal* little boy. No fun at all." Anna laughed, and my head whipped around.

The room was dim, only one wrought-iron lamp with a dusty rose-satin shade propped up next to the bed, on my left. Heavy wood paneling, a cobwebbed chandelier dangling lopsided from the ceiling, and a ceiling that looked like concrete. Graves and I were on a four-poster done in heavy pink velvet that probably dated from the Civil War. Other furniture was scattered around under moth-eaten dust cloths, and the door was a monster of iron and dark heavy wood.

It looked like a set designer for a really bad period movie had thrown up in here. Nathalie would have called the pink velvet *atrocious*.

Thinking of Nat pinched me way down deep in my chest. I hoped she'd forgive me. Hell, I hoped I'd see her soon and she could kick my ass for being such a bitch. I'd even sit still and take it with a big wide goony grin.

Hell, I'd even let her take me *shopping*. For clothes. Without complaining.

Anna was near the door, crouched down. Every other time I'd seen her, she'd been perfectly polished, fashion-model finished.

Not now.

Her red-gold ringlets were a tangled mess, there was a dark nasty bruise on one high flawless cheek, and her pretty red silk dress was ripped up, torn petticoats showing through the rents. Wine-red ribbons trailed through the rat nest of her long hair, her boots were scuffed, and the silk stockings were full of ladderlike runs.

She was taking the goth Lolita thing to new heights, I guess.

But the way she crouched, hugging herself and rocking slightly, wasn't right. And she was paper-pale, not to mention shaking like she had what Gran would call the delirium tremens. The shudders went through her in waves, and she was sweating, too. Little pearly beads of perspiration dotted her flawless skin, almost glowing in the dimness.

She was still beautiful, even all messed up like this. I probably looked like I'd swept up a barn with my hair, and I had that odd dirty feeling you get from sleeping in your jeans. It always pinches; denim is so not pajamas.

"Jesus." I eased up on Graves a little, swallowed hard to clear the sudden sourness on my tongue. The bed creaked a little as we shifted, like a rowboat in a shallow river. "What happened to *you*?"

"This." She lifted her tangled ringlets, and I saw the fang marks on the white column of her throat. My vision sharpened, and my skin was suddenly two sizes too small. Hard little bumps of goose-flesh stood up all over me.

The marks were white and worn-looking in the middle, bruised all the way around like an enthusiastic hickey. She dropped her hair over them after letting me have a good long peek. "Isn't it obvious?"

"I thought we were toxic—" I began.

"Oh, yes. But *he* could stand the poison long enough to sink his teeth in, and now I'm too weak. And *he's* stronger." She shuddered, turning even paler, if that were possible. "He'll eventually drain both of us dry so he can walk in the daylight." Anna laughed again, and her rocking back and forth sped up a little. The floor creaked slightly as her high heels dug in. "I thought I was so clever. So very very clever. You're Elizabeth's vengeance on me, after all these years."

Yeah. My mother's vengeance. Please. Anna had fucking *shot* me because my mother "stole" Christophe. Leon had maybe betrayed me to the vampires because of something Christophe did to him years ago. Just great. Just *wonderful*.

Jesus Christ. Was there anyone around who didn't hate me or think they loved me because of something that happened before I was even *born*?

As soon as I thought that, though, I knew there was one person. He was hanging on to me right now, terribly battered but alive. I'd gotten him into this, and here we were.

You'd better start thinking fast, Dru. But my thinker was kind of busted. I shook my head, curls falling in my face, as if that could jar my brain into working. "My mother's dead, Anna. We're here; we might as well get on with it. Where the hell *are* we, really?" *And Sergej brought me here for snacking later. Me and Anna, in the freezer like good little rodents for a snake to choke down. Ugh.*

"I think we're in Jersey." Graves hissed an in-breath as he moved slightly, and I loosened up a little more. "Of course, if I owned this place and Hell . . ."

The laugh that bolted out of me felt wrong. But it helped a little, before falling lifeless in the dead air. "Are we underground? It feels like it."

"Dunno. Think it's a warehouse. I was underground for a while. In a . . . a cell." Graves shivered. Gooseflesh roughened up his marred skin, and I got the idea he would be pale if it wasn't for the bruises. "They would come down at random times, ask me questions about you. Things they . . . Hey." He leaned in, his eyes burning. "Nice earring. I wondered where that went."

My fingers came up. I touched it, the skull and crossbones. "I . . . yeah. Thanks."

"Shhh!" Anna stopped rocking. "Shut up!"

Graves flinched. We stared into each other's eyes, those shadows gathering in the depths of the green, and for that one moment I saw right down to the bottom of him. He talked a good line, and he was really brave.

But at bottom he was just as terrified as I was.

Danger candy filled my mouth with thin, rotting, waxen citrus. The taste was oddly attenuated, fading. Feathers brushed my skin, and I heard wingbeats. "Vampires," I whispered.

Graves shook his head. He pulled back, his fingers sinking into my arm, and dragged me off the bed. My legs buckled, but he held me up. "Maybe," he whispered back. "Maybe worse."

It was probably a mark of how screwed up my life was that I didn't ask what could be worse than vampires. I didn't want to know, so I let him pull me around. My legs trembled. The rest of me wasn't too steady, either.

He shoved me back into the corner next to the lamp. Then he turned around, and the cuts across his back made me feel sick all over again. The light was scorching, making my eyes water, which didn't make sense. It was just a night-light-dim bulb shielded by a thick dusty shade; it shouldn't have stung me so bad.

I heard movement now. Stealthy little footsteps, taps, too fast or slow to be human, and something about them told me there was a hallway outside our door. A long one.

"Shit," Graves muttered. "Lot of them this time." He propped me against the wall. "You okay?"

My legs firmed up. I nodded, brushed hair out of my eyes. Blonde slid through the curls, and they clung to my fingers. *What the hell?*

Anna rose slowly, as if her joints were resisting. If she felt anything like I did after Christophe had bit me, I could understand why. And Christophe hadn't taken more than he absolutely needed, I guess.

I only borrowed, little bird, I did not take. Remember that.

I owed him an apology bigtime, but I didn't want to think about that while I was propped against the wall behind Graves.

Anna's eyes glowed blue, her fangs peeping delicately out as she glanced at us. I leaned against the wall, the cold of it scorching through my T-shirt. The wood was slick and freezing, hard like it was glued over concrete and slightly sticky the way paneling in a long-empty room will get. I cast around for anything that might serve as a weapon, but there was nothing except the wrought-iron lamp base. Hitting a vampire with our only source of light didn't seem like a good idea.

But there was nothing else. All the other furniture was too heavy to lift, and if there'd been anything else in here, Graves probably would have already picked it up. I reached out, touched the lamp's long slim length. Yup, it felt like iron.

Anna's lip curled. "You're going to defend her, *loup-garou*? It's a lost battle."

"You just do your part," he returned, just as sarcastically. "I'd rather go down fighting."

"Wait, we have a plan?" This struck me as need-to-know information. "What's the plan?"

"There is no *plan*. There's only improvisation." Anna straightened, and I supposed now was not the time to tell her she sounded a little bit like Christophe. She put her shoulders back, lifted her chin, and turned on her heel to face to door. Swayed a little bit, but settled into a ramrod-stiff posture. She'd looked about ready to fall over before. What was this? "I am *svetocha*. I do not *submit*. Not if I can help it."

"Oh." I sounded just as mystified as I felt. But I seconded that part about not submitting.

"You with me, Dru?" Graves squared his shoulders. I tried not to look at his messed-up back.

Always. My fingers closed around the lamp stalk. "You better believe it."

The footsteps drew closer still, tapping and sliding. That oddly thin wash of danger candy filled my mouth, I considered spitting. It could be a comment on the décor instead of a completely useless gesture, I supposed. I tried breathing deep and swearing internally at my legs to get them to starch up a bit. My bones ached, but all in all I felt better than Anna probably did.

Nobody had been sucking *my* blood lately. And yeah, she was a total bitch and had shot me.

But nobody deserves . . . *that*. I remembered the dragging weakness and the pain as something was torn out of me by invisible roots, something I wouldn't hesitate to call my soul, the very core of what made me *me*. I got the idea Christophe had been as gentle as possible about it.

Something told me Sergej wouldn't be. If he could get close enough to me. And he'd already gotten close enough to strangle me into unconsciousness.

The sounds rushed by outside the door in a tide. Little whispers, tittering laughter, tapping feet, a scraping like diamond claws on a sheet of glass. Pain speared through my head, twisting, and I pulled the touch back in a hurry. I hadn't even known I was using it, or that it would spread so far. But contracting it like a fist inside my head took effort, and I was sweating and breathing fast, the world wavering in front of my still-smarting eyes.

"Dru?" Graves, his head half-turned. His eyes were dark now. "You okay?"

"I . . . I just . . ." The ache was back, spearing into my bones. "I hurt all over."

"You're cresting." The contempt in Anna's tone could have dripped out and splashed smoking on the floor. "You have picked the very worst time to bloom. Right now you're at your most vulnerable, and of the most use to *him*. Not only can he drain me dry or keep me as a hostage, but he can drain *you* and possibly become the King in truth. He will walk in sunlight, and there's not much we can do about it."

Great. Blame me for it, sure. "Cresting? Like, the last step before I—"

"Before you become what everyone around you is waiting so breathlessly for. Fully bloomed and oh-so-ready to please." She tilted her head, her tangle hair falling in a cascade of red-gold curls. "A nice tractable little *svetocha* so blinded by Reynard she'll leave her own friends in the clutches of—"

"You want to shut your mouth." Graves, but it was a new tone for him. Flat, terribly adult, and thrumming with a *loup-garou's* command-voice. I'd heard him hold a whole room of wulfen back with that voice, but he'd never sounded like *this* before.

Like he was two steps away from kicking the shit out of someone, and not caring how bad he hurt them.

I didn't blame him, but it was a bad idea right now. I gathered myself. "Let's not do Sergej's work for him, okay?"

As soon as I said it, I knew I'd made a mistake. There's a reason every hunter I'd ever known wouldn't ever use a sucker's name out loud. I'd said it before, usually when he was a safe distance away. But here?

Bad idea.

Anna whirled, her blue eyes wide, and a low evil laugh slid through the darkened room. My fingers cramped on the lamp, and he just resolved out of thin air in the darkness.

He wasn't so tall, even if he was broad-shouldered. A little short-er than Christophe, but you wouldn't dare call him small. The ice around him made him seem way bigger. Loose, artistically mussed honey-brown curls fell over his face.

He looked just the same as he had in the Dakotas, no older than me. Seventeen tops, old enough for a scruffy little beard but still smooth-cheeked. It was the eyes that gave him away, black spreading out from the hourglass-shaped pupils, threading in little vein-lines from lid to lid. It made the whites look filmed with gray, so you could maybe mistake them for cataracts if you didn't know any better.

But those pupils could suck you down, leave you gasping for air on the floor while his fangs met in your throat. There was something hiding under the gelid darkness.

Something old. Something terrible.

Something *hungry*.

Sergej folded his arms. His watch, a huge chunky gold thing, was too horribly tasteless to be anything other than a genuine Rolex. He wore, of all things, a navy-blue Drunken Pixies T-shirt and jeans. And it was horrible, but now that I was looking for it, I saw how his face worked together, how beautiful he was. That face could have been taken from an old coin displayed in a museum or chipped from a statue found in a grotto somewhere, turned toward the wall because it was too . . . much. Too unreal-gorgeous.

Like Christophe's, and unlike.

It was *horrible*. Perfect poreless skin with a hint of coppery color, those curls, and those eyes full of cold tar-oil that could make you slit your own wrists if you had to stare into them long enough. The tar would close over your head, and it would be a relief to feel the sting of a blade.

He just stood there, next to the wall, between two shrouded shapes that could have been couches but instead looked like beasts with their hindquarters raised, ready to spring. My breath plumed in suddenly-frozen air, and steam lifted from Graves's shoulders in tiny finger curls.

Sergej examined all of us. When he opened his mouth, his pleasant tenor was even creepier than a horror-movie baritone would've been.

"The sweetest of all are the little birds. Hello again, Lefevre's child." He grinned, the spaces between his words just the same as Christophe's. And faintly, a little bit like Augustine's when he forgot his half-Brooklyn, half-Bronx Bugs Bunny and got a little tipsy, swearing in gutter Polish while he laughed with my father, bottles clinking against glasses and—

NO! The touch swelled inside my head, battering aside the pressure of his eyes. The place inside myself where the touch had been ripped loose echoed in a far bigger space than it usually did, a huge stone cathedral instead of the quiet little room where Gran's spinning wheel sat by the stove.

I dragged the lamp base toward me, my stiff fingers creaking as the bar actually bent in my grasp. Shadows shifted crazily as the light and the shade both moved, and I swear to God Sergej actually leaned back a little on his heels, his hourglass pupils flaring and shrinking.

For half a second, he looked surprised. Anna shot me an indecipherable glance, and I knew what she was going to do before she did it. I opened my mouth to yell *no, no don't*, but she didn't listen. She launched herself at Sergej, screaming like a banshee, and Graves shoved me back against the wall.

Sergej just disappeared. Or, no. He moved so fast he literally blinked through space, one moment standing there, the next turned aside. One slim strong hand flashed out. A sharp high *thwap* smacked the walls, and Anna flew. She hit the paneling above the bed with a sickening crack and slid down, landed in a tangle of red silk and splayed pale limbs.

How did I hold him off before? I searched for the heat and balm of the aspect, but it was hard. What a time for it to get even *more* unreliable.

She lay slumped there, and I grabbed at Graves's shoulder, my fingers sinking into bruised flesh. "Don't. *Don't.*"

Because the growl was rippling out from him in concentric rings of bloodlust, and a crackle ran through him. *Loup-garou* don't get hairy, but they do bulk up when they get angry. The bruises glared, and some of the marks on his back broke open. Blood slid down his skin, slipping between the flickers and valleys of muscle definition, and the hunger hit the map of veins inside my body *hard*, pulling like it intended to rip them free. My fangs slid out, my jaw aching, and that syrup-smell of baking cinnamon rolls drifted up, like those places in the mall that sell big sticky piles of sugar rush. They smell so *good*, but I can't even go near them without my teeth aching and my blood sugar crashing in sympathy.

The aspect blazed free, like all it needed was the bloodhunger to wake it up. I felt it move through me like a storm front on the plains, one you can maybe outrun if you keep the accelerator mashed down and the radio turned up.

And Sergej *backed up*. Just a half step, but still. He cocked his head, those curls falling over his forehead and that proud nose wrinkling, and I wondered for a brief second how the hell Christophe's mother—she had to have been human—had ever not noticed how utterly *alien* he looked. Especially when he snarled, his lip lifting and the fangs lengthening, upper ones touching his chin and the hiss filling his chest.

The door creaked. I pulled Graves back, my fingers slipping in blood and sweat and whatever else was coating him. He leaned forward, tense, but didn't shake me off. The thin tendrils of blood running down his back looked black in the uncertain light, and the lampshade swung as I dragged it. I couldn't see where the cord ended, and if I yanked it out of the wall, we'd be in here.

With Sergej.

In the *dark*.

The door swung inward, its hinges giving a squeal that belonged in a bad B movie. Still, it was a relief, because outside in the hall was bright electric light. It speared my eyes like a fork digging through jelly, but I saw a shadow. The touch rang like a gong inside my head, and I knew who it was.

"You agreed," Leon said quietly. Funny, he sounded just the same. Sarcastic, politely rude, and utterly normal.

"Leon?" His name slipped out. I couldn't help myself. "Leon, please—"

Sergej's head half-turned, and he stared at the door. Graves was still growling, and the unhealthy fever in him scorched my fingers. I blinked furiously, swallowing hard against the bloodhunger, its rasp like a cat's tongue at the back of my throat. The hunger squirmed inside my veins, just looking for a way out, I shoved it down and clapped a lid on it.

Or at least, tried to clap enough of a lid on it that the thin trickles down Graves's back didn't smell so goddamn *good*.

Leon stared from the door. Now that my eyes were adjusted, I could see that even if he sounded okay, he looked like hell. Dark circles ringed his eyes, his fine lank hair was mussed, and he was in the same clothes he'd been wearing however long ago, when he'd waltzed into my room and started convincing me to leap into this trap. One sleeve of his T-shirt was torn, and dark stuff was splashed on his jeans.

It looked like dried blood.

"Our agreement," Sergej said, enunciating with precision but lisping a little around his fangs, "was provisional."

Leon smiled. It was a rather gentle smile, and it bared his own fangs. He wasn't looking at Sergej. He was staring directly at me, his eyes grieving holes. They darkened even through the aspect on him, and Graves's growl dropped another octave as his shoulders hunched in front of me. More blood slid down his back, and I could tell from the shaking in him that he was working up to something big.

"I delivered, didn't I?" Leon's hands curled into fists.

"Any *ephialtes* could have done the same," Sergej hissed.

"There's just one problem." Leon stared at me, like he was willing me to figure something out. My fingers sank into Graves's skin, the prickle along my fingertips and the fierce pain in my wrists telling me the claws were sliding free. I didn't want to make him bleed more, but I was powerless to stop it.

"Problem?" Sergej laughed. It was a horrible sound, wrongly musical, lisping distilled hatred. His tar-black eyes shone. "I see no problem, Leontus Iulius. I see everything as it should be, the disobedient children brought to heel."

Keep him talking, for Christ's sake keep him talking! I ran through everything I could possibly do in this situation, came up with nothing that didn't involve my own gruesome demise. Tried again.

"Except Reynard." Leon's smile widened a trifle.

Sergej's face congested. That's the only word for it, the twisting up and the color rising from his neck, an ugly flush. I guess vampires *can* blush; you'd think the way the hemoglobin strips out of their blood would kind of preclude that. Maybe that's why he looked purplish instead of red

It was damn ugly.

The touch tingled inside my skull. A fresh wave of bloodhunger pulled on all my veins, and my heart gave a funny leap before starting to pound. Sergej's purple deepened, if that was possible, and he began to choke.

"Oh, Eleanor," Leon whispered. "Forgive me."

And he leapt straight for me.

CHAPTER TWENTY-FOUR

Things got confused.

I remember jerking on the lamp, metal shrieking as my fingers bit down hard enough to bend it. The plug left the wall with a pop, sparks showered, and the lightbulb shattered as the sudden motion ripped the shade free. A photographer's flash, then leaping shadows. The lamp actually whistled as I spun it, a sound like a train in the distance, soupy through the clear plastic goop hardening over the world.

The heavy, flared base hit Leon squarely in the face with a sickening *crunch*. I wanted to yell *I'm sorry!* And maybe I did. Someone was screaming, Graves let out a roar, and Leon pitched across the room in slo-mo, curling up like a bug, his lank hair flying and flashing gold for a moment. That dart of golden light hit the wall, a single clean spot of color in all this murk, and I *shoved* Graves aside through the hardening air. My fingers slipped against the gunk on his skin, my nails slicing hair-fine cuts across his skin, just like hatpin scratches on Gran's kitchen table. The lamp base flew off, describing a high perfect arc, and Leon's body hit Sergej right in the middle of his leap with a sound like a good clean break on a pool table. The sucker's face was still plummy and distorted, a mask of grinning hate, and I was already moving.

Faster, faster, but with precision! Christophe yelled inside my head. My grasp firmed on the lamp's post, the electric cord whipping off with a small cracking sound, also drawn out and weird since I was going so fast.

Graves folded down, tucking and rolling, and Anna was suddenly *there*, bouncing up off the bed like a jack-in-the-box. She alone seemed to be moving at normal speed; she was heading for Sergej — and right into my line of attack.

My left hand snapped forward, the hex building and tearing free of my fingers in a blue flash that lit the entire room like a camera, freezing time. It hit her square in the solar plexus, stopping her dead, and the *woof!* sound she made as she tumbled down to the floor in a heap would have been funny if I hadn't been so goddamn busy.

The ground spun away from under me and the lamp flicked down, hitting the floor and striking up more blue sparks as the force of the hex snapped back along my fingers. The bar spun up after giving me additional lift, I could feel the metal flex as I pole-vaulted, and the instinct that had taken me over was clear and cold as the look in Christophe's eyes sometimes.

I could also swear to God I heard Dad's voice, not in my head but from my left, as if he was crouched there watching. *You only get one shot at this, Dru-girl. Make it count.*

The top of the lamp had snapped off, and now I had a slim iron spear. The lamp base hit the far wall, crunching and crinkling as the force of its impact buckled it, and I had to get the tip up in time, straining against physics and the regular time holding everything else in the room in its clear-glass net.

Another crashing impact, and my feet hit the floor. The aspect blazed hotly all over me, ruffling my hair, and the hunger yanked every vein and artery I owned like it was going to pull them all out in a tangled spaghetti mass. I had a brief, mad, Technicolor vision of Benjamin crouched over his plate of noodles and sauce, and the world spun around me as if it was oiled.

Sergej's nose almost touched mine. A gush of hot black pattered softly to the floor. I had him pinned, the spear driven through his chest and into the wall behind him. He twitched, hot breath touching my cheek, and my stomach cramped hard.

I've heard that if you get it going fast enough, even a straw can punch through steel plate. If you get going fast enough, even a plain old iron lampstand can go through a vampire's chest. Up on the left side, too, a heart-shot.

Did I do that? My hands gave an amazing flare of rubbed-raw pain. I stumbled back, tripping and saving myself with an instinctive sideways leap. It was a good thing, too, because the spear tore free of the wall with a screech and Sergej fell, his claws slicing empty air. He would have landed right on me if I hadn't moved. The lamp pole hit the ground and he toppled sideways, landing with a heavier thump than I would've thought possible.

The world caught up with a subliminal *snap*. My sneakers slipped, I was falling, couldn't stop myself, and training shrieked inside my head to *stay on your feet, goddammit, he might get up again, it's never sure with a sucker, stay UP—*

Graves's hand closed around my upper arm. I let out a half-shriek and he ducked, the punch whooshing past his filthy hair and my claws scything free. *Claws, that's why my wrist was hurting, it's the claw structures building in there. Go figure. Hooray for me.*

"Easy!" he yelled. "Easy! Friend! *Friend!*"

My heart triphammered, even my throat and wrists pulsing hotly. The shriek died halfway; I swallowed and blinked. "Jesus," I whispered finally. My fingers tingled as the claws slid back out of sight. The urge to throw up or pass out rolled over me in a big black wave; I held it off with grim determination.

"Nope." Graves set me on my feet. His eyes blazed now, and how could I ever have thought they'd darkened? They were emerald lasers now. "Dude. You killed him with a *lamp.*"

Sergej twitched. Both of us jumped nervously. Leon had slid down the wall, spilled off the bed, and landed sitting up. His eyes were closed, mouth ajar, and a trickle of red slid down from his nose. Another trickle traced down his chin. The side of his chest looked funny. Bashed in, like a stove stroked a good one by a massive sledgehammer.

He'd hit Sergej pretty hard. Something that hard, going that fast . . . dear God.

He's not getting up anytime soon, Dad's voice whispered inside my head, soft and flat, telling me what was what. *Get movin', Dru-girl.*

Anna coughed. She scrabbled weakly against the floor, her shoes scraping a little. Sergej twitched again, and I flinched. My throat was on fire with the bloodhunger, my ears alive with little scraping whispers and the thudding of Graves's pulse, galloping along and somehow shouting *loup-garou, loup-garou.* Anna's pulse was high and fast, slightly further away, murmuring her name over and over as it echoed through her flesh. *An-na. An-na. An-na.*

The scraping sounds were vampires, and they were all over the house. There were a *lot* of them.

"We've got to get out of here," I whispered. The electric glow from the corridor still stung my eyes.

"No shit. You think?" He dropped his hand and coughed, rackingly. Under the mask of bruising, his face was alight. "Jesus, Dru. With a *lamp*."

It was all I had. I cleared my throat. Looked again at Leon. He didn't look like he was going to move, either, but I didn't want to take any chances. My legs felt like rubber noodles. The rest of me felt like it could light a match just by standing too close. Even my hair tingled.

I tested my knees, found out they would hold me up, and stepped cautiously toward Anna. She was making a hurt little sound in the back of her throat now, like a kitten knowing it's about to be drowned.

Leave her, Dad might've said. *She'll slow you down. You look out for you first, Dru-girl.*

Yeah. Looking out for number one had made Anna into what she was, hadn't it.

"What the—" Graves grabbed for me, but I shook him off. "Dru!"

"We can't leave her here. She jumped *him*, she's *svetocha*." *And I am not like her.* I took another step, my foot slipping in a lake of thin greasy black crud. Sergej was producing an amazing amount of fluid. No heartbeat from him, too. If I'd hit him in the heart, it might immobilize him until one of his buddies pulled it out.

Or maybe not. He twitched. The iron spear made a little *skreek* sound as its tip dragged along the floor.

"Dru." Graves sounded like he'd been punched. "What about him?" His finger jabbed out, pointing at Leon.

I can't carry more than one, dammit. "I don't know. Can you carry him?" I felt bad even asking it. He was bleeding all over, and I'd made it worse.

Graves snorted, green eyes now so bright they almost cast shadows of their own. The Other looked out through those eyes, and if I'd been less worried about a ton of other stuff, I might've been a little, well, concerned.

Because the Other didn't look like he really cared what happened as long as he got to hurt someone.

Graves shrugged. Halfway through the motion he stopped, as if it hurt. "Don't know if he needs it. He *smells* dead."

I didn't ask how he knew what dead smelled like. "Then leave him." The words stung my throat. "Worry about the living first." It was the same tone Dad used when he didn't want me to argue. Had it burned when he said it, too?

Graves looked at me like I'd just made some sort of embarrassing bodily noise, but he helped me heft Anna up from the floor. She didn't even fight, just hung between us like wet washing. I swayed, so did Graves, and the chances of us getting out of here were so not good.

Especially since Sergej picked that moment to move again, the iron spear scraping harder. Still no pulse from him, though. Maybe it was his nerves dying?

Oh, God, way to get the gruesome going, Dru.

I aimed us for the door, and Graves and I started dragging Anna. The pointy toes of her boots slid along the hardwood, and we had to lift her over the threshold and into the brightly lit hall. I blinked, my eyes stinging and watering.

The scream came out of everywhere, a wall of noise so massive it was almost soundless. It shook the hall, dust pattered from the low ceiling, and I almost dropped Anna because I wanted to clap my hands over my ears. It wouldn't do any good—the sound burrowed *inside*, scraping and twisting.

It came from the room behind us. I knew, without knowing quite how, that it was Sergej.

The king of the vampires was probably pretty pissed.

The noise stopped all at once, as if someone had hit the pause button on a CD. The house quivered above us, dust settling. It was a short hall, and at the end were stairs going up. Blank doors on either side, marching away; we were down at the very end. No other exits.

Shit.

But then I saw a long dark shape on a brass hook, and I breathed out in wonderment just as the entire house above us exploded with the soft scrapings, brushings, weird tapping footsteps of vampire activity.

Graves's coat. My bag. The *malaika* harness and the *malaika* I'd been wearing. All hanging right there next to another iron-bound door.

I slipped out from under Anna's arm, made it there in three long strides. "Amen. *Amen*, hallelujah, and pass the friggin' butter!"

"What?" Graves, left with Anna, almost went down in a heap. I grabbed my bag, flipped it open, and checked it. Extra ammo, no gun. But there were the rolls of cash and everything else. I ducked through the strap. "Hey. Is that my coat?"

I grabbed the harness. Buckled it on, my fingers suddenly sausage-clumsy, got the bag on over it. Grabbed his coat while I rolled my shoulders, trying to make everything fit right. It was heavy—ammo in the pockets, but still no gun. "Yeah. It looks better on me, though."

"You wore my coat?" Was he blushing under the bruises? Hard to tell. I made it back to them and grabbed Anna's arm, slinging it over my shoulder. "Oh."

"Put it on." *You might need it; it's cold outside.* I didn't say it, though. Who knew if we would *get* outside? I didn't even know where we were, and the vampires above sounded like a kicked ant-hill. "Careful, there's ammo in there."

"You think of everything, Miss Anderson." His eyes gleamed green for a brief moment.

It wasn't so hard to drag Anna now. I pulled her along, and her feet were actually trying help, pushing weakly at the concrete floor. Graves caught up after a couple steps, the coat now flapping around his knees. He ducked under her other arm, and we made it almost to the end of the aisle before Anna hissed at us to stop.

"Door," she slurred, and pointed her bruised chin at the last right-hand door before the stairs. "Open . . . that . . . one."

No fucking way. Who knows what's behind it? But the thing that decided me was shadows falling across the top of the stairs. "Is it locked?" I whispered.

Graves pointed. He wasn't looking too good, the bruises glaring and the rest of him yellowy and cottage-cheesy. His mouth hung open a little, and he wasn't so handsome right now. Matter of fact, he looked half dead himself.

I followed the line of his pointing. There was a key hanging on a hook, a big iron number. "Well, shit," I muttered, and tried to take more of Anna's weight, dragging her over to it. If Graves's legs gave out, I decided right then and there, I was carrying *him*. I wasn't willing to leave Anna behind if the two of us were ambulatory, but if it was a choice between them, it was really *no* choice.

The key went in the door. The footsteps spilled closer, I glanced at the stairs. More flitting shadows. If this didn't hold an exit we were pretty fucked. I had *malaika*, sure, and I could hold off a few suckers—but if Sergej managed to get that lamp out of his chest, we were looking at bad times down here in the basement.

The door swung in. It was dark inside, and for a moment I thought she'd got us to a room with some sort of exit. Then something moved, and I twitched.

It was a dirty, dark-eyed, very pretty *djamphir* boy in the ruins of a red shirt. More movement. Four of them, all in those red shirts, stared at us like refugees from a weird-ass convention or something.

I stared back, my right hand halfway to my *malaika* hilt.

Red shirts. It was Anna's Guard. I swallowed dryly.

"Milady!" the one near the door whisper-screamed. He looked like *hell*. Graves was pretty beat up, but this kid looked savaged.

Well, this kind of alters the situation a bit, dontcha think?

Anna lifted her curly head. "Blaine." She coughed. "Help . . . us. All of . . . you. Help *her*, too. I. Command." Her head dropped, curly hair sliding forward, as if the words had taken all the starch out of her.

They scrambled to their feet, and I tensed. Which of them had been around when I'd cleaned Anna's clock at the Prima? Which ones had watched me, waiting for me to be alone? I remembered two of them, holding guns on Christophe after Ash had saved me from the suckers yet *again*.

I used to think that if someone was in the Order, they wouldn't sell anyone out to the suckers, because they *know* what suckers are like. I guess I was wrong. So my right hand kept going up to my *malaika* hilt, and I was already calculating how to get Graves out of here and—

"Yes, ma'am." Blaine studied me, top to bottom. Getting even closer, the pitter-patter of little sucker feet. Once they hit the stairs . . .

I glanced over Anna's hanging head. Graves's steady green gaze met mine, and the Look that passed between us was worth a couple hours of conversation at least. The immediate communication felt so good I could've broken down and cried right there. Instead, I blinked back the stinging and watering and glanced back at the Blaine kid. The other redshirts—Christ, hadn't any of them watched *Star Trek* and figured out this was a bad thing to wear?—were suddenly ranked behind him, and the naked hope on their young-old, bruised, and bloody faces was almost too much to take.

No wonder they did anything for her.

"I've got standard-issue ammo," I found myself saying. "No gun. But I've got *malaika*, too. We're trapped down here, Sergej's got an iron post through his chest but I don't know if it'll keep him down."

"*Mon Dieu.*" Blaine stepped forward. "Hans, Charles, take Milady. Kip, the gun rack at the end of the hall?"

The sharp-featured one with curly dark hair nodded and brushed past us out into the hall. The two who looked like twins stepped forward to take Anna, and as soon as we handed her over I grabbed Graves's arm and stepped back.

Blaine actually looked pained. "Milady . . ." He glanced nervously at Anna, who hung bonelessly, as if she'd used up the last bit of her pep. "We're not the enemy. You've rescued Milady; we owe you thanks."

"Yeah, well." I coughed a little, bloodhunger rasping. "Let's just get out of here. Do you have a plan?"

"We don't need one. Not with you and some ammo." A fey smile brightened his battered face. "But as a matter of fact, I *do* have a plan."

It was a good thing. Because the first wave of vampires hit the stairs then, a cascade of tip-tapping feet and dark-spangled hatred. Graves whirled and leapt out into the hall, I followed, and the *malaika* slid free of their sheaths with whispering little sounds. Anna's Guard moved out behind me, and I was hoping Sergej wouldn't jump on our backs when Blaine was suddenly next to me. He let out a battle cry that scorched my ears, and we were fighting for our lives.

CHAPTER TWENTY-FIVE

Dead vampire bodies littered the stairs, twitching and crackling as the curly-headed one ripped the throat out of each. I gasped, leaning against Graves, my mother's *malaika* held carefully away—they were bastard sharp and dripping with thin caustic black ichor. One of the twins held Anna up, murmuring to her in what sounded like French, his lips next to her temple. The others were equidistant around us, a guard pattern. Blaine leaned against the wall, his ribs heaving and vampire blood all over him. His fingers flicked as he reloaded his 9mm, chambered a round. "We need to move," he husked. "There will be more soon."

"At least we made it up the stairs," the twin who wasn't holding Anna said, grimly but gingerly scrubbing at his face with one hand. "Thank God for the ammo. Milady." And he nodded at me, like I'd done something unreasonably, surprisingly spectacular.

The aspect was still boiling-hot all over me, but I couldn't get enough air in. "Thanks," I managed, sarcastically enough to make Graves move a little, restless.

"How the hell do we get out of here?" He had vampire blood all over him too, and it smoked on his torn coat, the heavy organic material reacting to its acidic spill. He was looking even worse, dead white under the bruises. But his eyes were bright, the shadows gone, and he was hanging on.

"This way, as soon as Milady can move." Blaine glanced at Anna. "Charles?"

"She's fading." The one murmuring at Anna stopped long enough to share a Significant Look with Blaine. The curly-headed one hopped up the stairs. I heard other whisperings in the warehouse, but none from behind us. That was the good news.

The bad news was every one of us was deadbone-tired and I still didn't know where an exit was. Or if Anna's Guard would leave me and Graves in here to rot.

Or if they would maybe help the vampires out a bit.

On the other hand, the vampires were back to choking and falling down when I got close to them, so I was actually not doing too badly. And with Graves behind me, I didn't worry so much about getting shot in the back.

I wish I was kidding.

Anyway, there wasn't much for me to do in the middle of a whirling dervish of fighting *djamphir* except keep my eyes open and step up with *malaika* and my toxic little self whenever any of them got into trouble.

But the ammo I'd brought was vanishing fast.

Blaine let out what could have been a sigh, if it hadn't been so sharply frustrated. "We'll strike for the place they brought us in. Kip?"

The curly-headed redshirt pointed down the hall, away from the skittering little sounds drawing closer all the time. "They're getting close."

"Let's move. Milady?" Blaine actually looked at me, eyebrows raised. He was bleeding from the corner of his mouth and low on his right side.

"Just get us out of here." *And once we're outside, you guys are on your own. You can take care of Anna and everything will be swell.* I tilted my head, listening. The silence behind us was stupendous, massive. The skritching scratching pitter-patters in the rest of the house ran together like raindrops on a windowpane, and I had a sudden Technicolor vision of vampires slipping through halls, smears of hatred moving with eerie blurring speed. They were shocked by Sergej's scream, maybe, and just now shaking it off? Like an anthill seething with activity while a swollen thing in its depths lay twitching and unable to direct it. The image made my gorge rise. Blood-hunger trembled its filaments all through me.

"Let's move." I couldn't talk right; my fangs were achingly sensitive and I tried to keep them behind my top lip without scratching myself on them. Graves was shaking, a high unhealthy heat bleeding off his skin. Once I got him outside, there was getting off the grounds of wherever we were held and getting transportation, then holing up for long enough to recoup, and . . .

My brain trembled like a weary horse. If my thinker busted all the way now, we were dead in the water, Goth Boy and me.

I couldn't let that happen.

One problem at a time. "Come on, Graves." I took an experimental step forward. He came with me, his chin dipping, dirty hair falling in his face. We looked like kids after a terrible catastrophe, which I suppose was true enough except for the shadow of age in Blaine's dark gaze. He was the only one who *felt* a little older, and it was weird. But I guess Anna liked the younger ones.

Easier to control.

We set out down this hall, which looked industrial in an old-fashioned way. Concrete, and full of fluorescent glare that tore into my brain through my eyes. It *was* a warehouse, I figured out, and felt a jab of tired pride as the touch nestled down in my skull again. The old-timey beams and plaster and golden light was behind us, and I had the sudden uncomfortable thought that the whole hall down there had been like a stage set, somewhere for Sergej to play a little game.

He seemed to like playing nasty games. So did Anna. But given the choice between them, Jesus.

Guess you made that choice, didn't you, Dru?

The twins held Anna up, and the curly-headed one drifted behind Graves and me. I didn't like that at all, and I kept the *malaika* out. Of course, he had a gun, and silver-grain ammo, and—

The touch flared inside my head. "Wait," I whispered, and pulled Graves to a halt. He leaned on me a little harder than before, his balance moving around like he was drunk or too tired to keep himself fully upright.

That was a bad sign. But still . . . I heard something.

"What?" Blaine had halted. Anna shivered uncontrollably, her hair running with copper highlights even under fluorescents.

Go figure; that lighting makes everyone look sick, especially beaten-up *djamphir*. But it just made her hair look even more beautiful, even tangled and gunky as it was.

"Something's going on." I closed my eyes against the stinging glare. My God, the world was just too bright. If this was blooming, leave me out of it. Except the vampires falling down and choking part. That was okay.

"Dru." A cough, and Anna tried to raise her head. "Have to. Talk to you."

"Shhh," the twin on her right said softly. "We'll have you safe in no time, Milady."

I didn't have the heart to tell him he was lying. Maybe he knew.

"Dru." Anna let out a soft moan. "Come . . . here."

"We've got to move." It was the same high, queer, breathless voice that was all I could use when the touch was telling me things. "They're massing. We're risking leaving a blood trail. And . . ." I struggled to concentrate. "Something else. Something . . ."

"Dru." Anna coughed again. It didn't sound good. She spat, a gob of something bright red that splattered on the floor. "Damn. You. Come. Here."

"Milady—" Blaine eyed me like he was considering dragging me over to Anna.

Graves stiffened. I solved the problem by taking a couple of steps forward, bringing him with me. At least it might get us moving again. I was beginning to catch my breath, and the itching under the heat of the aspect warned me.

I realized I wasn't tasting the danger candy just as Anna lifted her head. Thick red dribbled down her chin, and her blue eyes shone feverishly behind a raccoon mask of puffy bruising. The flat copper of her blood was full of carnation spice and terrible pain. I wasn't sure how she was holding herself up, even with the help of the twins.

She inhaled, deeply. More blood slid down her chin. I tried not to stare.

"I won't last long." Another deep breath, and she winced as if the effort hurt down deep. The blood was goddamn *distracting*. "Neither will you. So . . . you have to do something."

When did this become my job? But I nodded. Made little fluttering motions with one fist full of *malaika,* trying to get the guys to move. We could talk just as well while escaping here, couldn't we?

"Drink." Anna coughed again, and her head dropped. She raised it with an impatient, tired little shake. "You have to. Drink. From me."

What the . . . Then what she said hit home. "Oh, *hell* no. No."

"Milady!" Blaine sounded shocked. What was it with older *djamphir* sounding like prissy maiden aunties? "You can't—"

"Damn right she can't, let's just get *out* of here!" If I hadn't been holding Graves up, I would've hopped from foot to foot impatiently.

"No!" Anna actually jerked in their arms. "I am *dead*! *He* made certain . . . of that. Blaine. Kip. I consign you to her care. Obey . . . her."

What the hell? "Anna." I put on my best no-nonsense tone, striving for just the right amount of Gran's *we'll have no foolishness here* and Dad's *I got other places to be so let's move.* "I am so not going to do this. Let's go."

"Milady—" Blaine had gone chalk-cheesy. The curly-headed one pushed past me, and I would've rolled my eyes if I'd had the energy. "We *cannot*—"

"Don't. Argue." Anna stared at me. "Save them, Dru. Please. They're . . . good boys. They . . . deserve care. Now drink. I don't . . . have much left. I'm trained . . . you're not." It was painful to hear her gasping for breath.

Nobody deserved that. Not even her.

The world stilled itself. My head jerked up. Noise, in the distance.

Rapid popping gunfire. The walls trembled slightly, and Graves and I both flinched as the sound of a distant explosion reached us.

And all of a sudden I knew who it was. "The Order. They're coming to rescue us."

CHAPTER TWENTY-SIX

We dragged Anna into a small utility room off the hall. The argument now was whether to wait for the Order to find us, or get outside. I knew what I was voting for, but we had serious problems.

Graves leaned against the wall. His eyes were half closed, darkening rapidly, and his breathing had taken on an asthmatic wheeze. He needed food and rest, *bad*. Bulking up and getting ready to tango with Sergej had depleted whatever reserves he had left. Accessing the Other is hard on the body's energy factories; it's why wulfen are so seriously about munchies all the time.

Anna was still bleeding. It wouldn't stop; she couldn't heal. Something internal had been broken when Sergej hit her, and weakened as she was from his feeding on her . . . Jesus. Plus, the twins didn't look so hot either. One of them was limping, and his right arm hung at a funny angle. Blaine was paper-pale, and Kip—the curly-headed ghost-quiet one—was breathing heavily, like even walking was an effort.

I didn't feel so great myself. The heat of the aspect was starting to fade, and the *malaika* were getting heavy. If another wave of vampires came at us, I wasn't too optimistic about the whole thing.

Especially if they didn't choke and fall down when they got near me. Which all added up to a Very Bad Feeling About All This.

Anna shoved the limping twin away. She drew herself up, her knees visibly shaking, and glared at me. "Come. Here."

I shook my head. Curls fell free, the blonde receding from them. My entire body ached sullenly under the aspect's flaring and fading. "No dice, Anna. Don't trust you."

Her eyes all but snapped sparks, and the blood running down her chin wasn't just a trickle. "You didn't . . . leave me . . . there." Little crimson droplets sprayed. "Come. *Here.*"

I glanced at the door. Kip had propped himself against the lintel, keeping watch on the hall. It was clear, but for how much longer?

"Not leaving you to you-know-who is not the same thing as this, Anna." The *malaika* were so heavy, dangling in my fists. "Not gonna come near you, and especially not going to—"

She collapsed. The twin she still held on to cursed, going heavily to his knees. "Milady," he whispered, and his face looked like a three-year-old's for a single, wrenching moment. "Don't leave us."

My stomach turned over, hard. I knew I was about to do something incredibly stupid, but it didn't matter. The chances of the Order reaching us, or us making a usable break for the exit we were heading for, were pretty damn slim.

And God only knew what would happen if Sergej somehow got that spear out of his chest.

"Hey." I half-turned. Blaine was staring at me. "Help me get my *malaika* up."

"Perhaps . . ." He wet his lips. Even his tongue was too pale. He'd lost a lot of blood, too. "Milady, perhaps you could . . . share your strength, with Milady?"

I shrugged. "What do you think I'm gonna do, suck *her* blood? No way. She can take a little from me, then Graves can get me out of here while you get her out. And for what it's worth, I'd keep her away from the Order for a while too. They're pretty pissed off."

Not like I thought Bruce and the rest would do anything to one of their precious *svetocha*, but Anna had played them like fiddles before. I'd be an idiot if I gave her the impression she could just waltz back in and start her little games again. Especially since I was looking at taking a powder in a big way; I didn't want to end up with a bunch of her loyal *djamphir* chasing me, for Chrissakes.

It made me feel dirty to think that way. Dirty and tired way down deep inside, the way I imagine adults must always feel.

How do they stand it?

Blaine's shoulders sagged. He helped me snap the *malaika* back into the harness; I glanced up and found Graves had closed his eyes, his Adam's apple moving as he swallowed hard. "Hey. Jesus, you all right?"

Another explosion. It sounded closer. Just how big *was* this place we were trapped in? A complex of warehouses instead of just one? If we were in Jersey, it could be any of a hundred places. How had they found me?

How many of the Order were here, and were they dying or getting hurt trying to get to me? Or to Anna? Was Christophe out there? Guilt hit me with a sick thump, right in the stomach.

"Fine." Graves coughed. The coat hung scarecrow on him, flapping a little as he moved. "Get whatever you're gonna do over with, Dru. Then let's blow this Popsicle stand."

My smile felt traitorous and unnatural, but it helped. A little.

"Watch out for me, okay?" There was no point in keeping it a secret.

He half-opened his eyes, and instead of bright green they were mossy now. But he looked at me, the corner of his mouth lifting in a silent snarl, and one of those instants of communication passed between us, a zing like biting on tinfoil.

As long as I'm breathing, his look said, and I nodded. Let out a shaky breath, my eyes prickling with hot, useless tears. I shoved the urge to cry away. It wouldn't do any goddamn good.

It was hard to get close to her. I kept seeing her face, distorted as she screamed and fired an assault rifle at me. I kept hearing her last words to my mother.

Don't let the nosferatu *bite.*

She scared the hell out of me. Even wounded, even bleeding, I was pretty sure she'd have something up her sleeve.

The gunfire was getting nearer, echoing oddly. The touch kept trying to bolt free of my head and show me what was going down, but I was too tired. I needed all my energy for staying upright, and besides, I didn't want to know. If I was going to die messily when Sergej and reinforcements busted in here, I'd kind of prefer it to be a surprise.

I mean, *ideal* would be no dying at all. But that was looking less and less likely.

Anna was gasping. Under the blood and the bruising she was a bad color, a sort of pale yellowy-gray. The faint ghost of her polished beauty still clung to her, and that made it even worse. She would struggle to get in enough air and let it out with a little hiss that tore right through my chest, because I remembered that sound from Gran in the hospital, the night her owl showed up and the one person who hadn't ever left me behind slid away from life for good.

Why are you doing this, Dru? There's got to be a better way to prove you're not like her.

Except there wasn't. And I even hated myself for thinking like that.

Go figure.

I lowered myself down to my knees, slowly. "Anna." Swallowed, hard, hoping Graves hadn't closed his eyes. Hoping he was watching. "You're going to have to bite me. I, uh. There's just no way—"

Her hand shot out, grabbed a hank of my hair, and *pulled*. I let out a short scream, toppling over, and her fingers were slender steel visegrips. She had my head, and I didn't know where she was finding the strength. My palms slammed onto the floor, but it was too late.

Because my nose was buried in her blood-drenched neck. And the hunger woke with a snarling roar, dyeing everything around me red.

CHAPTER TWENTY-SEVEN

Sweet. **It was** so *sweet*.

I'd been pushing the hunger down, keeping it at bay, for a long time now. Christophe said I was stronger than it. But I wasn't. Not right now, with the rich copper in a haze around me and my entire body aching and the aspect bursting over my skin in a wave of sizzling. My lips, smashed against Anna's cold neck, opened, and the fangs slipped free.

I tried to rip myself away. Her fingers closed on my nape, iron-hard. "God *damn* you," she whispered. "Drink. Drink so you can save them."

I wasn't listening. It was like someone holding a kitten's nose in a dish of milk. A hungry kitten.

No. Not hungry.

A *thirsty* kitten.

My fangs slid into her skin so easily, and a gush of hot perfume filled my mouth. Anna was saying something, whispering in some foreign language, and the touch turned it into words inside my head.

"Hate you," she was saying. "*Hate* you, Reynard, and you deserve it."

It made me sick. She even *tasted* bad. You know how you think perfume is going to taste good because it smells so good? But it doesn't; it tastes like alcohol and acrylic.

Don't tell me you haven't tried it.

The worst part of it was the touch, lighting up the inside of my head like the Fourth of July. Whispering, hinting, *showing* me things.

Anna watching as Christophe crouched easily, all his attention on the street below. Her heart hurt, a sweet sharp pain, and she studied his perfect profile again. He wasn't paying attention, which meant she could look all she wanted. "Why are we up here again?"

She just wanted to hear him talk. But he gave her an irritated glance, the rest of his face set and only his eyes sparking. "Pay attention, svetocha." And the sting as the barbs behind the words hit home—she folded her arms, swallowing the sudden pressure in her throat.

She smoothed the skirt. It was exactly the right red, complementing her skin, and she'd learned the patience necessary to do up all the tiny buttons. Just see him ignore her in this—she made certain her eyeliner was perfect, and admired the heavy ruby drops in her ears. They sparkled just like she did.

But when she reached the Council chamber, there was a surprise.

The other svetocha sat sobbing in Bruce's chair, and Christophe knelt by her side, looking up into her face. The rest of the Council gathered around, identical worry on every face. The other girl was nothing special, a curly-headed mouse in torn blue jeans and a white shirt that seriously needed laundering. She stank of nosferat and fear, and flinched when Christophe moved to touch her shoulder.

Anna stood in the doorway, her jaw suspiciously loose. He had never tried to touch her that way.

"They just . . . kept screaming," the girl said dully, and Christophe leaned forward to catch her words.

"All's well, ksiezniczko." And Reynard was murmuring, not the curt monosyllables he affected with her, oh, no. He was trying to be soothing.

Soothing. To this sobbing little bitch, whoever she was.

Anna hunched in her bed, shoulders shaking. The racking would not stop; her arms wrapped tightly around her chest, tears slicking her fevered cheeks. She rocked back and forth, but quietly, so the djamphir on guard at the door wouldn't hear.

She would die before she let them hear. Christophe's words, clear and hateful, tolled in her head like church bells.

You, Anna? I could never love you. You love yourself far too much to need my help.

It isn't true, she keened to herself, rocking, rocking. It isn't true! I need, I NEED you . . .

But he was gone, and she was crying, and there was no comfort in the silken bed or the clothes on their hangers or the expensive perfumes and lotions racked on her vanity. Even the admiring, jealous eyes of the other Kouroi were not enough.

There was a hole in her, and it twisted . . .

The next mouthful hit the back of my throat and went down in a long, rasping gulp. Her fingers slipped out of my hair, and I tore myself away. Scrabbled back, crab-walking on my palms and sneaker heels, the *malaika* tangling inside their sheaths and scraping the concrete floor.

The *malaika* hilts hit the wall. I gasped, scrubbing at my mouth with the back of my hand, and Anna's eyes were half-closed. Her head lolled on the slender stem of her white neck.

I'd bitten right where Sergej had. Every inch of skin on me crawled with loathing. My stomach cramped hard, closing up like a fist. I understood a lot more about Anna now than I ever wanted to.

"Milady?" The twin holding her felt for a pulse. "She's . . . she's alive. Barely."

Oh, thank God. Thank you, God. New strength surged through me. The aspect came back, smoothing away all the aching and spreading blonde through my hair like a fast-forward at a pricey salon. Bloodhunger scraped at the back of my throat, the walls between me here and now and the past suddenly paper-thin. The touch threatened to spill me into a whirlpool of Anna's memories, time fracturing and splintering as the hall outside turned a dark wine red, filling up with danger.

"Shit." Kip chambered a round. *"Incoming!"*

I *heard* them, tasted the hate flying like clouds of bees around them. The lights were too bright, but closing my eyes didn't help because the touch showed me everything anyway, as if the walls were clear and I was a glass girl full of red liquid—an unholy mixture of perfumed blood and pure, deadly rage.

Christophe's blood wasn't like this, I thought, and another iron cramp of nausea hit me. There wasn't time, though, because Kip was already out in the hall, firing and screaming like he intended to make this his last stand.

It just might be, Anna's blood whispered in my veins. *There's too many of them, and he's wounded.* Training rose up, lattices of information and reaction snapping together inside my head. There was so *much*—I'd barely scratched the surface with Christophe.

Thinking about him was like lighting a match in the room full of explosive gas my skull had become. I rocketed to my feet, tearing the *malaika* free of their sheaths. Another explosion, this one so close it rocked the entire hall, and I sucked in an endless breath.

"Get out of here!" I yelled, and piled out the door.

CHAPTER TWENTY-EIGHT

Even if **Anna** hadn't been keeping up with her training, she'd still *had* it. And somehow, it was that training burning in my head, jerking my body around like a puppet, faster and sharper than I ever thought I could move. I shoved past Kip, who flew sideways and hit the wall; there was no time to feel bad about it because the vampires were coming. Smoke filled the hall, and for a moment I was back in the reform Schola as it burned all around me, hearing someone scream my name and watching the paint bubble up on the benches in the tiny little dead-winter garden.

The past touched the present, doubled over like the Möbius strip everyone makes in fourth grade, and Anna's high tinkling little laugh burst out of my mouth as I hit the first sucker with a crunch. He started choking as my right-hand *malaika* flickered, a gush of thin black acid spraying as I finished the slash and threw myself forward again, a whirling dervish behind the *malaika* blades. The swords were *singing,* a low sweet sound as they cut the silken, smoke-laden air, and that laughter coming from me took on an edge as the vampires fell.

Foot forward, knee precisely placed, swing of hip up as the wooden blades became living things. They danced with me, attack and defense shared in concentric rings of reaction. I blurred as if I was doing my *t'ai chi* on fast-forward, laughing like crazy because it felt so good.

Instead of being terrified, I was *fighting back*. It felt goddamn wonderful.

More gunfire, but I didn't worry about it. What I worried about was the knot of five *nosferat* in front of me, all male, Anna's training ringing inside my head recognizing a standard attack pattern in confined spaces. Two blond, two dark-haired, all black-eyed with the hunting aura and brimful of raging hate; the first two crouched and sprang as a second pair gained altitude, leaping and hanging in the air as the muscle inside my head flexed.

It was so *easy* now.

I skipped back two paces, wanting the extra room to build up speed. Behind me, screams slowed down to distorted mumbles; particles of smoke hung in the air, tiny crystalline flakes. Sneakers digging in, vaguely aware of my breath coming tearing-hard, the lump of heat in my stomach glowing red, I realized what I was about to do and almost, *almost* paused.

But you can't stop in the middle of a fight. You move, and you're either standing at the end of it, or on the dirt. If you're *on* the dirt you might as well be *under* it. That's why fights don't have rules.

My feet slapped, I lunged and left the ground. Gran's owl called softly through the slowed-down mishmash of confusion around me. For a few brief seconds I knew what it was to have hollow bones and feathers, to fly on silent wings, wind slipping past your ears with a low sweet sound like riding a bike down a long hill. Twisting, one foot flashing out to crack against the skull of the first sucker. Another half twist, *malaika* sweeping up as my wrist flexed, and it went through the second sucker's neck with a *tchuk* like Gran thopping her ax through a bit of dry-seasoned cordwood. An arterial spray of rotting acid described a perfect curve, but I was already up and over, my left foot kissing the wall to push me sideways again, shoulder dipping and my other *malaika* whistling until it carved through the third sucker's face at full extension. The third sucker went slack, body tumbling, and my right foot touched his back, neat as could be, as I pivoted and brought both blades across *en parallel.* They both bit deep on the fourth *nosferat* as he was in midair, one almost severing his hand and the other tearing out his throat with a flick of the wrist.

I wasn't done yet. Landing, the body under me absorbing rib-snapping shock, knees loose, my left-hand *malaika* stabbing down through his back. Another meaty thud, had to pull back at the last second so as not to splinter the blade or break the point. A blurted sound behind me, but I was already whirling, and the first sucker— the one I'd just kicked in the head—ran onto my blade at full tilt. He started choking, too, his face congesting and runneling with dark ash as hair-fine cracks ate through his skin.

Hawthorn poisons them fast. So does a *svetocha* once she's bloomed. Or maybe it was Anna's ability added to mine, a calculus of toxicity?

But maybe she wasn't very toxic to suckers, just to other *svetocha.*

My mouth filled with bitterness. The *malaika* jerked free, my hand twisting it precisely to break the suction of muscle against the blade. It gave with a wet splorching sound under the all the noise around us, and I winced.

I looked up, and there was Graves, his irises gone black for a moment before sparks of green struggled in their depths.

Behind him, the twins held Anna, who didn't even look alive. She just . . . hung there. I could still hear her pulse, thudding sluggishly and pausing like a train heaving uphill. Blaine's jaw had dropped. Kip leaned against the wall, clutching at his bloody shoulder, his jaw set and his dark eyes alight as he stared at me.

I hate being stared at. I realized what I'd just done.

That wasn't the worst, though. The worst was seeing Graves's mouth pulled down like he was disgusted. He was looking at me like I was a new sort of bug that had skittered out from under a rock.

One he wasn't sure was poisonous or not. Except I *was.* To suckers, at least. I was a murderous thing. A killer with fangs.

Like something Dad would have hunted.

I'm still me, I wanted to yell. Smoke poured down the hall from the direction we'd come, and I could hear shouts and screams — the glassy cries of *nosferat,* drilling against the brain; wulfen howls high and chill and silver; and *djamphir* battle cries. There was one hell of a pitched action going on down there, but they were working this way.

Graves opened his mouth to say something, but I saw everything right there in his pain-darkened gaze. He *was* disgusted. He'd seen me suck Anna's blood, and seen me do . . .

. . . this. The sucker bodies were rotting fast, and the smell was massive. Nausea hit me like a dodgeball in the stomach; I clamped my lips together and felt my fangs scraping lightly.

A *svetocha*'s fangs are relatively dainty, yeah. But they're meant for the same thing a sucker's are, and I'd just used them.

Graves inhaled. He'd gone completely white, and his mouth dropped open. Blaine's eyebrows went up, his entire face a comic illustration of surprise. Kip raised his 9mm slowly, like a boy in a nightmare.

My body was wiser than I was. It dropped into a crouch, but too late. Graves's warning was wasted.

CRUNCH.

He hit me from behind, flinging me forward, and I felt bones break. *My* bones.

Sergej had gotten the lampstand out somehow, after all.

CHAPTER TWENTY-NINE

Tucking. **Rolling. Great** gouging pain in my side. The aspect burned, and I stopped short, lying against the wall. The *malaika* clattered, both my fists clutching reflexively. I hadn't lost them.

Which was good, because Sergej, a huge hole in his flapping T-shirt, drenched in black blood and with his face a purple-red, hateful leer, was already on me. I jerked, my right-hand blade blurring up and missing him by a fraction as he bent back. He looked like he was about to do an overenthusiastic back walkover, spine creaking and crackling, the tip of the blade whispering past his chin.

I was somehow on my feet now, the wall at my back and red agony jolting up and down my left-hand side as broken bits of rib grated together. The aspect turned to liquid fire, peeling back my skin and grinding in as each break in my bones sang a hallelujah chorus of pain.

Sergej spun the length of iron lamppost, its end making a low hard sound as it tore through air. His mouth opened, but a roaring

covered any sound he might've made—it was the sound of fire as a
cool draft slid past us.

There was an open door somewhere, and the fire down the hall
was sucking at it like a calf at a mama cow's teat.

Sergej snarled, his face turning even more alarmingly purple. I
didn't dare glance past him, but I'd guess the boys had gotten Anna
out of here. Graves was probably gone, too, thank God. At least I'd
done what I'd set out to do.

Now I just had to face down the king of vampires, the one who
had killed my mother. Kill him, if I could.

Yeah. Right. I'd settle for just escaping.

Screaming and gunfire through the roaring noise. Sergej choked,
but he scuttled in quick, swinging the length of iron still dripping
with thin black fluid. My right arm still worked; the *malaika* flicked
out like a snake's tongue, deflecting the arc of his attack and slicing
inward. If I'd been just a little faster it would've opened up his belly,
but my left side seized up with a mother of all cramps, bones grinding together, and I screamed.

The sound cut through all the other chaos. The draft of cooler
air coming from behind Sergej—he was between me and escape,
just great—swirled and flirted uneasily. Heat touched my back.

Nosferatu crispy-critter really quickly; open flame or direct sunlight are really bad for them. But I wouldn't put it past him to wait
for the fire to be too much for me—I couldn't move my left arm,
my breath came in coughing gasps, and if he could get over getting
stabbed in the heart and still have this much juice left a little thing
like an entire fucking burning warehouse wasn't going to put much
of a dent in his day, you know?

Sergej darted forward again, the aspect bit down in my left side
like there were metal jaws meeting in my flesh, and I battered his

attack aside with my right-hand *malaika* again, with a thunder crack of pain and effort.

Over the roaring and the gunfire, another sound penetrated. "DRU! DRU!"

My name, screamed over and over again. I knew that voice. *Christophe. Oh, God.*

I didn't take my eyes off Sergej. He shifted his weight, and I did too, Anna's long-ago training echoing in my head. Her blood burned in me, whispered, tried to show me more of *her*. The touch pushed it back, making a fist inside my head so I could concentrate. He was going to come at me again, and I didn't know if I could hold him off. The smoke thickened, tearing at my eyes just like the fluorescents. Who knew when the lights would give out, too? Something about the sound of the fire told me it was Serious Business.

Sergej dropped back a step. Two.

I stared. The aspect gave one last crunching flare of pain, then, amazingly, I took a deep breath. Smoke rasped against the blood-hunger; hot tears slicked my cheeks as I blinked furiously. The agony retreated, turned into a deep bruising ache, and I raised my left-hand blade. Held the *malaika* in second-guard, naturally as breathing, and straightened. My face settled, eyes narrowing, and I had the sudden lunatic idea that I looked like Dad.

Fury boiled up inside me, pushing aside the pain. The hunger fed on rage, feasted on it, and this time I was a clear glass girl full of red wrath, but it didn't own me. I stood in the middle of all that anger, a ribbon of cold steel inside me, and felt something inside me shift like a key clicking over in a lock.

Sergej stepped back again. Under the dirty honey-gold curls, he looked almost . . . my God.

My God.

He looked *frightened,* his eyes completely black now, widening—but the force in them wasn't reaching through to crush all independent thought. Fine thin threads of gray crawled out of his eyes, fanning like crow's-feet toward his temples. A great gout of black stinking blood pattered down from his chest, slicking his jeans and boots, and for a split second I saw something else far back in his gaze.

Recognition.

Serves you right, you bastard. Do you see them? Do you see both my parents in my face? You're not the only one. Come and get me. Come on.

The *malaika* twitched, my weight shifting forward just a crucial millimeter, playing through the very first initiation of the attack.

This is where the first mistakes are committed, Christophe's voice said, dry and pedantic, inside my head. Why hadn't I absorbed his training when he forced me to drink his blood?

But I couldn't think about that. Because something blurred behind Sergej. A flash of black cloth, pain-darkened green eyes—

—and Graves skidded to a stop, lifted the gun, and started firing.

The first shot went wide. For the rest of my life I will swear, on a stack of Bibles if I have to, that I saw it as it whistled past my head and blew a chunk out of the wall behind me. A little more to the left and Graves would've shot *me.*

The second took Sergej high up on the shoulder from the back, just as the king vampire was whirling to face this new threat. The bullet blew out through the front of his shoulder, fragging and sending splinters, not to mention spatters of black acid blood, everywhere.

And I leapt. The hot hard lump of Anna's blood in my middle was shrinking, and either the aspect was cooling off or the radiant heat from the fire down the hall was getting much more intense. Either way it was bad news, and we had to finish this, now.

My heart swelled up like a balloon. Graves braced himself, his coat flapping around his knees in the backdraft, and made his triangle, aiming carefully. He didn't look particularly hurried, and I could see each bruise on him, smell the blood streaking him under the coat, and almost *taste* the colorless rage fuming off him as well. His lips skinned back from his teeth, and for a moment his eyes flashed bright emerald again. The wulfen Other filled his face with unholy light, and my heart made a funny jumping movement like it was going to break out of my ribs and fly straight toward him.

Sergej twisted back around, bringing up the iron spear. It was too late; I was already inside the critical zone, malaika both slashing in the *crux au courant* pattern. Christophe had only shown it to me once, but he'd taught it to Anna over and over, drilling her like he someday knew this would happen.

The blades bit. I was a little off, but not by much. One slashed across his face, grating against bone, and the other scored down his chest and bit into his midriff. The iron spear cracked against my shoulder in a flash of crimson pain; I went flying. Hit the wall on the other side, I was a regular old pinball, landed on my feet but my left-hand malaika went tumbling free. The fluorescents flickered, and there was a living glare from behind me.

The fire had found us.

Chapter Thirty

Graves turned on his heel, firing smoothly as Sergej barreled past him. I couldn't hear the shots over the roaring. I meant to bend down and scoop up my *malaika*, only made it halfway before my knees gave out and hit the floor with a jarring thud. My fingers closed around the hilt just as my teeth snapped together, fangs piercing my lower lip, and I tasted blood again. Thankfully, it was the sweet crimson of my *own* blood, not someone else's. The bloodhunger retreated to a tired glow, and I leaned back. The wall suddenly seemed incredibly comfortable.

Graves was suddenly *there*, looming over me. His face contorted; he was shouting. I stared up at him wonderingly. Even under the filth and blood and the ashen-gray tone to his skin, he was beautiful. I'd only seen bits of it before, but now that all the flesh was pared away from his bones he was . . .

He reached down and grabbed my arm. "*MOVE!*" he roared, a *loup-garou*'s command voice breaking through the crackling rush of the flames. "*DAMMIT, DRU, MOVE YOUR ASS!*"

I found enough starch in my knees to stand up again. His fingers bit into my biceps, and I suspected I'd be feeling this all over tomorrow.

Assuming we lived to see tomorrow.

He dragged me down the hall, gun held low in his right hand. My *malaika* tips dragged; I couldn't lift them but I didn't want to leave them behind. We stumbled together, and the fire licked closer. Glass shattered behind us, and the draft got stronger. Air swirled around us, lifting my hair and teasing at his coat. The hall stretched like infinity; he slipped and I pitched aside, my dumb body weight keeping him upright; he returned the favor by yanking on my abused arm and almost getting the *malaika*'s edge against his leg.

I didn't realize we were running until we rounded a corner and saw the door. It had been busted off its hinges, and the wind around us became a scream. We plunged through the door and into sudden relatively-cool darkness full of little tiny kisses of spring rain.

I dropped the *malaika*, dug in my heels, grabbed Graves's arm, and *pushed* with all the weary strength I had left. We went flying, rolling, his arms around me somehow and wet dirt squelching, as an amazing belch of red-yellow flame shot out of the open door. I lay on my side, cold water seeping into my jeans, and considered passing out.

No way. Still too much work to do.

But I just lay there for a few seconds, Graves in my arms, his head tipped back and his throat working as he swallowed several times. He was definitely hugging me tighter than he had to, and every time he gasped in a breath, he would exhale and his arms would tighten more.

Like he was afraid someone would take me away.

My arm was twisted underneath me, and I was exhausted. Even

my toenails hurt. Even my *hair* hurt. The pain was a river, and I just lay in it.

"Dru. *Dru.*" He was saying my name. He had his face in my dirty hair. I hugged him back as hard as I could. The fire roared like the sea, and I could see the side of a warehouse. We were on the verge of a greenbelt, wet bushes dripping under the fine misting rain, and the night was painted by leaping flames.

There were still sporadic gunshots. I didn't hear Christophe screaming anymore. The thought sent a hot bolt of guilt through me. Thick black smoke was heaving itself up into the sky.

"Dru," Graves repeated raggedly. "Dru. Jesus. *Dru.*"

"Um." I could find nothing to say. My fangs were still out, achingly sensitive. "Graves." *Or should I call you Edgar?* A thin bubble of hysterical laughter welled up inside of me; I ended up letting out a wheeze that turned into a series of smoke-tarnished coughs.

"Jesus." Was he shaking? I couldn't tell, because I'd turned into mud. I could've just laid there and waited for morning with no trouble at all.

Except it was going to get cold, and we couldn't stay here.

"Graves." The word rasped against the bloodhunger, quivering on the back of my palate. No more danger candy; why had it failed me this time? Had the blooming gotten rid of it?

Worry about that later, Dru.

He hugged me even harder. "Jesus. *Jesus.*"

I coughed again. "Got. To. Get out. Graves. We've got to get *out* of here."

Something rustled in the greenbelt, under the suck-back draft of the fire. Graves tensed, and weary annoyance filtered through me. *Oh, Lord, what now? Take a number, I'm done for the night.*

But we did have to go. And someone was in the bushes.

A shadow loomed over us, orange light reflecting oddly from his irises before he crouched. Soot smeared over his face, his long greasy hair was singed, and he was barefoot. He pushed at my shoulder with those long pale fingers, and a happy grin lit his dirty face.

"Bang," Ash whispered. White teeth flashed, just like the skunk stripe in his hair.

"Holy *fuck*." Every muscle in Graves's body had turned to stone. "What the—"

"It's Ash." I even *sounded* tired to death. It was hard to talk. "We've gotta get out of here. Just us."

"Bang!" Ash repeated, and pushed at my shoulder again. Nudging at me, like a dog.

I nodded, pushing my chin down and bringing it back up. The wet we were laying on was seeping into my hair. "Bang," I agreed wearily. "Help me up?" I freed one hand, and his slim strong fingers laced through mine.

"He changed back?" Graves made it to his feet slowly. He didn't bother brushing off his coat. "Jeez."

I patted myself down. No bleeding, just aching. My ribs on the left side seemed fine enough, except for hurting like mad bastards. The lump of heat in my midsection from Anna's blood was gone, and her whispering inside my head had faded to a ghost-mutter, as if I'd just cleared a haunted house and was hearing the echoes. I had my bag, and my *malaika* lay on the ground.

Think, Dru. Think now, and think hard.

First things first. "Help me clip my *malaika* in." I swayed. "Then let's get the hell out of here."

"What exactly are we going to do?" Graves just sounded curious, and I hoped he'd forgotten he was disgusted by my fangs.

It didn't matter, I told myself firmly. He'd come back and

unloaded most of a clip into Sergej. Whether he was disgusted or not didn't matter.

Not now.

"Catch a cab, ride a bus." I considered it for a moment as Ash steadied me. He looked *damn* happy, all things considered. "If all else fails, you get a crash course in how to steal a car."

"You sure do show a boy a good time, Miss Anderson." Graves hunched his shoulders. His irises flashed green again. "I'm starving."

He sounded, of all things, *hopeful.*

"Bang," Ash agreed, nodding vigorously. That made it unanimous.

The weight of being in charge, of deciding what to do, settled back on my shoulders. Like it had never left. "Transport first." I tried to sound absolutely certain. "Then food. Then we find someplace to sleep."

Graves bent over, straightened slowly with my *malaika*. The fire painted his bruises with garish immediacy, and I couldn't read his expression. Ash bounced a little next to me, like a hound who's just done a good deed and expects a pet or two.

"Good job," I managed. "Good job, Ash. Get us out of here and somewhere there's transportation, okay?"

"Bang-kay. Kay. Okay." He nodded vigorously, and pointed at the greenbelt. There could have been a million vampires hiding in those shadows, and for a moment the urge to just collapse right where I was and let the Order find me was overwhelming.

Then I squared my shoulders, stood still so Graves could snap my *malaika* back in, and found out I could walk.

EPILOGUE

scanned the hotel parking lot one more time and shut the door. Stood for a moment with my head hanging. The thought of warding the walls just about threatened to keel me over.

I'd paid cash and used an old fake ID, a leftover from traveling with Dad. The clerk barely glanced at it, his eyes lighting up when I shoved the greenbacks over the counter. He went back to watching the flickering television playing some show about tattoo artists, and I'd taken the key gladly and shuffled off.

"Come on, this won't stay hot. Or even warmish." Graves touched my shoulder.

Both the boys had carried up armloads of fast-food bags. That's one thing about the big city—they don't even blink when you go through a New Jersey drive-through at 3 a.m. in a stolen car with two hungry werwulfen and get sixty bucks' worth of burgers and fries, not to mention six large chocolate milk shakes.

Ash was already snout-deep in a double-bacon cheeseburger, try-ing to eat it and suck on the straw to his second milk shake at the same time. Graves had a handful of french fries and was already looking way more peppy. If he could get enough food in him, the bruises would heal down and he'd be all right in twelve hours or so.

My brain was tired. It felt like I was thinking through mud. Sergej. Anna. Christophe. *Did I really do all that?* I blinked, picked up a gigantic burger in its crackling paper wrapping, and swallowed hard.

The rock in my throat didn't want to go away. I just swallowed past it. I ate mechanically, and for about fifteen minutes the only sounds were slurping, munching, and Ash's happy little humming sounds as he chewed. Graves ate steadily, his eyelids at half-mast over his pain-darkened irises and his shoulders hunched.

After a while, Graves stopped. Looked at me. We stared at each other for a long moment, and I braced myself as much as I could. Kept chewing. Washed down the flavorless cud with a bullet of tooth-aching cold-sweet milkshake.

"So what are doing now?" Graves's eyes were lighting back up, the shadows retreating the more he ate. He looked at me like I should know.

Well, I did, sort of. Out of all of us, I was the one most used to planning things like this. Escapes. Scenarios. Dad had drilled it into me, I'd spent a whole childhood preparing.

Responsibility settled into me like a weight of cold iron. "Now we sleep. Then, in the morning, we find a car we can use for long distance."

He absorbed this. "We're not going back to . . . to them? The Order?"

"Why, you want to get handed over to you-know-who again? While they lie and keep me from coming after you?" I sighed when Ash looked at me, his dark eyes round like I'd just shouted.

I hadn't. I just sounded angry. Bitter. Old.

Older than I was, at least. I wished for some water to wash the taste out of my mouth. It was like ashes and old blood, that taste, and it wasn't nice. All the cheeseburger and milk shake in the world couldn't cover it up.

Graves nodded. His face pulled against itself, lines appearing like he was aging right in front of me. I've seen that look before, when Dad drove through the bad parts of town and I made sure the doors were locked. It was on the faces of kids who huddled in the cold, staring at passing cars and hoping they wouldn't stop—or hoping they would, because the kids were hungry.

So, so hungry.

"So, um. You . . ." Graves looked down at the pile of fries in front of him. "You came there. Alone. For me."

Yeah, and you're disgusted by the fact that I'm half sucker. So am I. "Let's not talk about it." I stuffed another wad of cheeseburger into my mouth. Chewed sloppily.

Ash looked at Graves, back at me, like he was following a tennis match. Half a fry hung out of his mouth, and he looked so sad and afraid it was almost enough to make me start yelling.

I dropped the remains of my burger and stood up, my chair scraping back from the cheap table. "I'm gonna get cleaned up."

There was only one bed in here, but it was queen-size. The bathroom was nothing to write home about; I could've cleaned it better with two rags and a bottle of spit. But it was cheap, it was safe for tonight, and we needed rest. *I* needed sleep. I needed just a few hours to figure out what the hell we were going to do.

I hadn't thought much beyond rescuing Graves. If Sergej survived he'd have an even bigger hard-on for me, the Order was going to be looking for me, and every sucker who caught wind of us would try to tear us to itty-bitty pieces.

At least the shower was on the hot side of lukewarm. I peeled my filthy clothes off and decided not to worry about not having clean ones for a few minutes. Stepped under the water, trying not to *ewww* too loudly when my feet slipped a little on greasy, not-cleaned-so-well plastic.

Dried blood and dirt sluiced off. My hips felt funny, and I was soaping myself up when I realized something had changed. I arched my back a little under the spray, and I wasn't just imagining things.

The chesticles were bigger.

I lifted my hand. The claws slid neatly from my fingertips, amber-colored and pretty dainty. *Svetocha* got claws when they . . .

I scrambled out of the still-running shower. Swiped condensation off the mirror. Looked at myself, hanging on to the edge of the counter while I dripped all over the yellowing linoleum. My jaw actually dropped, and I actually *saw* my canines lengthen a little, sharpening.

Holy . . . I couldn't feel anything but weary amazement.

My face was slightly different, heart-shaped now, and with my hair wet and slicked back it was easier to see how I looked like Mom. My cheekbones stood out like a supermodel's, my collarbones looked fragile, and the whole architecture of my face had changed by just a few millimeters.

It was official. I'd bloomed.

And now we were on the run.

I stood there, holding on to the slightly greasy counter while the shower ran, and watched the tears roll down my new, sculpted cheeks.

finis